AS WE FORGIVE OTHERS

AS WE FORGIVE OTHERS

A Northern Gothic Mystery

Shane Peacock

Cormorant Books

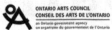

We acknowledge financial support for our publishing activities: the Government
of Canada, through the Canada Book Fund and The Canada Council for the Arts;
the Government of Ontario, through the Ontario Arts Council, Ontario Creates,
and the Ontario Book Publishing Tax Credit.

LIBRARY AND ARCHIVES CANADA CATALOGUING IN PUBLICATION

Title: As we forgive others : a northern gothic mystery / Shane Peacock.
Names: Peacock, Shane, author.
Identifiers: Canadiana (print) 20240364317 | Canadiana (ebook) 20240364333 |
ISBN 9781770867628 (softcover) | ISBN 9781770867635 (EPUB)
Subjects: LCGFT: Detective and mystery fiction. | LCGFT: Novels.
Classification: LCC PS8581.E234 A91 2024 | DDC C813/.54—dc23

United States Library of Congress Control Number: 2024934024

Cover and interior text design: Marijke Friesen
Manufactured by Friesens in Altona, Manitoba in September, 2024.

CORMORANT BOOKS INC.
260 ISHPADINAA (SPADINA) AVENUE, SUITE 502,
TKARONTO (TORONTO), ON M5T 2E4

SUITE 110, 7068 PORTAL WAY, FERNDALE, WA 98248, USA

www.cormorantbooks.com

"To forgive, divine."
Alexander Pope

For Sophie,
my mystery.

1

Gone North

ON THE MORNING the stranger came to his door, Mercer was at the window looking south, Alice's presence, like a radiance without a source, like something he couldn't grasp, still in the bedroom behind him. He wasn't seeing the bleak landscape though, the snow lying in rigid sheets in the frigid fields in the grey and white world around his old, rented farmhouse; he was remembering the drive north, heading here to this exile, his mind crumbling, alone yet talking out loud to his wife and children as they disappeared in the rear-view mirror, and speaking to the young man he had assaulted too. He was asking every one of them if there was forgiveness for him.

There had been times these last few weeks when he swore he could not see any colour up here. This morning was no different: the sun had struggled to appear. But then, two circles of light cut through the greyness — coming toward him along the lonely mile from the main road. The headlights shimmered as they moved, winking at him when they reached his lane, turned down it, and then eased onto the gravel driveway. It was seven-thirty in the morning.

He still didn't sense any danger. He didn't think of the Glock 38 he used to keep in his shoulder holster, turned in that last day in New York. He watched the car, just one person in it, approaching him in the middle of nowhere. His thoughts were still with Christine and their kids, and with his victim, whose scream still woke him up at night. He had not written anything in his journal for days. He needed to do that. It would help him come to grips with things. Someone had suggested that. Just write it out. What he had written though, seemed like stories, not reality.

He had no idea that morning, in this quiet and monochromatic place, that another story, full of colour and pain, was coming his way. The stranger in the car was bringing it to him.

He moved to the window that looked out toward the barn and driveway, once the vehicle had come to a halt. He watched closely. He was trained for this. The woman got out of the car, a mid-sized Toyota, blue like the ice on a pond at certain times. A blue and white licence plate. She closed the door quietly and stood still for a moment, then sighed and marched toward his front door. In her grey coat, she did not stand out against the snow or the grey everything else. She walked slowly, her head tilting upward, her breath forming puffs of clouds in the air.

Mercer pulled back from the window and made himself small behind the curtain. He listened for her footsteps on the long walkway that led to his door. They were barely audible — he hadn't shoveled since the last snowfall. It was funny how the snow muffled things here, how it made it more difficult to anticipate the approach of another human being. People in these parts were weightless; they were watching though, scenting one another, sizing each other up.

Her knock, which was not heavy, resounded through the old house, like the drum at the beginning of a Shakespeare play.

He stayed behind the curtain. The knock came again. Then

he heard the door creak open. No one locked doors here. He was trying to fit in.

"Mr. Mercer?"

Silence.

"Mr. Mercer?"

He heard her shut the door behind her. That was strange. She was in his house. For some reason, he thought of the scene in his favourite Lovecraft story where blood began to drip between the floorboards of the upper storey, dropping in crimson splats on the floor beneath.

"Yes?" he called out.

"Oh, you're home. I'd like a word with you."

If you weren't sure if I was home, he thought, *then why did you come in?*

He fixed his dark hair, still thick at his age, and tightened his bathrobe. *How many people actually wear these things nowadays?* He had nothing on underneath. Alice wanted him naked quickly each night, though she was all politeness and small talk until they reached the bedroom. It was always his bed. They hadn't been to her place yet. Perhaps that wasn't so unusual since they'd only been involved for a few weeks. *Should he be involved?* It was her, he told himself, the unprepossessing Alice, who had made their relationship happen, wasn't it? Aware that he was still technically married, he had resisted, hadn't he? Christine had told him to leave, in as many words. He smoothed out his robe and looked down at his feet. He was wearing slippers. *How many people do that these days?*

"I'm coming."

She didn't say a word as he came down the old staircase, his left hand on the carved banister. Seventeen wooden steps. He had counted them many times.

The woman was standing in his big country kitchen, an unremarkable sort. Somewhere in her thirties, she wore a long coat with black scarf, no toque or mittens. Her left ring finger was naked. She was slim and pale, brown hair cut short. A pair of wire-rimmed glasses sat halfway down her long nose, the lenses still slightly fogged. A little red button on her lapel read "I own my own body."

"How are you doing today, sir?" Her words were much more formal than her demeanour. She seemed anxious.

"I'm fine," he answered carefully. "It's early. You woke me. Do I know you?"

"No, sir, you don't." She regarded him for a moment.

"And?"

"You used to be a detective? In New York City?"

"How do you know that?"

"Small community, word gets around." She offered a slight laugh, but it seemed forced, like many of the expressions presented by people around here.

"I don't mean to be rude, but may I ask what you want?"

"Right to the point, eh?"

"You are in my house and —"

"No, no, I get you. This is a little unusual, to say the least." There was silence again. She seemed to gather herself. "I'm here to report a murder," she finally said and examined his reaction, watching him.

He wasn't sure what to say. For an instant, he felt a bit of a thrill and wanted to reach for his police notepad, ask her to sit down.

"I don't do that anymore."

"Well, this is important."

He wondered if she had actually said that, if she was real and standing there in front of him. "The taking of a life is always important. So, if you've seen evidence of a serious crime then you should report it to —"

"It hasn't happened yet."

"I'm sorry?"

"I thought we were the ones who always said that." She tried another laugh but when he didn't respond, she continued. "There is a man who lives with his wife not far from here and he is going to kill her. I guarantee it."

These people were insane. All of them. Even Alice. On the surface, they, and the country they inhabited, were so similar to home — normal — but there was something underneath that just wasn't right. In some way, they terrified him. Decent people but bereft of regular emotions. In a way, they seemed bereft of humanity.

"That doesn't make any sense. You can't report a crime before it's happened."

"I know."

"And I think you should leave."

At home, he would have had his house gun, a lighter model than at work.

"I can tell you her name."

"Good for you." He stepped toward her, holding out his hand in the direction of the door.

"Elizabeth Goode. She lives over in her family's place just across the field."

He put his hand on her arm. She glanced down at it.

"You need to get going."

"His name is Andrew. Andrew Eakins."

"Good for him." Mercer applied some pressure to the small of her back, turning her.

"I can tell you how he will do it."

That gave him pause. Just a little. It made the hair rise slightly on the back of his neck. He reached for the door, opened it, and nudged her over the threshold.

"She will be gone, just gone, suddenly!"

Once she was out on the step, he pulled the door closed and put his ear to the wood, listening. He could tell she was still there, just inches away.

"Men treat women badly," she said.

That bothered him.

"Oh, there are exceptions," she continued, "but not many, perhaps not any, really. Most women live in fear of their male partners, in one way or another. But this woman is in grave danger. You have the means to do something about it and you choose not to. Remember that. It will be on your conscience because you knew."

"Go away, please."

"Do you care about how men treat women, Mr. Mercer?"

He didn't answer.

"Do you, Mr. Mercer?" Her voice was rising. Thank God, they were way out here in the country.

"I care," he said to himself, then slipped the bolt in place with a quiet crack.

"Contact the police. There's a station in town," he said through the door

"They will do nothing. They know who he is, and they will do nothing. They do not have the imagination to grasp any of this. I thought you might ... being from the States and all."

Mercer didn't know what that meant. He stood silent for a long time and so did she. He could hear her breathing. Finally, she trudged back toward her car. This time, he could hear the footsteps, the force with which she drove her boot heels through the soft snow and onto the concrete. They faded as she reached the car. Then he heard the door slam, the car reverse and turn, and could sense the anger in the way she pressed on the accelerator as she went up the lane. He walked to the south end of the house, into what the old folks who had once lived here had called the sunroom. There was a big picture window there in a cramped space, facing south too, as if hoping for better things. He watched her car go down the sideroad, silent now, until it vanished.

2

Secrets

IT WASN'T UNTIL a couple of days after the strange woman's visit that he discovered that Alice was a police officer. They had known each other for several weeks by then and had been physically intimate many times but he had no idea what she even did for a living. When he'd asked her, she had evaded the question, though once or twice she had teased him, saying, "Guess who I am, guess what I do." When he said a schoolteacher, then a secret agent, she had laughed and turned away. It was odd because he had fessed up to his identity from the beginning.

He only discovered who she was, or at least her occupation, when he got up to pee in the middle of that night and saw that a black notebook with POLICE stamped on the cover had fallen from her jeans, resting there beside her clothes and underwear. The notepad was exactly like his, he knew instantly what it was, and it made him curious to say the least. That was what made him open it.

"Disappeared. Female. Possible homicide. Husband suspect. Country residents."

It was right there at the top of the first page — a recent crime, perhaps noted just the previous day. Mercer could only see a few words, but that was enough. He felt his balance go. He caught himself with a hand on the bedpost and after a few seconds turned toward Alice, sleeping outside the sheets again, unglued from him for the moment. He often thought there was something unusual about her, but that had been the case with so many people he had met in town and around here. Now this. He slipped silently over to his side of the bed and looked down at her. She was so ordinary with her clothes on; so different without. He often had the strange sensation that she had been sent to him, right from the moment he met her.

HE HAD ONLY been here for a bit more than a month at the time. It was mid-November, and the snow had not yet fallen. It was a warm night dropped into the middle of bitter ones, for an instant distracting everyone from what was just around the corner. He had little in the farmhouse, mostly just his clothes, and was keeping to himself. He had put a few beers in his fridge, slightly alarmed at the high alcohol content, picked up some groceries now and then, and occasionally bought eggs at a roadside stand from a lady who once offered him homemade bread when she learned he was from "out of town." It was an awfully friendly thing to do, though she didn't take his hand when he offered his.

Sometimes, he wondered if he was punishing himself, half starving his every need. That night though, he decided to slip into town to eat. He'd seen a family restaurant on the main drag —

called King Street, like every main street in every town he'd passed through on his way here.

He had chosen to live in this area because it was near enough to a big city if he needed it but far enough away in the country to allow him to disappear. It promised to be cold too, and only friendly if he wanted it to be, so it was perfect. He had lied to the border guards, said he was just staying a couple of weeks. It wasn't entirely untrue. He had no idea how long he would be gone. Perhaps the rest of his life. He had to slow down, get away from the horrors of New York and his job, from what he had done to that young man, from the way he had treated his wife and children. Mostly, he had to vanish. Christine had said what they both had been thinking for years: they needed time away from each other. It had torn out his heart to hear it said aloud. Christine's voice had been hard, and she would not look at him. He left within days, resigned the next time he went into Manhattan, turned in his badge and the Glock 38. He had to be somewhere that was nowhere. This northern place had seemed perfect.

"How you doin' today?" said the woman at the door of Connie's Home Style Grill, before he was fully inside. She had a menu in hand already, as if she had spied him from a distance. The name tag on her chest said she was Jennifer.

"Just one?" she asked, a smile firmly in place.

"Yes."

He had learned, within a couple of days, to keep his voice down. He had stopped in a bigger restaurant by the side of the interstate (or whatever they call them here) when he'd first arrived and was almost alarmed at how quiet it was, even though there had to be at least a hundred customers inside. Then a family had come in, all American drawls, chairs scraping, their orders and conversation booming across the restaurant. Even to him, it seemed almost rude.

There was only one other customer in Connie's that night.

Alice.

He barely noticed her at first. Her head was down at her food when he came in. Trained to survey a room, he checked her out with a glance. The younger, maybe darker side of him didn't consider her a prospect and the detective tossed her aside as a threat. Hunched over her meal, she wore a loose blue sweater rolled halfway up her slender but solid forearms, the insignia of a hockey team in patches on each shoulder. She was dressed down, covered up on purpose. She looked up at him briefly. Oval face, either grey or hazel eyes, little or no makeup. Her hair was what he would call dirty blonde, tied back tightly in a ponytail. As was a detective's habit, he observed the length of her arms, torso, legs, and came up with a description and size. About five foot four, perhaps 145 pounds, maybe a little more. It was hard to tell. Her jeans were baggy, flared at the bottom in an outdated style.

"How's it going?" he heard her say, after he sat down at the table across the aisle. Jennifer had flitted off, saying, "I'll be right back with water; you just take your time."

He looked right at Alice. She appeared to be tired but fighting it. Her greeting had seemed forced, as if she felt compelled to be friendly, but her heart wasn't in it.

"I'm all right."

"Weather's not the best, but it'll get worse."

"Not looking forward to it."

"You from out of town?"

"Out of country."

"From the States, I'm guessing?"

"Yeah, America."

"We don't say that here, but if you want to be from *America*, then no worries. We all have our own realities."

It occurred to him that if you'd read what she just said, typed out, it would look almost mean, but it didn't sound that way coming from Alice's thin lips, not in the least. She smiled when she said it.

"The more basic your order is here, the better. Get something like the soup of the day or a burger. That's always a good way to go."

"Thanks. I'll bear that in mind."

She went back to eating. He ordered the soup, the house burger, and a milkshake. Jennifer walked away, softly singing a song about a town he'd never heard of, and constellations of stars.

He watched Alice peripherally. No wedding ring. She was checking him out, noting his face, his hands. Based on her many glances his way, it appeared she now wanted to engage with him. But not saying so.

"Would you like some company?" he finally asked her, after Jennifer set his meal in front of him, along with a big ketchup bottle.

For an instant there was an expression on Alice's face that was almost like panic. She caught it though and paused. "For sure," she finally said. It was an odd acceptance, a sort of yes and no at the same time.

He couldn't smell any perfume as he slid in across from her with his plate.

"What part of the States?"

"Lived in New Jersey. Worked in New York City."

"Nice."

"Not really."

"I was in Manhattan once, enjoyed it. Saw a show, some big star in it, can't remember his name now. What did you do there?"

"Detective for the NYPD. Homicide Squad."

"Whoa."

"How about you?"

"The important stuff? What I do when I'm not working?"

He smiled. Perhaps the first time he had done that since he arrived.

"Sure."

"I like to go to movies, hang out with a few friends, barbecue in the summer, curl in the winter."

"Curl?"

"Curling. It's an exotic sport."

This time, he actually laughed. He had seen curling on television during the winter Olympics. The commentators said it was a complicated game. Seemed simple enough to him.

Jennifer sidled up to them with a blank look that also somehow broadcast her interest in the fact that this local had either invited a stranger to sit with her, or was being seduced by him. It was apparent that she knew Alice, though she seemed a little wary, as if her fellow citizen had some sort of reputation.

"How are yous two doing?"

"Fine," said Alice without looking at her.

"Can I get yous anything else?"

"We're good," said Mercer.

There was a long pause after Jennifer went back to the front counter. Alice and Mercer grinned at the same time. She ate another french fry and a little streak of ketchup flecked her cheek like a wound.

It was shocking to him that Alice came home with him. She really did not seem like the type, not even close. He wasn't the type either. He had slept with just one woman other than Christine in the last twenty-five years, a recent brief affair with a younger police officer that both he and she regretted, or at least they both said they did.

"Staying long?" Alice had asked him at the restaurant.

"Not sure."

She seemed to like that answer.

"What hotel are you at? Which one of the two? We have some real charmers here. Maybe I can suggest something better: a B&B."

"No, I've rented a place, an old farmhouse, and the whole farm, about ten to fifteen minutes out of town. Didn't intend that, but it was available and quiet. They're selling it. Apparently been in the family for generations. They just want someone to rent it for a stretch. They like the American cash, I guess."

"So ... you are definitely staying for a while, or at least a little while?"

"Yeah, I guess so."

He had never made more eye contact with a woman without making much eye contact. Her gaze never lingered more than a few seconds. She would look across the room when she talked or at the ceiling or out toward the front door.

"I can probably tell you a bit about that house, if you like. My family is from around here, know everyone and every home, been here for about seven generations, one of the oldest families in these parts who aren't Indigenous."

"You're welcome to drop by sometime." That felt like a forward sort of thing to say to a woman he had just met, even for a loud American. He had made it clear he was alone in the farmhouse.

She looked down at her half-eaten burger. It was red in the centre, and she liked to take big bites. "How about tonight?" she asked, picking it up.

It was hard to say who was more nervous. In fact, it was hard to tell what Alice felt period. It wasn't that she was robotic, she just didn't project a great deal of emotion. At the house, she kept the conversation to information about the area and the farm itself. It came out in short sentences, no elaboration, the tone of her voice flat. Only the very odd word carried any sort of inflection or emphasis. He heard his own voice bouncing off the walls like it was coming out of a megaphone, even when he tried to speak quietly. Each sound he uttered seemed almost exotic and yet unrefined next to hers, despite her plainness. The combination of their voices was thrilling, though, as it mingled in the air.

When she kissed him, he wondered why he responded. He hadn't asked her to come, not directly, not that night, but she had gotten into her car and followed him all the way out here, down dark country roads. Fearless. Or might she have been afraid? He didn't know, though he hoped she wasn't. Why was she doing this? Why was he? He needed affection, for sure, and he needed a woman too, badly. He wasn't, however, attracted to her, not in the usual way. There was something about her though, some mystery that needed solving and yet something he recognized too. But still, he couldn't understand why this unremarkable person with the unwashed hair, no scent of any sort, and appearing a little big in the hips and flat in the chest, felt so enticing. The attraction was not just in his head either.

He felt guilty too, even though he and Christine were now separated, and they had not been intimate forever, it seemed. Their marriage had been breaking down for years.

She had told him to go.

When he kissed Alice back, everything about her changed. She came alive. This was the female New York police officer tripled, young Christine doubled. She immediately started removing their clothes. Uncovered, her body was strong and shapely. Her face still a little lined in places, dark circles under her eyes, her features still blunt, but the rest of her a shocking surprise, tattoos and all. They touched, her pale hand on his darker chest electrifying and knowing what to do. It made him wonder about how he measured up. He was nearly fifty now, and though tall and still muscular, far from perfect. It had been hard to tell Alice's age at first. He had assumed in her mid-forties but now he wondered if he was wrong. Why, he asked himself again, did she want him? She did though, every inch of him.

And then she was gone. She vanished that morning the way she did every time after that, a magic act that he could never solve. He would sleep like a log and awaken to a quiet house.

NOW, HE STOOD there over her in the middle of the night, her police notepad in his hand, a crime that seemed a good deal like the murder the strange woman had foretold, noted in slashing red ink as plain as blood. He stared at her. It struck him that he should be writing this down.

"YOU KNOW WHY this soon has to end," Christine had said to him with tears in her eyes, the last night he came home in Jersey. His son, Keith, had left for college two weeks before. Their daughter, Stevie, was in her third year and came home infrequently and when she did, she rarely spoke to him.

"They don't hate you," Christine once told him. "They just don't know you. Neither do I anymore."

He always offered the excuse of his job in a clipped sentence or two: the horrible things he had to deal with daily, his responsibilities, the vicious things people did to each other in New York and the pace of everything there, his need to wind down when he got home and be alone. Why did he not simply sit down with her, really talk, and take her into his confidence? Why had he not told her his secret? So often, he would go to his study and pretend to work, while his wife and children laughed and shared their days elsewhere in the house.

Christine was right. He had allowed himself to spiral, glued to his own concerns. He had wasted the time he should have spent with his wife and family. Memories of Christine in her youth, of the love and admiration in her eyes, haunted him now. Why had he just thrown all that away? He had thought that here in this lonely place, far from his routines, he would soon find himself, the human being not the detective, but he had been wrong about that too.

ALICE OPENED HER eyes.

"Come here," she purred.

"Just a second, need to pee."

"I guess I can allow that."

He had moved the notepad behind his thigh and when he turned toward the bathroom, let it fall back onto her clothes.

When he returned to bed, he had every intention to draw her out about her work so he could confirm if what he had been told by his strange visitor had, in fact, come to pass. But once he slid under the covers his intentions dissolved. When he awoke in the morning, she was gone.

3

Tell Me

HE WENT NORTH into town around noon to find her. He knew the police station was in an old brick building that looked like it had once been a big Victorian schoolhouse, right on King Street Circle — where King made a loop in the centre of town — not far from Connie's Home Style Grill. Most of the downtown had retained its nineteenth century buildings, three-storey structures with Victorian facades on the upper levels, even as many of the windows and doors on the street-level shops had been altered over the decades. Some stores already had their Christmas lights out. He sat in his car across the Circle for two hours hoping to catch her coming out of the station. The engine had to be turned on several times to keep the windshield from frosting up and himself from freezing into a block of ice.

A woman passed by on the street, slim, in a long grey coat with black scarf, and it made him sit up. He thought she glanced his way, thought he caught the glint of wire-rimmed glasses, but couldn't make out her face, and to follow her would mean risking missing Alice. Was he being overly dramatic about all of this?

Obsessing, as usual. For at least the tenth time that morning he told himself that the crime written up in Alice's notepad was not necessarily the one the stranger had predicted. But he knew he had to at least look into it.

He barely recognized Alice when she appeared. She was the sort who blended into crowds and this time she was part of a trio of uniformed police officers. The two women were about the same height, had the same hairstyle, and even walked the same way, though the other did look older than Alice, heavier, with a darker complexion and hair. The man, well past forty, balding, with thinning brown hair peeking out from under his tipped-up cap, strode ahead of the women and was clearly doing most of the talking.

Mercer got out, crossed the icy street, carefully made his way through the snowy centre of the Circle where a small tree decorated with about a dozen red Christmas bulbs had been erected, crossed the treacherous road again on the far side, and then stepped through a little gap in the snowbank so he could meet the trio on the sidewalk. He almost slipped when he looked up from where he was placing his feet to focus on Alice, then almost slipped again, and slowed his pace. She noticed him from a way off and stopped for an instant, allowing her colleagues to get ahead, but then caught up with them.

"Well, hello there," she called out as they neared, putting on a smile for him.

"Whoa!" said Mercer. "So this is what you do? This is a surprise."

Mercer was wearing two layers of sweaters under his tan Burberry coat, the one that looked elegant and permanently pressed, had fixed himself up for the occasion, combed the grey into subtle streaks in his black hair, and donned his Perry Ellis shades, which he took off now. He had decided not to mess the hair with a hat, so his ears were already growing red. His wife had told him that his shoulders appeared wider in this coat — almost a compliment, something rare from her over the last few years. His best pair of shoes, Italian made, shone somehow in the dark cloudy day. He looked more than a little New York.

"Yes, this is indeed what I do," said Alice. He could tell that she knew he had tracked her.

"Hi," said her female colleague, clearly expecting an introduction. "Weather's not so bad, could be better."

"Oh," said Alice, "this is Hugh Mercer. He's from out of town. New York PD, in fact … homicide."

"Something we should know?" asked the man, taking a step toward him. Just under six feet tall and around two hundred pounds, his gut was evident under his jacket.

"Nope," said Mercer, "I'm just here visiting. I'm sort of retired." He stuck out his hand and they shook. The man's fingers were short and stubby.

"Leonard Ferguson," said the officer clearly.

"Pleased to meet you."

The other woman cleared her throat.

"Oh," said Alice, "this is Salma, uh, Constable Haddad. Sal, actually."

The woman gripped his hand firmly. Maybe five four, weight 155, heading toward sixty years old. Alice was the baby here. "It's a pleasure," said Sal and then looked down.

"So, how did our Sergeant Morrow here get to know a NYPD man, homicide guy, to boot, without our scoping out the situation beforehand?" asked Ferguson.

"Let it go, Fergie," said Alice.

"No, I think we —"

"Let it go."

Ferguson hesitated for a moment. "Oh … kay."

"I'll see you guys later," said Alice.

Sal steered Ferguson away, glancing back at them over her shoulder.

"You caught me," said Alice, after they had walked without saying anything for nearly half a block. "Cuff me and do what you will."

"Why didn't you tell me?"

"Oh, I don't know, it just didn't come up in a serious way."

"That's not an answer that would stand up in court."

They walked on in silence around the Circle, Alice looking away. She seemed to be moving slower than when he had first spotted her. Perhaps she was being considerate, not wanting him to lose his footing again on the icy surface. Finally, she sighed. "I would have told you eventually and you would have found out before long anyway. But I just kind of like to keep my professional life separate, when I can. It's a small town."

"That was pretty spectacular evasion on your part though. How long have we known each other? Three weeks, maybe a bit more? And you kept *that* quiet. Kept it from a detective too. Good job."

She smiled and for a moment, he thought she might put her arm through his, but she didn't. It occurred to him that she had never made any show of affection outside his house, in fact, outside his bedroom.

They passed a few banks, a couple of restaurants, a convenience store, and a sports memorabilia place with hockey sweaters hanging like threats in the windows.

"Hungry?" he asked.

Connie's was just ahead, where King Street straightened out again on the other side of the Circle.

"Always."

They found a booth at the back of the restaurant. It took him about fifteen minutes into their meal to get the conversation where he wanted it to go. When Alice spoke about Salma Haddad and what a good person she was, how she sometimes felt bad after they arrested hard-luck criminals, Mercer struck.

"So, how's police work in general in this area?"

"Well, it's work, you know, though not like yours." She took a swig of her milkshake. "It's fairly boring around here."

"No murder and mayhem?"

"That's New York."

"No one has ever committed a serious crime in these parts?"

"I didn't say that."

"How many homicides last year?"

"One. Two if you count the rural areas. Many years there aren't any though. They're usually pretty cleverly done when they do happen, to be honest. Keeps us on our toes."

"This year?"

Alice paused. "None," she finally said.

"You don't sound too sure about that."

"Well, we may have one."

"May have? That's a strange thing to say. What do you mean?"

"Just what I said. Something's happened and ..." She trailed off.

"When?"

She hesitated again. "Recently."

"Very recently?"

"Look, Mercer, this is confidential stuff. I can't say much."

"Well, you know what I do, or did, and I have to say, I was good at it. Solved nearly every serious case I had, and I had boat-loads."

"I can imagine."

"You are looking at a decorated NYPD detective, top of the service in just about the toughest precinct anywhere. So, if you want to bounce anything off me —"

"That wouldn't be —"

"It's not like I couldn't help."

Alice squinted at him. "This thing, actually, just happened." She sighed. "It's pretty weird." She slurped the last bit of the milkshake, trying to get everything out of the bottom of the cup. Some of it sprayed above her upper lip and he could see tiny droplets on the light hair there. "It'll be in the paper in a day or two, probably online this evening, so I suppose there's no harm in telling you a bit."

"I'm all ears."

She sighed again. "The victim's name is Elizabeth Goode."

He had learned to keep a poker face during investigations and that talent had seeped into his private life, but when Alice said the woman's name, he could feel himself go pale. She, for some reason, was regarding him closely as she spoke, which was unlike her. He saw that she had noted his reaction.

Mercer started thinking about how he had not informed the police that he had been warned that a homicide was imminent. His visitor, however, had just seemed like a nutcase. But then, he had seen Alice's notepad, and he still hadn't spoken up because he hadn't wanted to reveal that he had been snooping through her things.

"Elizabeth Goode lives with her husband on a farm not far from yours, actually. A man named Andrew Eakins."

Same man too, same location. This was getting a little disturbing.

"She and her husband went into town the evening before last, to a little place, a café, not equipped with security cameras."

Mercer wondered why she was adding that.

"And ..." continued Alice. Then she paused.

"And what?"

It was remarkable what a good storyteller Sergeant Alice Morrow was. He hadn't expected that. Detective Hugh Mercer sat riveted, seeing the characters, the location, wanting to know what was going to happen next.

4

Apparent Facts

TWO DAYS AGO, *late on Monday afternoon, Andrew Eakins and Elizabeth Goode got out of their car, leaving it seven stores from the Shelter Café on King Street Circle. Eakins had the keys. Half a dozen strides away, he turned to press the lock button, but she shook her head, smiled at him, and took his hand. Turning back, they nearly ran into a pedestrian, who adroitly sidestepped them and, of course, apologized, even though it was the couple who had not been watching where they were going. The two of them walked hand in hand to the café, which was opened about a year ago, by a newcomer named Jonathan Li. The Shelter features all kinds of coffee and beverages like chai latte and hot pumpkin spice drinks, as well as fancy baked goods. It took the locals a while to patronize it, but there were enough recent transplants from the city to keep it in business. Various rumours circulated about Li, who he actually was and why he wanted to start a business here. He arrived suddenly from the city, slept on a cot in the café sometimes while he renovated the space, then rented an apartment in town.*

Elizabeth and Andrew often came to the Shelter for a treat just before it closed on Mondays and Fridays because by then there was often hardly anyone there. As they approached, they passed another couple who had just left the café. It was 5:51 p.m. There was a little bell on the latticed glass door, and it rang as they entered. Li noticed the time, since these were likely his last customers, and he was hoping to close soon. Just one of the seven tables was occupied, and the music had been turned off. Elizabeth waved at Li who seemed to be in a sombre mood and barely responded. Elizabeth and Andrew quickly took off their winter coats, hers long and down-filled, his a puffy bomber-style, and put them on the backs of their chairs at a table in the middle of the room. The best window spot for two, near the door and always the first to be filled, was taken, and other tables still had not been cleared. The couple sat and took a second to decide what they would order. As they were talking, Elizabeth's cellphone rang. She picked it up and answered but there was no response, perhaps a wrong number. Andrew instinctively felt for his phone, which he kept, "like a woman" Elizabeth often said, in his back pants pocket. It was not there.

"I forgot my phone, honey," he said and got to his feet.

"Just leave it. We won't be long."

But Andrew Eakins was an anxious sort and having his cellphone in the right place and near him was important to him. An artist, his sculptures impressionist metal stuff on dark subjects, he never wanted to miss a call that might mean a sale or a commission.

"I'll be right back."

"I'll order, sweetheart. What do you want?"

"A chai latte and Italian banana bread."

"All right."

"Don't run off with anyone."

"Never," she said, and they smiled at each other.

Andrew Eakins was gone for about three minutes. When he returned, their table was empty. In fact, the room was deserted, except for Li cleaning up behind the counter. Andrew assumed Elizabeth had gone to the washroom, though he wondered why she had taken her coat. He sat at their table checking his phone, awaiting her return and their order. After five minutes, neither had come. After ten, he approached Li at the counter, who looked a bit impatient since it was past six now and Andrew was the only person left in the café.

"Don't we have an order coming?"

"Excuse me?" asked Li. "We? I was wondering why you —"

"Didn't my wife order?"

"Elizabeth?"

Li knew her name. She was friendly. Andrew was a different story.

"Yeah. Where is she?"

"She wasn't with you, sir." He couldn't bring himself to look at Eakins.

"Yeah, not when I came back in. I forgot my phone and had to go out."

"I'm not sure I understand what you're saying." Li tried to seem busy. "We're closing."

"Elizabeth. Where is she? Where's our order? We came in together."

There was a long pause. Li looked up from his work, right at Eakins.

"No, you didn't."

Andrew's face turned pale. "What?"

"I haven't seen Elizabeth. I was wondering why she wasn't with you."

Andrew turned back and looked at their table, then he marched down the little hallway toward the women's washroom, his boots *pounding on the wooden floor. He tried the door. It was unlocked. He opened it. Then he came back to Li.*

"I came in here with my wife!"

Li said nothing, though he looked a little frightened.

"What the HELL *is going on?" Andrew shouted. "Where is she?"*

Li picked up his phone.

"Who are you calling?" barked Andrew, even louder.

"Shelter Café. I need some help. Now," was all Jonathan Li said.

Sergeant Morrow and Constable Haddad happened to be in the store next door, off duty, and Sergeant Ranbir Singh, who took the call at the police station across the Circle, knew they were there. The constables walked next door to find Andrew Eakins trying to wrest the cellphone from Jonathan Li's hands.

Elizabeth Goode has been missing ever since.

"SO?" SAID MERCER. "Is it possible the café owner just didn't notice her come in? He was cleaning up, wasn't he? And then, after only being there for a few seconds, she quietly slipped out a back door when her spouse left. You know, running out on her husband. A domestic problem. Wives sometimes find ways to —"

"We find that difficult to believe."

"Why?"

"Because there are only two exits from the café. Either the front door or you have to leave through the kitchen. Li looked up when Eakins came in, since it was almost closing time, and he's pretty sure the customer was alone. Plus, we have another eyewitness, two of them in fact, a couple on the street, who saw Eakins enter the café the first time, by himself. It appears that Elizabeth Goode was never there."

"What about the other couple at the window table when Eakins first came in?"

"Yeah, the ghosts."

"Sorry?"

"They're only present in Andrew Eakins's version of the incident. Jonathan Li disagrees. He says the café was empty by then and we have reason to believe he may be correct."

"May be? But not sure?"

"Well, the couple who saw Eakins approach the café alone from the street said they were the last customers at the Shelter before he arrived, and that when they had left seconds earlier, the place was empty. Li knew these customers, so we called them immediately and thoroughly questioned them. They're locals, good people, no reason to make anything up. But we're considering all possibilities. If we can find the ghost couple, we could have the answers we need."

"Maybe Eakins just has a screw loose? And she's taking a well-deserved break from him?"

"He was angry, maybe a bit confused, adamant that the others were lying or mistaken, but he seemed very lucid to me, remarkably so considering what he said had just happened. He left and returned home to find her and when she wasn't there, drove everywhere he thought she might be, and then called us. She's gone, Mercer, vanished without a trace, for well over twenty-four hours now."

Mercer could hear the woman at his door say *"She will be gone, just gone, suddenly!"*

"So, the café is small, one front and one back entrance, and you have what amounts to three reliable witnesses, not counting the ghosts. Andrew Eakins comes into the café, goes back out, and comes back in. No wife at any point."

"I can tell you how he will do it."

"That is correct."

"Curious."

"No kidding."

"So why would Eakins make up something like this? That's your first question."

"Yeah, Sherlock, it is."

He felt a little sheepish.

"We have some theories."

"And?"

The most likely scenario, in Mercer's mind, was that Eakins had done something to his wife, then tried to make it look like she'd run off.

"They are not to be shared with former NYPD detectives, even highly respected ones — even ones who come with other benefits." The last bit was said almost apologetically, glancing down, as if she was unsure it should be said at all.

Why say it, he thought, *if you can't own it?* This was the same Alice Morrow who said rather startling things in the bedroom and made surprising suggestions with wide-eyed clarity in the heat of their encounters, things she had sometimes followed through on.

She brought her head back up and looked toward the door and the waitress. He noticed that her foot was tapping underneath the table and wondered how he could get her to say more.

"So, Andrew Eakins is your guy for now. He's the main suspect, one way or the other."

"So it seems, though Elizabeth Goode hasn't been gone for a full two days. There is no evidence of a crime yet. But, well, something is wrong here."

Mercer nodded. "*I'm here to report a murder,*" the woman at his door had said. "*He is going to kill her. I guarantee it.*"

"What do you know about Eakins?" he asked.

She gave him a blank look.

"I guess you aren't telling me that either."

"I've told you more than enough already. It's not like we can arrest him. There is nothing to charge him with at this point."

"But you've thoroughly questioned him."

She gave him another look.

They ate the rest of their meal in near silence. That was something he told himself he had to get used to if he was going to be with Alice. She wasn't a big chatter. You could even say she was secretive. It wasn't only her profession that she had kept from him. He knew very little about her, period. Mercer often found their silences uncomfortable, but today his brain was racing, turning over the details in his mind. He wondered too, if the café in question was one he had been to downtown — it fit the description.

He wanted to ask her if she knew anything about a thirtysomething local who matched the description of his visitor. In fact, he wanted to ask if this woman might have been one of the witnesses who had seen Eakins on the street outside the café. Or whether this woman might have been anywhere near the café that day. But he didn't. Alice wasn't revealing any more details, and he would have to explain why he was asking these particular questions. It would seem insane, anyway.

Alice finally spoke again once they were back on the street.

"I noticed you reacted when I mentioned Elizabeth Goode's name." Alice didn't look at him when she said this.

"Reacted?"

"Yeah, just a little. Do you know her?"

"No."

It was the truth, as far as he knew.

5

First Attempt

SHE DID NOT offer to kiss, even touch him, as they approached the police station and kept glancing around as if worried that someone might see them. She had maintained a good three feet between them as they walked, just as she had when they went to the restaurant. He had wondered then if keeping her distance had something to do with not wanting her colleagues to know they were together, but the other officers were now nowhere in sight.

He had noticed that almost everyone around here had an evasive way about them — the grocery clerks, the gas station cashiers, passersby on the street. Few ever said hello. They were polite as hell, ridiculously so, held doors for you even if you were twenty strides behind them, but they didn't offer friendliness outright. It seemed like nearly every individual he met would give you the shirt off his or her back, but they always appeared to be putting you off, as if they didn't trust you or had something better to do than interact. Could they sense he was a foreigner? Maybe.

"What time were you supposed to be back at your desk?" he asked Alice.

"Sorry?"

"That was a fairly long lunch. Is your chief of police lenient about your hours?"

She laughed and didn't say anything.

"Is he?"

"Why do you assume it's a he?"

"Is she?"

"He. Chief Smith. He's not likely to have even noticed I was gone. He's rather, shall I say, old, and hands-off." They reached the station. "Later," said Alice, and climbed the concrete steps to the station's front doors without looking back.

Mercer realized that all of their conversation had been instigated by him — she had simply responded to his questions. The only word that had escaped her was when he had slipped, for a second time, and almost tumbled to the sidewalk. She had seized him by the elbow in a grip that actually hurt, a moment that reminded him of how she clutched him in bed. "Whoops," she said, smiling, and quickly released him.

He glanced at her as she went up the steps now, in her short police parka and loose black pants. With her mitted hand on the cold steel door handle, but barely turning toward him, she spoke again, almost as if to herself. "Funny thing, we've had a number of disappearances around here. Probably our most common sort of serious case."

He looked up at her "Really? So disappearances, as in lost and then found?"

"Mostly just lost."

He shivered. "Maybe people have good reason to want to get away, change their lives."

"Or maybe they are being brutalized in a basement somewhere." Then she was gone, and the door swung shut.

Mercer stood looking after her for a moment before turning

toward his car. "*You knew,*" he heard the woman at his farmhouse door say. "*You knew.*"

Half a dozen steps away from the station, he slipped once more, and this time fell flat on his ass. He somehow kept his head up but burned his hands on the salt. There was salt everywhere you walked or drove here. A couple crossing the Circle rushed over and helped him get to his feet.

"Are you all right?" asked the man.

"That was quite a tumble," said the woman.

Mercer tried to respond with a quick pat of thanks on the man's shoulder, but the two of them immediately shrank back and looked him up and down as if worried about damage to his wonderful Burberry coat.

"I'm fine. Thank you," Mercer said, knocking the grit from the coat.

"Not at all," he heard them say in chorus.

He glanced up to smile at them, but they were already several strides away, waving at him with the backs of their upturned hands, moving quickly along the Circle, as if fleeing from him. It was more than a little creepy.

"He needs a good pair of insulated rubber-soled boots," he heard the man say.

MERCER DROVE OUT of town thinking about the woman who had come to his house. He relived that scene in detail, recalling the woman's car, her face, the tone of her voice. Both that visit and the bizarre nature of the apparent crime that followed did not seem real.

He had to remind himself why he had come here — to get away.

There was a deadness to the town's streets, just as white and grey as on his farm. The roads were walled by snowbanks. Even the Christmas lights didn't brighten things up. He passed by the requisite fast-food restaurants as he hit the outskirts.

Once out of town, he tried to imagine how the rolling countryside, dotted with farms and fields, might be beautiful in the spring, and perhaps even more so in what the locals told him were "actually" hot summers. Now though, it was endlessly monochromatic, broken by blocks of dark coniferous trees.

It took about fifteen minutes to get to his place. His days of fast driving were done. A speeding ticket was the last thing he wanted. He slowed even more as he passed through a little village, careful on the hills, remembering how he used to race up and down every undulation when joyriding on dates with Christine, loving the butterflies that teased their stomachs, thrilled by her giggles and the way she looked at him.

He turned left past the village and climbed the hill from which he would be able to see his farm, thinking that he should just look into the identity of the woman in the Toyota on his own. The houses along this stretch of road were as old as his place, mostly wooden frame structures painted white or a pale shade of something. He imagined the woman driving along here, the sun not yet fully up in the colourless morning sky. Who was she? How could she have known? He turned onto the long, frozen sideroad that led to his lane and farmhouse.

"Why did she come to tell *me*, of all people?"

The terrain here made him think of *In Cold Blood* — the book, not the movie. Books, to him, did so much more to unleash your imagination. It was all in your mind. In *In Cold Blood,* two murderers do their gruesome deeds at a farmhouse in the countryside where neighbours were too far away to hear the victims scream. It was the scariest thing he had ever read. It also made him think of Springsteen's *Nebraska,* both the album cover and the song, and especially that haunting harmonica. He no longer sang within anyone's earshot — Christine and the kids claimed he was tone deaf and always got the lyrics wrong. *Nebraska.* He tried to remember those words: something about the narrator going for a ride, and innocent people dying, a shotgun in hand and a meanness in humanity. This sideroad looked bleaker than Springsteen's mind, but then The Boss wasn't raised here.

Maybe I should get a dog. A big one. Rottweiler, male.

He stopped by the mailbox at the top of the lane. It was tin with a little red flag. The post had sunk a good two feet he figured, since now you had to reach down to open it when you stuck your hand out the car window. It creaked too. There was never much in it other than flyers and the odd letter for the old owners. They had passed away, just phantoms in the house now. Their kids, nearly retirement age themselves, were going to eventually sell the farm.

Mercer didn't get much email either. He had not told anyone exactly where he was living, none of his buddies, and not Christine either. He sent her the odd text to let her know that the father of her children was still alive; that was it. She didn't seem to care; her replies expressed no concern. She had wanted him to go. He rarely texted his kids. He just couldn't find the right things to say.

He looked down toward the house, sitting to the left at the bottom of the lane, set off by a huge leafless birch, a few apple trees, and a giant spruce, surreal and blue. A good American quarterback could throw a football from here to the house.

"Do you care about how men treat women, Mr. Mercer?" he heard the woman say.

By the time he was through the entrance and the screen door (still on somehow in the winter) had slammed behind him, he had remembered the letters and numbers on the blue and white plates on the mid-sized Toyota. He pulled off his coat and hung it in the closet just inside the door, then walked into the big kitchen and turned down the hallway past the staircase, heading south.

His footsteps reverberated in the hollow house. There was almost no furniture on either floor, other than one nearly empty bookcase in the living room containing a *Complete Shakespeare* he had perused a few times, a table and two chairs in the kitchen, and the bed, of course, in his room upstairs.

"Well, at least you have a stove and fridge," Alice had managed to say that first time she was here. "What's upstairs?"

Mercer slid down onto the smelly rug in the sunroom and dialed a number in New York.

"First Precinct, Manhattan. Sergeant Jackson speaking. May I help you." The woman's hard New York accent made his heart soar for an instant. She didn't answer the phone with a question. It was a demand.

"Lauryn?"

There was a long pause.

"Hugh Mercer."

"I need something."

"What a surprise."

"I'm looking for the name of the owner of a blue Toyota Corolla, I'd say somewhere between 2014 and 2016, licence plate TLCC 665."

There was another long pause.

"That's it? No *how are you doing, Lauri? It's nice to hear your voice?* None of that?"

There was a short pause.

"Just trying to keep it impersonal."

She lowered her voice. "Listen, Hugh, I went into what went on between us with my eyes open, and I understood why it couldn't continue, but that doesn't mean it didn't happen. If you are going to call me, you could at least pretend I'm a friend."

"You are a friend."

"So, start over."

Short pause.

"Hi, Lauri. How are you?"

She sighed. "I'm well and it's nice to hear from you. Where are you? Are you working privately? People around here think you've gone AWOL for life, or died, or something. Did something happen I should —"

"Away. In another country, actually. North. You can tell by the licence plate number. Four letters, not three. Christine kind of asked me to leave."

"Was it us?" She sounded worried for an instant. "Hugh, did you tell her?"

"No, she doesn't know. It was mostly a ... well, something we shouldn't have done, don't you agree?"

"Sort of, yeah. It was nice though."

"I'd never done anything like that before."

"Me neither."

"Do you mind running the plates for me?"

"Not really up on out of country, not my area, but yeah, I'll do it."

"Call me back when you have it."

"I'll text you."

She hung up the second she said that last word. She was a tough woman, up front, even for a New York cop. Maybe that was why he had let it happen. He had needed someone who was no-nonsense. She had played elite-level sports in college, and it showed in her attitude. He wanted something and so did she and they just did it.

He lay down on the rug for a while and waited, the brief bit of sun glowing through a hole in a cloud and the beam shining through the window passing over him for a moment. He fell asleep and woke up an hour later to find his cellphone still in his hand but no messages.

It's a dumb idea, anyway, he told himself. *Stay out of this.* He groaned as he got to his feet. It seemed like he did that all the time now — getting up, sitting down, lugging his sorry carcass anywhere, he always groaned. *You're here to get away from stuff like this, for God's sake. To get better.* He staggered down the hallway, his legs slightly numb, made his way upstairs to fetch his laptop, and came back down to the kitchen. He plugged it in and sat at the table.

Journal.

The first page was headlined "Hugh Mercer." He had written a lot of crap about how he had become obsessed with his job, how he was unable to forget the worst cases, and he had tried to write something recently about how often he had neglected his wife and kids, and what he could do to rectify it. *Christine, Keith, Stevie.* He had written their names out in bold letters to emphasize their importance. He had even mentioned Alice and some of what was going on between them and had actually wondered, in a brief entry, if she could be some sort of answer for him.

He had not yet committed to a word about his secret, and knew he had to write about it. It was just too painful though, this memory of beating that young man. Then asking his partner to lie about it. He had lost control of himself for an instant. Anyone can do that. But Mercer knew that his whole life was about catching the bad guys, about serving justice. Was any of that just? Was his home life just? Was *he* a bad guy?

He wasn't writing this down.

His phone vibrated on the table.

It's a rental said her text. *Hassan's Hertz. I'm guessing you know the town. Wow, are you ever in the sticks.*

He searched "Hassan's," found it on the outskirts, not far from the fast-food restaurants he had passed just a couple of hours before and headed for the closet.

"What am I doing?" He put the coat back.

He sat at the kitchen table with his laptop for several hours, unable to write anything of real importance about his situation. He knew he should root things out, delve into his childhood, his single-parent upbringing in poverty after his father lost his job at the bottle works in their little Virginia town for stealing a couple of cases of Coca-Cola. Accused and fired because of a miscount, not because he was actually guilty. His father's suicide. Little Hughie Mercer's vow to insist on justice in everything, to make it his life's work. His doubt now that policing had anything to do with justice. Instead, he made lists of facts about the people who were close to him, or were supposed to be. He wrote of how he admired Christine for the sacrifices she made to raise their kids, for going to law school after, and now for working to help people as a pro bono lawyer. Both their daughter and son intended to become lawyers too, of her sort. When Keith was little, he had loved to dress up as "Hugh Mercer, Detective," but that sort of admiration was long gone.

Mercer got to his feet, fried up a couple of sausages, ate them while falling down a rabbit hole or two on the internet, then caught some of the livestream of a New York Knicks game and went to bed.

IN THE MORNING, he drove to Hassan's Hertz before he even had breakfast. The man who greeted him was likely Hassan himself as he was the only person in the little trailer office and had the air of someone in charge. There were just four cars on the lot, at least visible ones, none of them the Toyota.

"How is it going?" asked Hassan, shivering in his sweater, his arms crossed in front of his chest as the blast of cold air from the quick opening and closing of the door filled the space. The smile on his face looked a little forced.

"Not bad."

"Cold enough for you? It'll be over before you know it."

"Yeah, definitely cold enough, and I hope you're right."

"Looking for a car? We have a very nice selection remaining."

"Sort of."

"Not sure I'm following you, sir."

"I wanted to inquire about one, first."

"Well, aren't you cautious."

"Let me cut to the chase. I'm inquiring about a car you lease, a pale blue Toyota Corolla, licence plate TLCC 665."

Hassan looked at him for a moment. "You know the licence plate?"

"Yeah. Because I like the car so much. Noticed it on your lot the other day. I'd like to rent it."

"This is a bit irregular."

These people were unbelievable.

"Why would you care, sir, if I may say so. I want to rent the car. I will pay you."

Money talks in America and Mercer was betting it would here too.

"That is all fine and very good, sir, but the vehicle is not here. It is out. I have never had a customer know the licence plate number before the actual rental of the product." He narrowed his eyes at his prospective customer.

"How long?" asked Mercer.

"How long what?"

"How long until the car is back?"

"I am not sure. I can check, but there are other lovely vehicles on the lot. I can give you a discount."

"I don't want a discount. I want that car."

"I see." Hassan did not make a move to check for the return date on his computer.

"Look, I'll be honest with you: I want to know who rented it."

"Why?"

"I will pay you one hundred dollars simply for the information. American dollars." Mercer's face was getting a little red.

Hassan just looked at him.

"I am a police officer."

"May I see your identification, then, please?"

Mercer, of course, did not have a badge. He had turned it in the day he left.

"I must see some ID."

Mercer reached into his pocket and took out his wallet. "I am an American police officer, New York PD, Homicide Squad, and this is important. Here's who I am." He pulled his driver's licence out of the wallet and slapped it on the table.

"Mr. Hugh Mercer, but it doesn't say —"

"Oh, for God's sake, call the police station here, ask them about me, ask for Sergeant Morrow."

"Alice?"

"Yes, Alice! Look, here's my union card!" He slapped it on the counter too. Hassan looked down at it.

"I am afraid that is not sufficient, sir. We have strict laws in this country, what we call the rule of law. I am sorry."

Mercer could read between the lines of what Hassan had just said. They didn't have the sort of freedom here that citizens had back home. It was much slower to get anything done. Lots of red tape. He had left his guns in America and hadn't bothered to get one when he came here. He'd been told it would take forever. He'd imagined that buying a house around here would be a long process as well. It was as if they weren't interested in your business, like they weren't enamoured of the idea of getting things done, and money out of and into pockets in a timely way.

"I will call Ms. Morrow for you, sir."

Hassan went into the back room and made the call. Mercer could hear him whispering. After about a minute of that, he came back out.

"She is not there."

"Not there? What about, uh, Constable Haddad or ... or Ferguson? Chief Smith, for God's sake. Surely he's around."

"There was only one lady on duty."

"One lady? This town must have five or six thousand people! They have one person on reception at the police station and that's it?" His voice was rising.

"Nearly seven thousand, actually, sir, and I believe there was more than one person at the station, but she called out your name, I could hear her, sir, and there was no recognition. She took a message."

"Oh, for fuck's sake!"

"Sir, that is not the best language."

Mercer whirled and pulled open the door, vaguely aware that in his anger and impetuousness, *so fucking American*, he had made the mistake of letting this man call the station, possibly informing them, informing Alice, that he was searching for a car with a specific licence plate. He left the door wide open so Hassan could enjoy the weather — the weather he said would be over before you knew it — and stomped to his car. Glancing up as he started the engine, he could see Hassan at the door looking out at him, at *his* car's licence plate, his mouth moving as if he were repeating the numbers. Then Hassan turned and shut the trailer door behind him.

6

Best Intentions

BEFORE MERCER WAS halfway home, his cellphone buzzed on the seat of his car.

"You are a fugitive from the law, Hugh Mercer. Turn the vehicle around and turn yourself in, my office, back of the shop, just the two of us."

"Alice. Hi."

"Do you have both hands on the steering wheel, Detective Mercer? Illegal here to talk and drive."

"Got the phone on speaker."

"That's illegal too, but I'll overlook it."

"That Hassan guy is an idiot."

"A nice man, actually, just doing his job."

"His job?"

"Whereas you weren't. Correct me if I am wrong, but I do not believe you are licenced to ask about licences here. Why do you need to know who rented that car?"

"It's a long story."

"I'm all ears."

He was not sure how much he should reveal, even now. It would look very bad that he had held something back. *To hell with it*, he thought.

"Look, come out for dinner tonight. I'll make something, get some wine. I'll explain why, in detail."

"Should I be afraid, alone with a fugitive from the law? A big strong man capable of who knows what?"

"Maybe."

"Sounds good to me. I'll see you at six."

MERCER WAS NOT a chef, to say the least. At home, his agreement with Christine had been that she would cook, and he would do the dishes. That had worked out well for the first few years while the romance was still in bloom, but soon it seemed to wear on them, or at least on Christine. She claimed that he did not keep up his part of the bargain and it was likely true, since there were many nights, when he was home that is, that he did not complete his chores. She noticed. Every time.

He could operate a barbeque though, and there happened to be an old one still functional at the farmhouse. He picked up some ribs and some sauce on the way home, a prepared salad, and some instant rice. He bought some flowers too, a small bouquet of red and pink, and set them on the table in a jug found in the kitchen cupboards. Then, he hooked up his little speaker to his laptop and put on some Aretha and Marvin Gaye — the music soothing him as it floated through the old house — and went to work, freezing his ass off as he rushed in and out of the house to check on the meat.

How could that woman have known what was going to happen? he asked himself again. *Why, in God's name did she contact me? How the hell will I put this to Alice?*

Sergeant Morrow arrived at about twenty-five minutes after

six. People never seemed to be on time around here, which was especially strange given that there appeared to be so little to do. She was still dressed in her police coat and uniform. She kept the parka's hood up even after stepping in the door, as if to keep a distance between her and her host. There was an awkward moment when he took the coat from her instead of allowing her to hang it up in the closet. The black jacket over the pale-blue shirt and tie did not exactly flatter her. As usual, she didn't appear to care. Her hair was tied back in a sloppy ponytail. She did a clumsy little sway of her hips to the music and blushed when he kissed her on the cheek. He never did that. She reached up to embrace him but then withdrew her arms quickly.

He felt as if he had made a mistake from the second Alice entered the house. It always gnawed at him when he committed a tactical error. Detectives are taught not to show their hand, not give out one ounce more of information than necessary. Only colleagues got the inside dope. Was Alice a colleague? It did not seem like it. She was an evasive woman who slept with him. That was it. And a police officer from whom he had kept vital information. He had asked her out here in a moment of need and curiosity, and now had to tell her everything. Or did he?

"So, tell me about what it was like growing up here," he said as they sat down to eat. "You've never said a word about your childhood."

"My childhood?" asked Alice. The warm expression on her face evaporated and for a second she looked almost frightened. "There's not much to tell." She paused, took a rib in her chapped hands and ravaged it. "Mmm. That's good."

"It's just that you never —"

"That's not why I'm here, is it?"

No, he thought, *you are here to get some information out of me and then take me upstairs.*

Alice reached for another rib. "The rental? The licence plate inquiry?"

"Oh, yeah."

"Yeah."

"Well," he realized he hadn't started eating. "It was a favour. Someone needed to know about that car."

"A favour?"

"Yeah."

"Where did the request come from? Here or from stateside?"

"Uh, from the NYPD."

Alice looked up as she reached for her third rib.

"Truly?"

"Absolutely."

Alice Morrow and Hugh Mercer were trained to spot lies.

"Why did the NYPD need that information?"

"Don't know, someone there just asked me."

"About a rented car in a little town up here?"

He shrugged his shoulders.

"So, back home, they know you're here?"

"One person on the force."

"How about your wife?"

She had never asked about his wife before, in fact she had never asked him many personal questions, period. Now though, she was grilling him as a professional police officer. He thought he detected a slight smile.

"Yeah, she knows I'm up here, somewhere around here."

"So there is one, a wife." She glanced at his naked ring finger. "I thought it looked a little pale below the knuckle." She laughed and bit into another rib. The sauce ran down her chin.

"I'll get that," he said and leaned forward with his napkin and gently wiped her face, his hand touching her lips. Her eyes were really quite beautiful up close, a different sort of grey. There was usually a kind of blankness in them, but as he touched her, they began to light up.

"Maybe we don't need to eat all of this." She reached up and gripped his hand as he was about to pull it back. "Not just yet." Her face flushed a little. He realized that she had not asked him if he had kids.

She led him upstairs slowly without ever looking at him.

"WE'VE ARRESTED ANDREW Eakins," she said breathlessly as they began to disrobe. "Obstruction of justice, that's all we could think of, settled on that because the testimonies of the café owner and street witnesses indicate that he was lying, so he's likely lying to us." They were down to their underwear. "Elizabeth has been gone for three days, so we had to do something. It's weird though, we can't find much about Eakins, his website doesn't even have a bio, there is only basic stuff about his work online, and he keeps refusing to tell us anything about himself, or even defend himself."

"So, what's next?"

She didn't answer.

"I'VE GOT TO go," she said afterward, kissing him just once and quickly and rolling out of bed. "I need to get some sleep. Got to be on top of my game right now."

"You could sleep here." He didn't really want her to, but he thought he should ask.

"I do that better at home. You're a distraction."

She was already sliding into her clothes. She always dressed in the dark, even after they did it with the lights on. She would either put on her things while he was asleep or after turning off the lights. He wondered why.

Within seconds, she was transformed, big black pants buckled, blue shirt tucked in, tie a bit askew. She flicked on the lights and looked back at him, still lying naked on the bed. For a second, her eyes roamed over him, all six foot two of him. It made him realize that they still hadn't finished their dinner.

"Bye," she said and flicked the switch off again.

He caught a glimpse of a bit of flesh where she missed a button on her shirt. The reflection in her eyes from the quick glare made her look almost evil.

7

Victim in the House

MERCER LAY THERE in his bed listening to Alice walk down the stairs, open the door and close it, move in that near-silent way through the snow, start her car, and head up the lane and down the sideroad. Headlights briefly cut across his window and his body and then pointed away. Dinner had been abandoned on the table. There was still music playing downstairs. He had set it on a shuffle of soul classics and then his favourites. *Nebraska* had played while they made love. Now, it was Neil Young. It had been pointed out to him that the singer was not an American, but came from up here somewhere. That was hard to believe. Or maybe not. "Helpless" played through the house now, that ethereal voice flowing up the stairs toward him, somehow seeming to increase in volume. It told of a northern place, a place of shadows and changes and somehow, comfort, big birds flying across what always seemed to Mercer to be cold and cloudy skies. He lay there in the same position he had been in when she departed, where she had left him after rolling off, almost as if she had smacked her hands together with accomplishment and satiation. He thought of her on top of him, looking down at him, an expression on her face akin to anger, as if she was taking back something that was hers. As he thought of her standing at the door of the bedroom, her features changed from Alice Morrow's to another woman's: the one who had come to his door. The anger in that face was undeniable. "*It will be on your conscience after it happens*," he heard her say. He thought of Alice's comment about people disappearing, brutalized in basements.

She's been gone for three days.

WHEN HE WOKE in the morning, he felt frustrated. He felt guilty too for still not having told Alice what he knew. He fried himself some bacon, ate a pickled egg with it, and drank some strong coffee. At home, he liked to read, but here he'd been doing very little, just passages from what made up his entire northern library — *The Complete Shakespeare* on the nearly empty bookshelf.

Instead, he texted Christine, then Keith, then Stevie. He simply told his wife that he was okay and hoped that she was too. Her response was quick: *I'm fine, glad you are. This is for the best.*

He did not know what to say to the kids. Finally, he typed the same thing to both of them: *I'm away for a while. How are you doing? Miss you. Love, Dad.*

He had been a good father at the beginning, spent time with the kids, reading them stories most nights, creating voices for each character and making the two of them laugh. He had been a good husband too, attentive, leaving Christine notes expressing his love where he knew she would come upon them. It had faded though, as time went by. Everything fades; everything goes from colour to grey.

When he had assaulted the suspect in the summer and came home with blood still on his knuckles, some stained on his wedding ring, he felt as though Christine and his children somehow knew. Police brutality was a subject Keith and Stevie had taken to discussing lately. Things seemed to descend even faster at home after that. He withdrew more, to work and to his home office. That was when Christine began to speak of them "taking a break."

He waited for an answer from Keith or Stevie. Nothing came.

Other thoughts were quickly swirling through his mind anyway: of Andrew Eakins and Elizabeth Goode, whose faces he imagined, the two of them entering that café. *Did they really come in together? Was she dead now, or worse? Did Eakins kill her? What a strange way to do it. What's his game?* And Alice knew something about it that she wasn't revealing. He was sure.

He paced around the house for much of the rest of the morning, wishing he could go outside. In New York, when mulling over a difficult investigation, he had often taken to the streets to think, and it had helped, but it was too bloody cold here, too bloody depressing outside. New York had been cold enough after Virginia. He wondered how the people here stood it.

The floorboards creaked and sighed as he moved from room to room. Perhaps he knew more about this crime than he realized. That was often true in a case — you could find leads, directions to take in an investigation, in the most minute and pedestrian of details, in apparently innocent things that people said. He considered his visitor again, what she said and the way she said it. "*Men treat women badly.*" That stuck out. She had stood there in his big country kitchen peering out from those wire-rimmed glasses, adamant that Andrew Eakins was about to kill his wife, make her vanish. How could she *know* that?

"What else did she say?" he asked himself.

Andrew Eakins and Elizabeth Goode lived "*not far from here ... just across the field.*"

He looked out the window. "What does that mean, exactly? Real close?" To the west of the house, the land, bare of any trees, rose gently to an old, unused lane, and then it rose slightly again on the other side. That field belonged to a neighbour and Mercer had often stared out at the dark roof of a house and the top of a barn visible on the rise

Alice had questioned his reaction to Elizabeth Goode's name: "Do you know her?"

Then it came to him. He had had another visitor, though just briefly. A woman too. From the farm to the west. It was the second or third week he was here, the first truly frigid day. She had appeared at his door out of thin air, rosy cheeked and friendly in that way they have here. She had walked across the fields and the knock on the door had startled him. Had she been Charlie Stark-weather at Caril Ann Fugate's door in Nebraska or Perry Smith or Dick Hickock in Kansas, shotgun in hand, she could have taken him without resistance. People didn't kill that way around here though, it seemed.

"I'm Libby," she had said. "I live just up the hill."

"Hugh Mercer." They shook hands.

A pretty woman, he had thought, though stiff from the cold, her red face peering out from the fur in the hood of her parka. Her hand, though it had surely been kept deep in a pocket, was frigid.

"I just wanted to quickly introduce myself. And hopefully warm up just a tad, before I walk back."

"Sure," he had said, "of course. Would you like some coffee?"

"Thank you, but no." She paused. "You Americans are always so friendly, no beating around the bush."

"Oh?" he said. She knew he wasn't from here.

"I lived in the States for a while." She did not elaborate. "May I come in?"

It had seemed to him that she was already in. "Yes, of course. May I take your coat?"

"That's okay, won't stay long, as I said." She pulled down

the hood and a toss of amber brown hair, almost red, came tumbling out. She seemed quite a bit younger than him, over a decade, maybe fifteen years. She was well-spoken, obviously intelligent. As she walked across the room, she pulled off the coat, revealing a sweater and expensive-looking jeans, put the coat over the back of a chair, and sat down. He wondered a bit about a woman, alone, seeking out a strange man in his house and seeming to think nothing of it. *It would have made more sense*, he thought, *if she had simply stayed at the door*. She had long lashes, and was wearing makeup — dark eye shadow, bright red lipstick — which made him think she had readied herself to make this visit.

"I have a husband, but I keep him indoors," she said out of the blue. That struck him as an unusual way to talk about a partner, even if joking. It almost made the husband sound dangerous. Why had she even brought him up?

"Is he not friendly?"

She didn't answer right away. "He's friendly enough," she finally said, "he's just being smart, in this weather, you know." Her voice had quavered just a little when she spoke.

"Most women live in fear of their male partners, in one way or another. But for this woman, it's extreme: she's in grave danger."

"Right. Stay out of the cold whenever possible. Smart man."

The rest of their conversation had been small talk, perhaps why he had almost completely forgotten about it, even though she had stayed longer than he expected. She had put her hand on his arm more than once. She liked men, a lot. Men can tell that, if they look for it. Mercer always did. She had known he was an American, perhaps even known what he did for a living down there. Word got around here, indeed.

Mercer got up and paced again. He remembered the woman's eyes. There was something about them that he could not place — black-brown and switched on as they were. It could very well have been fear. Whatever it was, she was hiding something. She had not mentioned her husband by name, nor had she ever said her own full name.

"But her name was Libby, not Elizabeth."

He wondered though, if those two names were the same.

8

Pursuit

MERCER NEVER USED to nap, but he had been trying to do it in this house. He needed to shut himself down from time to time, and right now he had to get away from this case, about which he seemed to be making things up. So, he went upstairs and lay down. But he couldn't relax. Everything seemed so calm on the surface around here, the way he needed life to be, but wasn't really calm at all — from Alice to Libby to Elizabeth to Andrew to the crime itself and every bloody person he met.

He turned over and found himself back on that street in the Bronx.

The murder had been a particularly awful one. The victim, who had been Stevie's age, had been found brutalized in her apartment. Mercer and his partner had been asked to help and staked out the place, then caught a young man who appeared to be snooping around the building. When Mercer accosted him, the man pleaded his innocence and they had no reason to detain him, but he tried to get away, lashed out with a fist, and Mercer exploded. He threw the young man to the pavement and began to beat him. Then he pulled out his gun, struck him, held it to the suspect's bloodied face and a desire to pull the trigger came over him. Only at the last moment did he stop. He got off, let the man go, and dissolved into tears, pleading with his partner to keep quiet about his conduct. There was no police inquiry into what he had done. A different man was later found to be the killer.

Mercer tossed on the bed. It wasn't a dream. It was real. Images of Elizabeth Goode came to him, chained in a basement, a gun at her head as well. He thought of his victim screaming and he heard Elizabeth scream too.

Mercer sat, sweating. He calmed his heartbeat, got up after another five minutes, showered, and got himself dressed — Burberry coat on, again making his shoulders wide — and combed his hair.

He drove into town with a plan. He was involved in this case whether he liked it or not, and he needed to get to the bottom of it. There had to be justice. *There had to be. He had to put things right this time.*

The Shelter Café was half full. Mercer had definitely been here before. He sipped his pumpkin latte and took small bites of banana bread, casing the place, and keeping his eye on Jonathan Li too. He checked for avenues of egress. There indeed was only one exit in sight: the front door, large and latticed, with a bell attached that rang when it was opened. That feature was in every little establishment in this town, it seemed. He imagined the unseen exit past the counter, through the door, at the far end of the little kitchen. He had positioned himself at a table in the centre of the room, where Eakins had sat, to observe what he could see past Li's head and shoulders as the man moved about preparing coffee. The half door in the counter was narrow, perhaps even latched from the inside. It might be a challenge to get through quickly — and maybe require help. He could see the table near the window where the ghost couple may have sat.

The café struck him as an anomaly in this town, a little fancy and big city. The few other early afternoon customers were what passed for somewhat hip around here — younger people mostly, focused on their cellphones, dressed in black leggings or college sweatshirts or designer hoodies. Everyone seemed to keep to themselves, occasionally glancing up at others. Conversations were quiet, so personal and hushed that it had the appearance of gossip. Was it possible that something could happen in here — something quick and criminal — and not be noticed? Li, a tall young man dressed in black pants and a black sweater, was the only person working, which seemed a little strange at this hour. The café likely had been closed for a few days after Elizabeth Goode's disappearance for the police to thoroughly comb things over. This may have been its first day back in business.

Mercer spent a good hour in the café and never once received any indication from Li that he wanted him to move along. Mercer had paid when he ordered, which appeared to be the way to do things, and had added a large tip, a gesture that seemed particularly to please Li. But other than that brief encounter, the owner barely seemed to be aware that he was there until he rose from the table.

"Anything else for you, today, sir?" Li asked as Mercer pulled on his coat. The comment struck Mercer as a little needy especially since he was obviously ready to leave.

"No, that was great."

"Thank you."

"You are a one-man show today?"

"Uh, yeah, Fatima got off at noon and Colleen doesn't start for another half hour. I am hiring now though. Do you want a job?"

Mercer was never sure about the sense of humour around here. It could be sarcastic, said with a straight face, even sardonic. Usually in a monotone. There often seemed to be more than one meaning to the things they said. This seemed to be a joke though, and Mercer smiled.

"Things getting back to normal?"

The smile left Li's face, but he recovered quickly. "All is good," he said. "I hope they find that woman." It seemed like a strange way to refer to Elizabeth Goode, since Alice had said that Li knew her. "Hope you are enjoying the weather," Li added, the smile fully back on his face. The day was so cold that the café's windows were frosted.

That was definitely a joke. "Absolutely," Mercer said. "Thank you."

"Have a good day." Li had unusually dark circles under his eyes for a young man. "Good to see you again."

Good memory, thought Mercer. The bell tinkled as he opened the door and stepped out into the cold.

It was just past four. He was ready for mission number two. Alice's work hours were regular, so different from what he had been used to. She left for home and then work early in the morning from his house, she had been going out for a noon-hour lunch when he intercepted her the other day, and whenever she dropped by his place, it tended to be around five.

Mercer strolled by the police station and checked the small parking lot that wrapped around to the back of the building to confirm that her car, a well-used little red Honda, was there. Then he walked to his own vehicle, parked across the Circle. He could see every car that came out of the lot. Mercer had learned to have patience on stakeouts. He was willing to wait this one out. Sergeant Alice Morrow was watching him now, in her own way, he was sure of it. He needed to know more about her, and this case, and you could learn a great deal by observing.

Alice came out of the police station with Constable Haddad at four-thirty sharp, looking frumpy in her police overcoat and big hard boots, trudging down the three concrete steps and waving goodbye in the parking lot. It was fascinating to observe her. Mercer wondered for a moment if it was maybe a good idea for everyone to watch their romantic interests for a while, completely undetected.

Following her was going to be tricky. There were so few cars in town that it would be difficult to stay unobserved behind her. He would simply have to follow at a greater distance than usual.

She was in her own car, so she was obviously going home. She pulled up to the Circle and turned right. He waited for a count of twenty and then pursued. Luckily, another car had turned out of a side street and slipped between them. She turned right again, onto King Street East.

She headed east along that main street for maybe half a mile, the car between them still in position, before turning left. He drove past, did a U-turn, then got onto her street, spotting her car turning into a driveway a good dozen houses and an elementary school up from the corner. The snowbanks were even higher in this neighbourhood. The houses were older, not very big. Hers was a little different, set back from the road, white stucco with green trim, two stories high with green gables. He stopped a few houses away, waited for a few minutes to give her time to get into her house, and then drove up to a spot directly across the street. He was surprised to see that there was another car in the driveway, an older model Honda, this one grey. It was already getting dark. He noticed that all the lights were on in the house, even in the upper storey. There was no way she'd had time to go through the house yet.

"What's going on?" he said aloud, inspecting the exterior of the building. "Does she have a partner? A husband? Another lover?" Three bedrooms, all lights on. "Children?"

There was a tap on the window. He started and turned with a jerk.

Alice. She made the "lower your window" motion. He complied.

"Can I help you?"

"What's going on?" It was all he could think of.

"You, Detective Mercer, are stalking me. That's what's going on." She did not look pleased.

"No," he blurted out. He tried a smile. "Just thought I'd come in through your window and surprise you."

"Fuck surprising me, sir. Explain, please."

He had had enough of her. He was going to be blunt. "Okay. I think you're carrying on an affair with me behind your husband or partner's back. You've been deceiving me too." He nodded toward the house with the two cars and the lights all on. "I don't appreciate being made a fool of."

She started to laugh.

"What's so funny?"

She leaned down into the window frame and brought her face up within a foot of his. "My husband, Detective Mercer?"

"Yeah. You have some explaining to do."

"I don't explain. Not to you or any man."

There was an edge to her voice that he had never heard before.

"Alice May?" cried a voice from the porch of her house.

As he and Alice turned to look, Mercer could see someone clearly through his open window. A woman he estimated to be in her seventies, lean and short, was standing outside the front door in the freezing cold in just a dress and a light sweater. Her arms weren't even crossed against the weather.

"Supper's on," the woman added. "Who have you got out there? Invite them in if they want to come, but get your butt in here before it's all gone cold. You know your father won't abide that."

"Your parents?" said Mercer, his mouth open.

"Yeah. Mom and Dad. I guess you're a dinner guest. Come on."

AS WE FORGIVE OTHERS | 61

Why was Alice coming here right after work, still in uniform? Why not slip home first to change clothes. Unless ...

"You live here?"

"Yeah."

She let him walk ahead of her as they went up the driveway and around to the back door, either to keep him from bolting or to save him if he fell on the ice. When they reached the door, she stepped in front of him.

"Act normal, be nice. You're good at that, being an American and all. But when we're done, you are going to answer some questions. Lots of them." She opened the door. "Smile."

9

Interrogation

DINNER WAS DELIGHTFUL as were her parents. There were no surprises: peas, corn, potatoes, and ham, some sort of mild spice cake with lots of white icing on it for dessert. Doreen and Ralph Morrow seemed to be politely interested in everything he said but when their inquiries about his home life met with short, evasive answers, they didn't probe. They didn't ask what had brought him north of the border. They didn't say much about themselves either. He gleaned that they had both been schoolteachers and taught locally, but what grades they instructed or even how they felt about their profession was never offered. They seemed intrigued by the fact that he was from New York and had worked for the police department there, Ralph even letting out a low whistle when that was revealed. They did not ask about their daughter's relationship with him.

"Well, I am quite aware that we do not have the excitement in these parts you do in New York City, but our Alice has had a few cases of slight interest," said Doreen. "I am guessing she has told you about some?"

It was said so lightly, so innocently; so cleverly done.

"Yes."

"A recent one. Most curious," added Ralph.

"Did you know the alleged victim?" asked Mercer.

"No, they don't," said Alice quickly.

Doreen leaned toward Mercer. "She doesn't like to bring her work home." She said it as if it were something to keep between them.

"We all know a little about this man who appears to have done the deed," said Ralph. "He isn't from around here." There was a slight scowl in his voice.

"More peas?" asked Doreen.

Mercer could hardly tell if he wanted to stay at the table or get away from it.

"I need to speak to Detective Mercer privately," said Alice to her parents when they were done. It seemed like an awfully formal thing to say to them, but they didn't bat an eye.

"Oh, yes, dear," said Doreen. "You two don't mind about the dishes now." *You lazy young people*, she might as well have added, a lovely smile on her face.

They went upstairs to Alice's room. His steps made the old staircase creak while she, not light-footed by a long shot, went up without a sound.

She led him along the narrow, carpeted hallway on the second floor. There were three bedrooms and a little bathroom up here under an arched ceiling, all the doors shut. Her door was an old thick one with an ivory white knob. She closed it once they were inside. There was music playing softly, hardcore rap music, which surprised him, unusual to hear at such a low volume too. Mercer noticed the little speaker on the floor just inside the door.

"Sit," she said. There was a chair pulled up to a desk with a laptop on it, but he moved past it to the bed and sat there. A little of the steel went out of her eyes when he did that. Still, she did not sit. She stood over him. The room was small with just the bed, desk, and an old dresser, a small closet with the door slightly ajar. There was a print on one wall, of a northern forest and a lake, a scene that looked a little surreal to Mercer, with darkness coming on as a strange sun set, a heavily shadowed tree in the foreground. The painting was signed by an artist with whom he was not familiar. There were a couple of posters on the other wall and a single ornate Victorian shelf over her bed with almost nothing on it. As he sat down, he saw his reflection in the oversized mirror attached to the dresser that was tipped slightly downward. He looked foreign in this room, out of place — his face scruffy with a few days of salt and pepper growth, his shirt a nice one with a button-down collar — a man on a bed with pink sheets and pillows and a warm red duvet. Before dinner, she had taken off her gun belt, jacket, and tie, and opened her collar.

"So?"

"So what?"

"We are going to go over this licence plate tracing thing again."

"Why?"

"Because you are acting strangely."

"And you aren't?"

"I'm not doing anything out of the ordinary, Detective Mercer, and you're trying to change the subject. You are in my jurisdiction now, there has been a murder, and —"

"I thought it was a disappearance?"

"A highly suspicious disappearance, and you are running licence plates and withholding information."

What does she mean by that? AND withholding information? Does she somehow know about the strange woman and what she had said to him? That woman had come alone on an early morning, way out in the countryside. No one else had visited him that day.

"What information would that be?"

"Come on. You are neighbours with Elizabeth Goode and Andrew Eakins. She came to see you."

"How do you know that?"

"She came to see you, yet you pretended to know nothing of her."

"How do you know she came to see me?"

Alice sighed. She turned to the desk and put her hands on the back of the chair. She wore two rings, must have slipped them on when she got home, one with a snake that curled all the way up the middle finger on her left hand and the other a wide gold bar on her right ring finger. He thought of the tattoos on each side of her hips nearly reaching her thighs — her own initials with hearts — they had surprised him. She stared through the little window that looked out onto the cold, snowbanked street.

"Detective Mercer, do you think we are fools here?"

"No."

"We have had interviews, plural, with Mr. Eakins. He is very tight-lipped, as I told you, and that's a problem, but we have a pretty good idea of his and his wife's whereabouts and activities over the past few weeks. She came to see you three weeks ago this past Tuesday, stayed with you from approximately nine to ten a.m., that's what Eakins figured."

"I —"

"Mr. Eakins wasn't too pleased about that. That was a long time for a woman to be visiting with you, Detective Mercer, alone in your home."

It was the first time that Mercer had ever detected anything remotely like jealousy in Alice Morrow. He did not think she was capable of it. Or was he imagining those feelings? There was silence in the room. A pause between songs. He could hear Ralph and Doreen's voices downstairs. Mercer knew he was going to have to come clean, about many things. A new song — about shooting a movie in someone's hometown — started to play.

"I'm waiting," said Alice.

He sighed. "I forgot. I forgot she came to visit. To introduce herself as a neighbour. She said her name was Libby. I didn't connect that to Elizabeth, not until later."

"How much later?"

"Just today, actually."

Alice turned and stood over him again. The music changed. Guitar chords were crunching now, drums pounding, a weird voice singing.

"She was an attractive woman, wasn't she?"

"Yes, I suppose she was. The whole thing is terrible. Look, I wish I would've remembered earlier, but I don't see how this has anything to do with the case. We just made small talk."

"For an hour?"

"Yeah. Honestly. Then she left and I never saw her again."

"Did she come on to you?"

"Sorry?"

"Sorry isn't your style, Detective Mercer, you heard what I asked you."

"No. No, Alice, she did not come on to me, nor I to her if you're interested."

"I'm not, believe me. It's her intentions that interest me. Though if something happened between the two of you then it's important that you are truthful about it."

That sounded like a threat.

"It was just chit-chat."

"Lots of it."

"Yeah, I suppose. She was very friendly, in her own way."

"What does that mean?"

"You know, the way people are friendly around here."

Alice smiled for the first time. He didn't like that. It was almost conspiratorial.

"I wasn't insinuating that she told you anything in particular that we need to know, it's just that we are trying to learn as much as we can about her, and here you are interacting with her and not admitting to it."

"That's not the case. I told you, I forgot."

"Did she seem afraid of her husband? Did she talk about him?"

Mercer considered how to answer that. "Mentioned him, briefly, said he didn't like the cold. That's why he didn't come along too."

Alice stood back a little, thinking. "Anything else you want to tell me?"

"About her?"

He realized his mistake the instant he said it.

"Yeah, that's what we're talking about, aren't we?" Now she looked him straight in the eye. "Is there something else?"

"What do you mean?" He knew how a defensive attitude or a guilty one manifested itself. He knew that when a subject was being interrogated, their voices changed a little when they lied. Eyes wandered too. He did everything he could to look steadily at her. She smiled again. She had seen his effort.

"What else, Mercer?"

"What do you mean?"

"Already said that." She leaned over and put her hands on his shoulders. "I think you have something else to tell me, Detective."

He took her hands in his and stood up. He was looking down at her now. That was better. He would need that advantage for this next part. He could see her eyes soften again as he stood there holding her hands, but then she pulled them away and stood back.

"The floor is yours, sir."

He looked away and rubbed his hands together. He needed to come clean. She was good, surprisingly very good, and she would likely find out everything anyway. But he wished that he knew more about Sergeant Morrow. Who was she, really? He glanced through the open door of her closet. There were more dresses and skirts hanging there than he would have imagined, some that looked short. Mostly however, there were jeans and sweaters, several police uniforms. He could see a movie poster on the wall inside, peeking out between the skirts. Tarantino. *Pulp Fiction.* Uma Thurman's bare feet in the foreground. He turned around and sighed.

"Someone else came to see me."

"Go on."

"A different woman, early in the morning of the day of the incident at the café. Came to the farm, alone too."

"You seem like a popular man for solitary women. Description please."

"An unremarkable sort, no name given, a local. Somewhere in her thirties. She was in a loose grey coat, which she never took off. I'd guess five foot four and slim. Short brown hair, long nose, wearing a pair of round wire-rimmed glasses that had slid halfway down her nose. No wedding ring. A red button on her lapel that read "I own my own body.""

That was the easy part. He wondered if he should just tell her what the woman said or see if Alice got it out of him.

"And why did she come to see you?"

He paused for a moment. "She told me that Andrew Eakins was about to kill Elizabeth Goode."

A look of incredulity crossed Alice's face. It took her a while to speak.

"And," she finally said, "this woman was driving a pale blue Toyota Corolla, licence plate TLCC 665."

"Correct."

There wasn't really enough space in the room to pace, but Alice started pacing. The silence between the two of them grew strained.

He knew what she was thinking. *This really is a homicide, or worse, and as strange as hell.* He hoped that was the least of what was going through her mind.

"Why do you live here?" asked Mercer, finally. "At home with your parents?"

"What does that have to do with anything? You, sir, have withheld a very important piece of information from the police." She was growing angry. "Why? Did you forget about it too?"

"The information isn't really that important, when you think about it. This woman, she just knew they had troubles in their marriage, maybe a history of violence, maybe she didn't know anything at all and was just nosey. That button indicated that she was a bit political. Maybe she had a hate on for Eakins or men in general. Who knows?" His words sounded hollow, even to him.

"She predicted it, Mercer, *on the morning of the day it happened!*"

"Yeah, but she isn't a witness, likely doesn't really know anything."

"We don't know that."

"I —"

"She isn't a local, probably doesn't know Elizabeth Goode."

"What? How do you know that?"

"Mercer, this woman rented a vehicle to drive out to your farm. Would a local do that?

He felt embarrassed. "I see your point."

"Why, in God's name, did you not tell me this? *Really.*"

"I don't really know why."

"That's not a good enough answer."

"I've been through a lot lately."

He had several times considered telling her about his situation, everything that happened back home, why he was here, but there had never seemed to be a right moment.

"That's what they all say."

Mercer wondered what exactly she meant by that. Who were "they?" Murderers? Was he a suspect? A possible person of interest? He knew that made some sense.

"My second question to you, Mr. Evasive Homicide Detective Who Knows All About How to Commit Perfect Crimes, Mr. Withhold Information, Mr. Lives Next Door to the Vanished Victim, is why did this mysterious woman come to you?" Alice's voice had gone up a notch. "Why did this Cassandra come your way with her crystal ball, and predict a murder, on the morning it happened? What was her intention and why tell you of all people?"

The murmur of voices downstairs suddenly stopped.

"We need to find her, your woman," added Alice, now quietly, almost to herself.

"I think you are reading too much into all of this. I can help you —"

"Oh, no, no, no." She actually took a step back from him. They both knew the old thing about those involved in a murder trying to stay close to the investigation.

"Alice, let's not jump to any conclusions. I'm just a burned-out guy from New York with a wrecked marriage and a family that is kind of alienated from me. I'm just up here trying to figure out some things, get my life back on the rails. I'm simply curious about this case; it's in my DNA. I can't help it." Now, that was something he should write down. "Look, I didn't know the woman named Libby who came to see me was Elizabeth Goode, honestly I didn't, and the encounter with the other woman kind of freaked me out, and I just held it in for some reason. I don't know why she came to see me. She was just a weirdo and what she said was just a coincidence, or that's how I thought of it. You can call the NYPD and ask about me any time." No one there knew anything incriminating about him, or would admit to it.

Alice did not respond. For the first time in the conversation, she looked a little guilty about something.

"You've already done that, haven't you?"

"Yeah."

"I am who I say I am."

"None of us are," said Alice in a clear voice. For the first time since he had met her it sounded like she was saying something that came straight from the heart.

He took her hand and sat on the bed with her. They stayed there for a moment, quiet.

"Or maybe I'm just a bad man," he said and kissed her. She responded, right there in front of the perfectly positioned mirror that reflected everything on the bed. Alice was reaching for him now. He could feel her strength again. She was allowing this to happen, maybe making it happen. The phone rang downstairs. They kept kissing.

"Alice?" called Doreen Morrow. "It's Sal. Says you have your cellphone off."

Alice stiffened and pulled back. She stood up briskly, doing up a button, even though only two were undone.

"Coming," she said loudly. She turned back to him. "You should go. And you are to stay in the area, cease making inquiries of any sort, and have no contact with anyone connected to this case."

With that she was gone out the door. He heard her downstairs on the phone, talking in a muffled voice, but excitedly relaying something. He stayed on the bed for a few moments, a smooth yet haunting voice now on the speaker singing about someone creeping into a house by the back stairs. Here he was in Alice Morrow's bedroom. Posters for concerts by bands he'd never heard of were grouped on a wall. A certificate over the desk: "Grade Eight, First in Class. Congratulations, Alice M. Morrow!" And a photograph of a young man, late teens. There was a stack of books on the bedside table. A well-thumbed copy of *The Girl with the Dragon Tattoo* on top, then *Lolita*, *The Handmaid's Tale*, collections of short stories by a female author he did not know, and several others. Was she that much of a reader? Some of the books were familiar, but he didn't know what the others might tell him about her. They had never talked about what they'd read.

She would have been intimate with him, taken him ... right here. In her childhood bedroom, her parents nearby.

He got up, walked carefully down the stairs, and went out the front door because Alice was on the phone in the living room and her parents were in the kitchen. He crossed the road to his car.

Elizabeth Goode has been gone for four days now, he thought.

"Yoo-hoo!" he heard a voice shout.

He turned and saw Doreen standing on the front porch waving at him.

"So lovely to have you, sir ! Please call again!"

These people were insane.

10

Help Me Help You

HE TRIED TO write in the journal that night but got nowhere. His thoughts kept turning to the case. At least Alice had not asked him that question: THE question always asked when you are somehow connected to a crime.

"What were you doing on the night of the murder?"

Over the years, he had thought of that as a tough one. How many people can actually recall what they were doing on a given night? It seemed to him that it would be more suspicious if someone knew exactly what they'd been doing right away.

What *had* he done that night?

The conversation with the woman in the rented car had disturbed him. Her accusations of the violence men do to women had dredged up his own neglect of his family and his professional failure. Failures he had fled from like a coward.

Mercer had been drinking. It came to him now. He had polished off a bottle of rye, alone at the farmhouse. That was never a good thing. He could handle a little wine, a little beer, but the hard stuff always had a bad effect on him. Sometimes, if he drank too heavily, he would black out — he had done some strange things with little or no memory of what happened.

Could he have done that the day of the murder?

He knew where the café was. He had been there.

A ridiculous thought, a self-accusation.

Once, when he was feeling particularly down, he went to see a therapist at the station in New York, whom the force provided for employees. Her gentle, non-judgmental way made him wonder if he was far too self-critical. He had made mistakes, but he was basically a good man, wasn't he? It was this therapist who had suggested he write things down.

IN THE MORNING, he drove into town to see Alice. This time, he parked his car right in front of the police station and marched up the stairs past the big rubber floor mat for snowy boots. The reception area was bright and friendly. There were all sorts of posters on the walls about things the local police were doing in the community, a bulletin board with notices about lost cats and dogs. There were even a couple of comfy fading green chairs for people to sit in while they waited, and two heated pots of coffee and tea, and paper cups on a stand. And it was quiet, just a murmur of conversation. The front counter, he noted, was not fitted with bulletproof glass.

The desk officer had her back to him, and he could see into the office, a hodgepodge of a half-dozen workstations and beyond them, a few doors leading into offices, including one that was closed, with "Chief Smith" written on the nameplate. The ceiling was high and the floor hard, so every voice, every movement of shoes along the surface echoed slightly, like whispers. He realized he could hear music too, and it was coming out of Smith's office, some sort of heavy metal played at low volume.

Alice and Sal were talking just outside an office door, their backs to him, shoulders almost touching. The acoustics were so good, or so bad, that he could hear every word. They sounded anxious, but denying it, trying to start their day normally, put their work off for a few minutes, work that he was sure Alice had now told Sal likely concerned murder.

"So," said Alice, "you're bringing the chicken and I'll have a beef stew. What about Fergie?"

"Nothing, just hauling his ass there, adding to his pot belly at the potluck."

"Too manly, I suppose, to cook something."

"Well, Michael doesn't do much in the kitchen either. Mahmoud and Aya do more."

"Maybe his wife will cook something for him to bring."

"He's taking her to Florida soon, isn't he? Payback time."

"She's out of work, I hear. Maybe she's got extra time on her hands."

"My mother would turn over in her grave if she knew I was doing this in a Christian church."

"Just IN the church, Sal, they're only providing the location, just sponsors like the police union, you're not worshipping there or anything. It's for a good cause. Nearly a dozen battered women a year in a town our size is way too many. One is too many. I'd like to be there when those clowns are at it, like to beat the shit out of one coward after another with a spade, and then sever their —"

"It's the church you go to, isn't it?"

"Yeah, I'm there most Sundays, with Mom and Dad, makes me feel a little less heathen. It's pretty liberal, pretty open-minded."

"So, they don't really believe in anything."

"As much as anyone around here believes in anything."

"If I could have a prayer answered right now, it'd be the identity of that woman in the blue Corolla."

They moved toward the office.

Mercer cleared his throat, loudly. The women immediately stopped talking and turned toward him.

"This might be where I come in." There was silence, so he continued. "Sounds like a lovely potluck, a good cause indeed. Maybe I can come? I can barbecue something."

They still didn't say anything, just stared at him. He let himself in through the door in the counter and walked toward them. The desk officer glanced at Alice and Sal, and when neither said anything about stopping him, she let him proceed.

"Well, first, let me say that I am very pleased that you were not talking about me, and second, maybe I can help assure you that the Corolla renter is of no real importance." He came to a halt about five feet away from them.

"I told you to stay out of this."

He noticed a photograph of Elizabeth Goode on the wall; in fact there was more than one. The search for her was intensifying. They would likely do a more thorough sweep of the area near the Goode farm next, perhaps reach out to other precincts nearby to see if there was any sign of her outside their jurisdiction.

"She told you," said Sal, though not speaking with much conviction. She fixed her hair.

"Yes, she did," said Mercer, "but I went home and thought about it, and I just don't get why you would turn down my help when I have so much to offer, and especially when I am kind of involved anyway. We all know how awful and difficult this is. I'm sure, as it deepens, there will be more and more to do."

"Well," said Sal, glancing at her colleague, "he does have quite a bit to offer." Alice glared at her. Sal quickly turned to Mercer. "I don't think she's going to change her mind, sir — as you know, that's a woman's prerogative." She said it almost under her breath, as if she were trying to keep Alice from hearing her.

"Let me ask you a question, Detective Mercer," said Alice. "Would you let someone, quote unquote *involved* in a case, work on it, down in New York?" She even made the quotation marks signs with her fingers.

"I think I would, Sergeant Morrow, if that person were an experienced homicide detective, and if I knew that anyone with common sense would not suspect that person of actually being involved in a murder."

"A disappearance. Still."

"Suspicious disappearance," added Sal. "Fifth day."

Alice's head whipped back to Mercer. "Common sense?"

At the sound of her raised voice, a chair squeaked, and Leonard Ferguson came to the door of his office. The desk officer had turned to regard them too. There was no reaction from the boss's office: the door remained closed and the music still a quiet, heavy metal pound.

"Whoa," said Ferguson, fastening his fingers into his belt loops and adjusting his pants up over his gut. "Nice to see you again, Chief Mercer."

"Detective!" said Alice.

"Right, Detective Mercer, good to see you." Ferguson walked across the room and offered his hand to Mercer, who took it, happy for any sign of welcome, even if from this horse's ass.

"I've been meaning to call you up, sir, and bring a brewski or two out to your place and swap murder stories. Get ourselves lubricated and get at 'er."

"You've never solved a murder, Fergie," said Sal.

"That, Constable Haddad, is a matter of opinion."

"No, it's not."

"Look, Alice," said Mercer, "give me a chance. Just give me a day or two to work with you and your colleagues here, just unofficially, and see if I can offer anything. If I can't, then shove me aside, no problem."

"Wow," said Ferguson, "you would actually work on a case with us, this murder in the café thing, I'm guessing?"

"Suspicious disappearance," said Sal.

"No, no, this is a murder all right, the kind you've dealt with every day in America, Chief Mercer."

"The United States," said Sal.

Ferguson ignored her. "It's murder sure as shit, and I think we both know who did it, though he's a tricky one. Aren't you going to let the chief here work on this, Allie?"

"Don't call me that, Fergster. It seems to me that you were doing something in your office. Best get back to it, don't you think? You won't be on this case. You're going on vacation soon, anyway. Heading south? Make like a snowbird and fly away."

Ferguson crossed his arms over his chest and didn't move.

"So, Alice," asked Mercer quietly, "did you do the licence plate search? Did it turn up anything?"

"Oh, it turned up something all right," said Sal.

"Constable Haddad," said Alice sharply, "please refrain from sharing police information with the public, especially with the not-even-a-citizen public."

"What do you mean by that, Constable?" asked Mercer.

She smiled at him, then at Alice. "I, uh, probably should not say. But let me just add, kindly and neighbourly like, that it isn't really your business, if you don't mind me putting it that way."

"Oh, for God's sake, Sal," said Alice.

"Well, there's no need to be rude to him."

"Exactly," said Mercer.

"Shut up, Hugh!"

"Alice Morrow," said Sal, "let's not be loud and unkind."

"I would like you to leave, Detective Mercer," said Alice, "and I will not ask you twice."

"Leave?" said Ferguson loudly. "She doesn't mean that, sir.

You know, I'm a big Yankees fan. Maybe you and I could —"

"She means it!" shouted Alice. "And get back into your fucking office, Fergie!"

There was absolute silence in the station, for a long time.

"Oh ... kay," said Ferguson. He rolled his eyes, then gave Mercer a smile and mouthed the word *hysterical* before walking back into his office.

Constable Haddad looked a little shocked at Alice's outburst.

"It's all right," said Mercer and turned to leave.

"I'll show you out," said Sal. "Least we can do."

When they got outside, the wind was blowing snow and it seemed as if the temperature had dropped a hundred degrees.

"Oh," said Sal, "it's a little brisk out here, must be south of ten below now." She hadn't put on a coat. She stood at the top of the station steps. He began to descend.

"Watch your feet, sir."

He started to slip on the second step. Salma Haddad reached down with one hand, gripped him by the scruff of his Burberry coat, and held him upright. He could not believe her strength. He had put her at about five foot three or four.

"Whoops-a-daisy!" she said, then leaned toward him, their heads almost touching. "The woman who rented the Corolla," said Sal, barely above a whisper, "used fake ID."

11

Beneath the Floorboards

MUCH LATER THAT evening, as Mercer was fixing a midnight snack, his cell rang. It was Alice. It struck him that he had never given her his phone number. He realized too that this was the second time she had called him: the first was when he was driving home after his confrontation with Hassan at the car rental service. He had been too riled up then to notice how she had reached him. Before that, she had always just dropped by.

"Hugh?"

She didn't often use his first name. Usually, it was Mercer or Detective Mercer; in fact often she would use the latter in bed. "Detective Mercer," she would say into his ear as she gripped his arms or shoulders and guided him toward her during an intimate moment.

"Hi, Alice. Look, maybe I was a bit too —"

"I've decided to let you work with Sal and me on the case."

She didn't add anything, just let that comment hang in the air. She had spoken in a tone that he didn't recognize, like she was acting.

"Oh. okay, that's great, real great."

"There will be conditions."

Silence.

"Of course."

"You will not be doing any solo work. Everything you do will be under supervision of Constable Haddad and myself. You will share everything you learn or even suspect with us. We will be in your confidence at all times. You are not officially on the case, just an advisor. Is that understood?"

"Absolutely."

"I will pick you up at nine tomorrow morning and the three of us will drive over to the farm where Andrew Eakins and Elizabeth Goode lived."

"I could walk over, meet you there."

Silence for a while. "You will be traveling with us."

"Of course."

"Too cold a walk for an American."

He laughed at that, but she didn't.

"And," she continued, "we will provide lunch for you at the station and then we will proceed to the holding cells and have you interview our suspect."

"You what? Really?"

"No, I just made that up."

He couldn't tell if she was being serious.

"I'm sorry, I'm not sure if you are kidding or not."

"You will be questioning Andrew Eakins. I'm guessing you've cracked a suspect or two in your day. See you tomorrow at nine."

"Okay, and uh, thanks, Alice, I appreciate this."

"No problem, Hugh, I'm looking forward to working with you."

"Well, we've worked pretty well together in the past." He was taking a chance saying that.

"Expecting more of that sort of work too, Mercer."

He could not believe she had said that. She said it in a grim voice that struck him as incredibly sexy. It felt like she was ordering him.

HE COULD NOT focus on anything other than her and the case after that. He went to bed and spent the first couple of hours in it trying to figure her out. Why had she changed her mind? He still really knew very little about her. At least, little that actually mattered. He had the funny feeling too, from the tone of her voice and her evasive manner, that she wanted him to work on the case not only because he might help her solve it but also because she suspected him of being involved somehow. Maybe not directly, but just ... somehow. He was part of it from the moment that woman came to his door. *A woman who was using fake ID.* Alice wanted to keep him close.

ALICE AND SAL appeared right on time the next morning. In the stillness of the day, he heard the cruiser almost from the moment it turned from the highway onto the sideroad. He stepped out his front door. As they approached, he could hear that they were playing music too, loudly, a song he knew called "Down by the River." When they got near, he could tell they were singing along: lyrics about someone shooting their loved one. They pulled up the driveway, the black and white cruiser framed by the grey barn and the white, encrusted snow. Alice was driving. She got out and came up the walk to the front door toward Mercer, leaving the driver's door open. Behind her, a creepy guitar line was taking over the song, attacking it, putting exclamation marks on the dark story it was telling.

"Hi," said Alice. "Ready?"

"Sure."

She turned her back and trudged toward the cruiser, her footsteps soundless again. He followed, the snow crunching beneath his feet. He had finally bought some short, slip-on rubber boots and had snapped them over his shoes. When he was halfway down the sidewalk, the music suddenly ended. Now there was just the sound of his footsteps. They got into the car, Mercer in the back like a criminal, behind the screen. The doors thudded shut. He hadn't been able to read anything in Alice's face, blank as it often was. Now he looked at the backs of their heads, caps off on the front seat: dirty blonde and raven black, tied back in ponytails. Constable Haddad turned around and smiled.

"How are you this morning, Detective Mercer?"

"I'm fine. You can call me Hugh, please do."

"Okay. I'm just Sal." She smiled again.

Alice swung the cruiser around, the tires crunching the snow until they reached the sideroad and then drove down it. At the end, she turned right, or west as they said around here, and accelerated instantly, speeding along the highway, braking and turning sharply on to the next sideroad. Hugh held on to the door handle to keep from tipping over.

The farm where Elizabeth Goode and Andrew Eakins lived was the same distance up their sideroad as Mercer's was along his. When they turned right, or east, past the black mailbox with "Goode & Eakins" in red lettering, Mercer could spot the weather vane at the top of his barn and the roof of his house in the distance. This house looked to be from the late 1800s, yellow brick, two stories, about the same size as Hugh's. The barn was located much closer to the house than at Mercer's, not much more than fifty yards away. It looked well-kept.

They got out of the cruiser and the car doors thudded again in the near silence. Mercer could see that the snow in the fields nearby had been trampled down from searches of the property. The house would have been checked too, but they were here to go over it more thoroughly.

"The old Goode farm," said Sal, "has been in the family for six or seven generations. That's the way around here, though it's changing. Lots of new folks moving here, over the last decade or so. Brown people like me too, finally!"

"How old is Elizabeth?" asked Mercer as they walked up the sidewalk to the front door.

"Oh, about thirty-three or thirty-four," said Alice.

Wow, thought Mercer, *they don't know their victim's exact birth date yet. That's different from back home. Details are important.* But he let it go. "So, where are her parents? She and Eakins didn't live here with them, did they?"

"Dead," said Alice.

She unlocked the door and they entered. They were immediately in a huge country kitchen with big windows, similar to Mercer's. The heat was on in the house, and it felt like someone was still there, just around a corner or hiding in a closet.

"Her parents died the same day, heart attacks. It was strange, found right here in the house, bodies near each other. About three or four years ago, or so."

"Any thought of foul play?"

"Heart attacks," repeated Alice.

"Elizabeth was away," said Sal, "came back for a while, took charge of the estate, rented out the house, and went away again. She was an only child. Then, about two years ago, she came back to stay, kind of all of a sudden. Folks round here were surprised that she returned. She was a high achiever, top student in high school and couldn't wait to get away."

"When did Andrew Eakins come onto the scene? "

"Not sure," said Alice as she took off her parka and put it on the back of a chair in the kitchen. "I'll do the bedrooms. You two cover the downstairs. We'll check out the barn again another day." She went into the hallway and up the stairs, silently.

"Not sure?" asked Mercer, turning to Sal. "That's it?"

"As I think Alice told you, Mr. Eakins won't tell us much, even about himself. He remains a bit of a mystery. He has a driver's licence, a social insurance number, but no birth certificate to show. Told us he is thirty-nine, name Andrew Eakins, that he did not kill his wife. Gave us details of the café incident and that bit about Elizabeth visiting you, and that's it. He just keeps saying the same thing, same nothing."

Mercer had the feeling that despite that, they knew a bit more about Eakins. "You need a lot more from him."

"Well, you're going to get to talk to him."

Mercer had dozens of questions for Andrew Eakins.

The two of them combed the bottom floor thoroughly, going through the kitchen, living room, dining room, sitting room, and both bathrooms. From what they could tell, Elizabeth and Andrew seemed like a normal, relatively young, childless couple. Their taste in decor and furniture was contemporary and of good quality, but nothing unusual.

Sal was conventional in her search: going through drawers in desks and living room furniture, pulling up throw rugs, looking in cupboards, and behind paintings. Andrew Eakins seemed to be a slippery character, and Mercer wondered if they might be dealing with a seasoned criminal, perhaps even a sophisticated killer, so he kept an eye out for hiding places used by more devious suspects. He searched in the little spaces at the ends of the curtain rods, felt for compartments in the couches, and stood on a chair and checked the light in the ceiling fan. He hoped Alice knew to go through the cartons of feminine hygiene products upstairs, always the cleverest hiding spot, one he had seen used many times.

They spent more than an hour searching and came up with nothing. The earlier sweep would have picked up any bills, mail, or documents to examine, and someone at the station would be checking bank and phone records, that sort of thing.

Mercer kept his eyes on the floor and the walls, searching for loose boards. Nothing. Finally, Alice came down the stairs.

"Nothing up there of significance," she said. Both Mercer and Sal had turned to face her. As she reached the wider tread where the staircase curved slightly before the bottom few steps, he saw a floorboard move.

"Right there," said Mercer, pointing.

"What?" asked Alice.

"A board on the landing moved beneath your feet."

He walked toward it, kneeled down on the bottom step, and felt around the board's edge until he found a spot to lift. It came up in his hands. There was a small compartment underneath and in it a Bible, a big one, King James version.

"Looks like a family bible. Let me see it," said Alice.

Mercer was reluctant to give it to her, but he picked it out and handed it over. She turned to the frontispiece. "It's old," she said, " and" — she flipped through the first few pages — "without any name or address in it."

"Could be the old Goode family Bible," said Sal. "A lot of the folks around here hold on to them, attachment to the past, I guess. I can't imagine why they'd hide it like this though."

"Yeah, that would make sense, I guess," said Alice, still examining it, "though it's strange they didn't write their name in it, and it's not published in this country. It's an American edition."

"Maybe in those days they were mostly published down there?"

"Hmmm," said Alice. She began leafing through it, looking for letters or even notes written into the margins. Mercer could see that there was a string bookmark inserted about three-quarters of the way along. His parents had been religious, Southern Baptist; he wasn't, though neither was he an atheist. He liked to think he had a little more imagination, more interest in the mystery of life; he knew though, from his youth, that this marker looked to be somewhere early in the New Testament.

Alice found the page.

"Hmmm," she said again, running her fingers down to a spot where verses were underlined. "Matthew 6:14 – 15." She said it like someone who knew her Bible. "*For if ye forgive men their trespasses,*" she read, "*your heavenly Father will also forgive you.*" She paused. "*But if ye forgive not men their trespasses neither will your Father forgive yours.*" She had read it with feeling and there was silence for a moment.

"Might I look at it?" asked Mercer.

"Knock yourself out."

The cover was heavy leather, black and thick. Mercer first examined the inside of the front cover, then opened it at the back. He could see, on the inside of the back cover, a second surface. Using his fingernails he picked at the black leather material that matched the binding. It was held in place by an adhesive around the edges, He carefully began peeling it off, stripping it all the way down. Underneath was a sheet of paper with a few lines scribbled in ink, some of the text smudged as if by water.

"*I murdered my wife,*" it read. "*I cannot deny it.*"

12

Murderer

IT WAS NEVER this simple. The paper was slightly yellowed, so, likely, it had been sealed in place long before the past week and Elizabeth's disappearance. The Bible could have been brought here and not even belong to the Goode family. The words probably referred to something else simply connected to this Biblical passage.

But Mercer also wondered if this note, found in this house, was somehow, in some way, the first light shining at the end of the tunnel of their case, a slight opening toward finding this woman, or her body. *Justice*. Now, he could hardly wait to interrogate Andrew Eakins.

THE SUSPECT WAS a slim, muscular man of slightly above average height, with fashionably cut sandy blond hair that sometimes flopped over his slightly tinted aviator glasses. *This guy could be a male model*, thought Mercer when he first saw him — a poor man's Ralph Lauren kind of guy, in a short-sleeved red shirt, designer jeans, and black running shoes.

The station had a small room where suspects could be questioned, but Mercer had suggested they do it in the cell. Alice said they never did that but let him go ahead. The location of an interrogation was important to Mercer, and when he discovered that Eakins was the only one being held in the cells, he thought an interview there might create a certain intimidating atmosphere. Mercer understood that his job was to get Eakins to speak, say anything really. He intended to use his size, his New Jersey accent, his NYPD pedigree to get this man to tell him something, make a mistake. Eakins was going to go through this alone — he had refused a lawyer, refused to ask for bail. He'd even brushed aside Legal Aid that Alice and Sal had tried to persuade him to accept.

It was going to be a curious interview for Mercer, because he was under observation too. Alice and Sal were sitting in on the interview, watching. They were definitely good at that sort of thing.

Before the three of them went in, he instructed them to open the cell door for him, so it was obvious he was the tough new guy brought in to make things happen. Though he wasn't a smoker, he had even asked for a cigarette so he could puff on it dramatically and make the air a little uncomfortable, blow a little smoke toward the suspect.

"There is a no smoking policy in our station," said Sal the moment he brought it up.

Mercer eyed Eakins through the cell door window. Alice and Sal had set the table in the centre of the room, as he told them to do, and arranged for his chair to be slightly higher than the suspect's. Eakins didn't appear to be a smooth operator, nor did he seem tough or hard to break. The man looked back at Mercer with a direct expression and a hint of fear. Mercer nodded gravely to Alice to open the cell door. He was hoping she could pull this off without rolling her eyes. She unlocked the door and then stood behind him with Sal as he approached the table. Eakins stood up.

Maybe a bit north of six feet. Mercer had made sure they had given him a thick folder, three-quarters full of blank sheets, that had been labeled HOMICIDE. It had taken some convincing. The women had argued that it was a bit over the top, that it wasn't even the actual charge, and it might frighten Eakins too much, but he got his way. Now he slapped it down on the desk and regarded the suspect.

"This is Detective Hugh Mercer, NYPD and —" began Sal.

"Why?"

"I'm sorry?"

"Why do you have —"

"Never mind why, sit down," said Mercer.

"Is this allowed here?" asked Eakins, still standing. Mercer thought that an interesting way to put it. What did he mean by *here*?

"Why," asked Mercer, "do you have something to hide?"

"I —"

"If you have nothing to hide then it shouldn't matter who asks you questions, should it?"

"I suppose not."

"Sit down."

Eakins sat and glanced at Alice and Sal who tried not to return his gaze as they moved over to the wooden bench.

"I will be conducting this interrogation in its entirety." Mercer ground his chair back and sat on it.

"They didn't call it an interrogation," said Eakins, looking to the two local police officers again. "They just called it a conversation."

"Well, they aren't the ones —"

"I didn't do this."

"Do what?"

"You know."

"No, I don't, perhaps you can help me out?"

Eakins indicated the Homicide file. "Murder my wife."

Mercer nodded to Sal, who took the Bible they had found in the Goode farmhouse, which she had held hidden by her side, and handed it to him. He let it fall onto the desk with an even more emphatic crash than he had produced with the thick folder.

"Interesting way of putting it."

Eakins looked down at the Bible and his eyes widened. Mercer opened it so the slip of paper was exposed.

"You've signed some things, Mr. Eakins. We think that's your handwriting. Your Bible too, isn't it?"

"That's not about —" Eakins stopped.

"Hmmm? Go on."

Eakins steeled himself. "I went to the Shelter Café with my wife, my dear wife, Elizabeth, and I went out for a moment. When I came back, she was gone. I don't know why the others are lying. Or they're just mistaken."

"But there's three of them, at least, three ordinary, good people, with no reason to make anything up."

"You need to find her, not accuse me of things."

"Sticking to the same story?"

"It's not a story!" His voice went up a notch.

"The same song and dance, Andrew."

"I have told you everything I know. I gave you all the personal information you need as well. My name, my social insurance number, my driver's licence."

"Really nothing more though, my friend, nothing of any real substance." Mercer leaned toward him. "Where you from, originally?"

"I am not the guilty one here. Someone has taken my wife or coerced her into going with them and they are doing God knows what to her while you keep asking me questions that aren't pertinent!" Eakins's face was turning red. His anger had boiled up quickly. He dropped his head. "She would not have run off!"

"Where you from?" asked Mercer again. "Because I think I know."

For the first time, Andrew Eakins looked rattled. He lifted his head.

"Look, I did not do anything untoward concerning Elizabeth. I love her. She definitely loves me." His hands were shaking. "I believe ... she loves me."

"I think I know where you're from," Mercer repeated, staring at him.

He did not know, but he had an idea. He prided himself on his ability to pick out regional American accents.

"Ever been to Pennsylvania, Andrew?"

"Pennsylvania?" His voice cracked.

"I'm guessing toward the east, kind of Philly but not in the city, somewhere out in the country, but not pure country either. Small town. Phillies guy or Eagles?"

"I'm not answering any more questions."

"You've been here for a while, flattened out your vowels a little, flattened out everything. These parts will do that to you, especially when you're living with a local woman, won't they? What did you do back there, in eastern Pennsylvania?" Mercer's expertise in accents did not stretch to the area where he now lived. The accents around here were so damn godawful flat. It was like they didn't come from anywhere.

"I wasn't just living with her, she was my wife. This interview is over," said Eakins and he stood up.

"She *was* your wife?" Mercer stared at him for a moment. "All right." Mercer stood up too. "But I'll be back."

"No, you won't!" shouted Eakins. "I have said all I'm going to say to you!" His hands were balled into fists.

"Interesting," said Mercer. "So, no desire to tell us where she is? ... Or worse? Tell us why she might run from you?"

The suspect just stared at his interrogator.

"Thank you, Mr. Eakins, you have been most helpful. This is a good start." He motioned to Alice and Sal to open the door. Alice actually did roll her eyes this time, which pissed him off. *Stay in damn character*, he thought. Sal and Alice followed him down the hallway to their offices.

"Well, that went well," Alice said and glanced at her watch. "I'd barely sat down."

"I'm pretty sure your man is not only from a small town in Pennsylvania, but he was also born and grew up there. He's hiding that, for some reason. He's hiding lots of things. How long has he lived here? I'm guessing you know a bit more than you've told me."

Alice didn't respond.

"Near as we can tell, about two years," said Sal. "Apparently lived in town at first, kept to himself."

"This is a man with a past."

"Whereas most of us have no past," said Alice.

"You know what I mean."

"He has anger management issues," said Sal.

"Yeah. Tried to bring that out. I'd like to talk to him again."

"We'll see," said Alice. "He doesn't appear to be up for that. Mostly you just antagonized him — for the entire minute you were in there." She had paused for a moment to hear him out but now she moved through the office toward the reception area, so Mercer and Sal had no choice but to follow. She opened the counter door there and held it so he could walk through.

"It was about putting him on edge," he said, "fast and emotional, see how he reacted."

"Thank you, Detective Mercer, you may go." She motioned toward the cold outdoors.

"That's it? No more discussion? I have some other observations that I'd like to share with you."

Her face and body language gave the impression that she had seen everything she needed to see, and had come to her own conclusions.

"Such as?" she asked, sounding a bit bored.

"Such as ... more about what I just told you, plus that Andrew Eakins doesn't seem like a deceitful sort, other than wanting to hide his past."

"Well, that's a pretty big thing," said Sal.

"I've interacted with all kinds of murderers, and he just doesn't seem like one. Evasive, yes, distracted somehow, prone to anger, but not a murderer. Just my gut telling me that. He seems kind of guileless, actually. I believed him when he said he loved her."

Alice said something under her breath. It almost sounded like "how would you know."

"But," said Sal, "crimes of passion can be committed by the best of people."

"True," said Mercer, "I'm just giving you my assessment of his character. I'm not saying that he definitely didn't do it."

"Well, thank you for all of that," said Alice. "You can go home now. Stay in the area though."

"Why would I —"

"We will be involving you again."

He smiled. "Great. What's next?"

"A long list. I'll brief you in the morning, here, bright and early. Then, we need to look for where the body might be."

13

Suspicions

MERCER WAS AT the station early the next day. In fact, the sun was not yet up, and he actually wondered if it was closed. The cold had frozen the door so that when he first tugged on the handle, it wouldn't open. He looked in and saw the night sergeant, a thick-set man in a black and blue turban that matched his uniform, peering out at him. The man motioned for him to pull in a certain way, but Mercer tried to no avail. Finally, the man sighed, got to his feet, came out from behind the counter, and opened the door.

"On cold mornings, you must pull and lift at the same time on this door, sir," said the sergeant. "Please, come in. The weather will be better, I assure you, but not for some time. One must be patient with God and with doors."

"Thank you."

He stood in front of Mercer, blocking his way into the station. Mercer noticed that his hand was near his gun. "My pleasure. May I help you?"

"Oh, my name is Hugh Mercer. I'm an American from —"

"Yes, I can hear that."

"... from the New York Police Department and I am helping Sergeant Morrow and Constable Haddad investigate a murder."

"Do you mean suspicious disappearance?"

"Yes, I stand corrected."

"Not at all. I am Ranbir Singh, at your service. But I am sure we will find the evidence to convict this fellow of a crime. It is more than six days now that she has been gone."

"Well, who knows, it may not be a fellow."

"Right," said Singh with a twinkle in his eye that said they both knew who had done it. "That is quite a story Mr. Eakins has told about his innocence, worthy of a great novelist."

"I suppose that's one way of looking at it. I'm meeting Alice and Sal this morning."

"It is a good thing that you have a reason for trying to enter the station this early. Now, I will not be forced to kill you." He stepped aside gravely and motioned for his guest to enter the reception room. *More of that deadpan sense of humour*, thought Mercer. "They will be here eventually, I imagine," continued Singh. "I am a punctual man, Mr. Mercer, and appreciate it in others. Sergeant Morrow and Constable Haddad, though, are not always paying attention to the clock. You may be seated."

Mercer sat on one of the comfortable green chairs and waited, looking at the posters for lost pets again, and the toys in the corner, placed there for children, the unlikeliest of criminals. He wondered if these toys were ever put to use.

It was about half an hour before Alice and Sal showed up.

"You see what I mean," said Singh.

"So I just put up my feet and watched Netflix," Alice was saying. "Apple crumble and tea, and a dose of Scandinavian crime."

"Oh, which show?"

"Can't remember the name, something Norwegian, or Finnish, not sure. Pretty gruesome: pedophiles and incest and sadomasochism mixed in by the end of things. Par for the course for those shows. Almost made me laugh."

"Scandinavians are weird."

"Think so?"

"Well, maybe not. Maybe it's more true to life."

"Reminds me of here most of the time, actually, like they're trying to imitate us, and coming up short. The ones set in the American Midwest even more so."

The conversation halted when they noticed Mercer.

"Good morning, Detective Mercer, lovely to see you," said Sal.

"Hi," said Alice.

Their coats were wide open, no mitts or headgear, and both were holding cups of coffee from a coffee shop chain that he had seen everywhere he'd traveled in the region. It seemed wildly popular. They both had doughnuts in hand too, from the same place, eating as they talked.

Last night, instead of trying to write in the journal, Mercer had started making a list of questions for Alice on his laptop. He had also searched for an Andrew Eakins of the right age in Pennsylvania, but found nothing. He knew, however, that he had to keep himself in check today.

"I wonder," he began, "if I might speak to your three witnesses?" There were actually four, if you included Eakins, six if you considered the ghost couple, though Alice likely would have told him if she'd found them.

Alice glanced back at him as she opened the counter door and nodded at Singh who barely acknowledged her.

"Good morning, Sergeant Singh," said Sal.

"Almost afternoon, Constable Haddad," said Singh.

Sal smiled.

If Mercer had hoped to learn more about Alice from her office, he was out of luck. It was almost bare — an old wooden desk with a photograph of her parents to one side, a laptop and stacks of folders, and a map of the region on the wall with a few pins in it. That was it. The walls were the same unattractive shade of green as the reception area.

She pulled off her coat, put it over the chair, set the coffee cup on the desk, and then bit a big piece out of the apple fritter before putting it down on the desk too, sans napkin. Sal took a big bite out of hers at the same time as she leaned against the map.

"I will let you choose one witness or person connected to the case to interview. One," said Alice, still chewing on the fritter. She picked through the folders and plucked one out. "You can read all the statements first. Let me know who you want to talk to, and then give me a full report on everything he or she says. These files don't leave the station." She handed them to him. "I'm trusting that you will pick a fruitful individual with whom to speak."

"Thanks," he said. "Where can I go through these?"

"He can use the chief's office, can't he?" said Sal. "He's away for a few days."

"The chief's office?"

"We have surveillance cameras in there," said Sal. Mercer could not tell if she was serious. Alice gave Sal a look and Mercer wondered if it was for saying something awkward or because she had given away the fact that they could watch what he did in the chief's office. For a second, he imagined that this was a part of a set-up.

"You will have time for that later," said Alice, nodding at the files in his hand. "Chief's office will be fine."

"What are we going to do first thing? Disposal site, I think you said?" He realized, as he said it, that he sounded awfully eager; loud and eager.

"Calm down," said Alice. She put her feet up on the desk, took a slug of her coffee, and then put all of the rest of her apple fritter into her mouth.

Sal laughed. "Need our sustenance first."

A figure swept by the door, then came back. Leonard Ferguson.

"Whoa!" he said and entered. "Hot on the trail, eh? See you got Captain America on the job, after all. Give 'er, big guy." He slapped Mercer on the back. "Howz it going, chief?"

"I'm good."

"Close the door, Sal," said Alice.

Constable Haddad got up and ushered Ferguson out of the office and closed the door on him. She turned back to the room, sticking a finger into her mouth to get a bit of doughnut out of her teeth.

"Okay," said Alice, "we are heading back out to your neck of the woods, Detective Mercer, to talk to the neighbours. We need to know more about Mr. Eakins. Did anyone see him on the day of the disappearance? Did they see Elizabeth? Did the two of them actually drive into town together that afternoon? We need to locate your mystery woman too, Mercer, though all we have is your description, your story."

Mercer didn't like the implications of how she said that. "What about possible disposal sites?" he asked.

"Oh, we've decided to leave that to others," said Sal putting her hand on the doorknob again.

"Others?" Mercer couldn't believe it. He and Alice and Sal needed to be on that job, not sloughing it off to others. There was likely no one else on this little force with expertise in these sorts of cases. Knowing how to find a body was of utmost importance. He hadn't seen Eakins as a murderer, but like Sal said, anyone can do anything in a moment of passion.

Alice stood up, tightened her gun belt, and reached for her coat. "Yeah, I'll ask Sergeant Singh to check out the Goode place for disposal sites. He just does a half shift as desk sergeant, so he'll be available all morning. Ranbir loves his job, seems like he never leaves. He can bring the cadet with him. Ferguson might even do some of the grunt work, if it comes to it. We'll have volunteers help with a sweep of the forest nearby as well."

"Singh and Ferguson? A cadet?"

"A youngster in training. We've got a guy now, good kid."

"You've got to be kidding me."

Sal had been starting to open the door.

"Detective Mercer," said Alice, "are you questioning my decision making? Or Sergeant Singh's capabilities?"

"No, it's just that I kind of expected that I ... or you and —"

"Close the door, Sal."

Alice waited until it was completely shut.

"Sit."

They all sat.

"Two points, Mercer. First, things will work smoother if you just go with the flow, pretend that Sal and I actually have some brains and are somewhat capable."

"Right. Sorry about that."

"No problem," said Sal.

Alice rolled her eyes at her. "Second thing: what about you?"

"What do you mean?"

"Did *you* see Elizabeth Goode that day? Or Andrew Eakins?"

"No." Mercer was taken aback. "Alice, I told you I only met Elizabeth Goode once."

"Met," said Sal. "Observing her from a distance is different. You lived next to Andrew and Elizabeth for nearly two months, surely you saw her or them more than once."

Mercer suddenly realized that it was true that he had lived near them for that long. But the relationship was non-existent, really, disturbingly so, just as with others in the area. He honestly could not recall ever seeing Andrew Eakins, and he had seen Elizabeth just that once.

"Observing her? What, do you think I was stalking her or something?"

"Well," said Alice with a sigh, "considering the one time you *did* meet her, you neglected to tell me for a long time."

"And you neglected to tell me that you were a police officer for longer than that."

"Are you two fighting?" asked Sal.

Alice stared at her for a few seconds and then turned back to Mercer. "So, Detective Mercer, what's the deal?" she finally said. "Did you see Elizabeth Goode or Andrew Eakins that day? Simple question. Take your time, think about it."

"No," said Mercer, "I don't need to think about it. I didn't see them that day. I keep to myself. So did they, apparently. Their sideroad is on the far side of their buildings. I can't see it from where I live. I wouldn't see them heading into town or heading anywhere."

"However," said Sal, "if you were driving in to town at about the same time, on your own sideroad or out on the highway, you could have seen them going down their road. Take a moment to reflect."

"Didn't see that."

"Ever hear any noises from their place? Loud arguing, a woman's scream?"

"I don't think I would hear anything like that from inside my house. It's nearly a mile away."

"Six-tenths of a kilometre," said Sal. "Walked it off. That's far from a mile."

Mercer had no idea if that was true or not. "I wouldn't hear anything from inside my house," he repeated. He tried not to sound pissed off, but this was ridiculous.

"Wasn't saying that," said Alice. "But you'd hear something like that if you were outside, up near the top of your lane, say, near the mailbox."

"That's a rare thing. I try not to go outside too much here."

Alice stifled a smile.

"Okay, let's go," she said.

The women stood up. The file was still on Mercer's lap. Alice held out her hand and he gave it to her as he got up and she dropped it on her desk. As they turned to go, Alice in the lead and Sal holding the door for the others, Sal leaned toward Mercer.

"Folks are nosy around here. Someone will have seen something. Or say they did."

14

A History of Violence

THERE WAS A farm on the highway close to the turnoff to Mercer's sideroad, and another house just a lot over from it, occupied by the farmer's retired parents. A couple lived at the end of the Goode's sideroad too and there were a few homes farther north up that road, in a forested area.

"We need to talk to all the neighbours, eventually," said Alice as they got into the cruiser. "We will do it together, just in case one of us picks up on something the others don't notice."

Or, thought Mercer, *so I don't hear something you think I'll keep from you.*

They drove out to the area with Alice behind the wheel, moving beyond the speed limit most of the way, a local radio station that played oldies from the early 2000s blaring so loudly, and the two women singing along so fervently, that Mercer was sure any call on their police radio would go unheeded. During a song called "Girlfriend," about stealing someone's boyfriend, brash and full of shouts, they really got into it. Mercer had never seen this side of Alice, or Sal. The moment they reached the first home though, they turned off the tunes and were all business. Both of them put on their caps, did up their uniforms and coats, and pasted serious expressions onto their faces, slamming the cruiser doors emphatically too, as if announcing to the folks inside that the law was here. Mercer's legs ached from being crammed into the tight space in the back seat. He had to move quickly to catch up to the women.

Mercer had offered to follow in his own car and that seemed to him to make a lot of sense since their first stops were right by his house. The other potential locations for interviews — and they hadn't told him exactly how many they would do today — would be at homes nearby too. Going in the cruiser meant they would have to take him all the way back into town after the interviews and then he would have to drive all the way back out to get home. It seemed ridiculous, but Mercer had seen where questioning Alice's plans had gotten him so he kept his mouth shut.

The first stop wasn't at the farm on the highway — they went right on past it to the newer home just around the corner, accessed off the sideroad. A family, the husband in his early forties and his wife in her late thirties, with five kids, occupied the farm. This newer house belonged to his mother and father.

"Common thing around here," said Sal to Mercer as they trudged toward the front door, "or at least used to be, for the old couple to either move into town or build their own house on the back end of the property and give their farm to the son. Used to always be a son, anyway."

Though just a bungalow, the house was large, especially for just two people. It sprawled along a hill at the end of a rapidly ascending driveway, as if situated here to have a good view of the movements of any visitors. In fact, Mercer could see a woman, white-haired with a blue tinge, peering out the large, curved window after the cruiser doors slammed. Santa's sleigh sat in the snow on the front lawn, "Merry Christmas!" in unlit neon lights circumnavigating his belly.

"Met these folks yet?" asked Sal.

"No."

"But they are the closest people to you."

"I guess I just thought they'd say hello themselves someday, kind of like I thought Eakins might, I suppose. Isn't that how it works most places? Residents make an effort to say hello to newcomers?" He didn't add that only psychos would think otherwise. He had seen this older couple several times, getting out of their car as he drove past, eyeing him.

"Ebb and Delilah Morton," said Alice as she reached for the doorbell.

"Ebb?"

"I think it's for Ebenezer. Don't know of anyone who has ever asked. She's not really Delilah. It's a nickname, I guess she was a little wild in younger days, and it stuck."

There was a long pause after the doorbell buzzed. Mercer wondered why. The people inside clearly knew they were here. It was a little milder today and icy rain started to fall, pelting down on the women's caps and on Mercer's head.

"Shows respect to talk to the parents before you speak to the younger ones," said Sal after a while, rocking on her heels.

That's not much of a plan, thought Mercer. *Talk to the ones who might give you certain kinds of information, then to the ones who might add to it.* He kept quiet though.

"What's the hold up?" said Alice aloud to herself. "Come on, Del."

She rang the doorbell again.

About a minute later, it opened.

The woman with the blue-tinged white hair appeared before them with a smile as wide as the door. She was wearing brown slacks, a white sweater, and a cheap looking necklace that read "World's greatest grandma."

"It's Ralph and Doreen's gal, Ebb!" she called out toward the innards of the house. "In full regalia!" There was a faraway sort of snort of response. She turned back to her visitors. "Alice, isn't it?"

"Yes, Delilah, it is."

"How are you dear?" She asked with a bit of an edge, as if she didn't care what the answer was, as if she knew something about Alice Morrow that she didn't like. Still, she projected a stolid friendliness.

"I'm fine."

"I hope there isn't anything the matter out this way? You and your friend, all done up in your outfits like this."

"It's about the Elizabeth Goode situation."

"Oh, my, yes, that was terrible. Murder! One of our own, one of our neighbours, murdered. My!"

"We haven't established that it was murder yet, Mrs. Morton," said Sal.

Delilah glanced at her and then back to Alice.

"It is more along the lines of a disappearance," continued Sal.

"Suspicious disappearance," added Mercer. "Almost a week ago now."

"I know you, don't I?" said Delilah to him, looking at him for the first time.

"Yes, I live at the end of the sideroad."

"In the old Powell place!"

"Yes."

"They were lovely people. The best. They don't make them like that anymore. Why are you here with the police, sir? Are they concerned you might know something about this, living just across the way? Involved somehow?"

There was a slight pause, during which Alice and Sal said nothing.

"No," said Mercer. "I'm —"

"Delilah, may we come in, ask a few questions?" asked Alice.

"Why, of course, dear. Noticed you approaching. I've put the tea on, and we'll have a biscuit. I've roused Ebb from his nap too. Likes to sleep on the loveseat, you know, but I have him upright now. May I have your friends' names?"

"I'm Constable Salma Haddad."

"Haddad?"

"Yes."

"Don't recognize that name. Where are you from, dear?"

"Lived in town for more than thirty years, now."

"Oh?" She turned to Mercer. "And you, sir?"

"Detective Hugh Mercer. I'm from New Jersey, and New York City, ma'am. I worked for the police department there. I've offered my services in this investigation, and living nearby makes me of further use, I guess."

"Yes, we knew you were an American." She sighed and smiled. "Well, won't you all come in? Boots off on the mat, please."

Mercer noticed the hole in Alice's left sock as they walked out of the vestibule with its grey linoleum and onto the thick blue shag rug of the living room, a naked big toe pointing out, the scarlet nail polish he recognized.

"I see the boss has allowed you in," said an old man in a checked flannel shirt with blue suspenders and jeans, slippers on his feet. His ball cap read "Massey Ferguson." He didn't get up. "Have a seat."

"Well, Ebb, you know Alice, and this is Constable Haddad. Do I have that right?"

"Yes."

"And the man who lives in the Powell place. Mercer's his name, from the States, as we suspected." She spoke loudly when she addressed her husband.

"Ha!" said Ebb, slapping his knee with a liver-spotted hand, loud too. "Knew it. Well, get on in here, make yourselves at home, all of you, welcome to our neck of the woods."

"He's a policeman too, New York City, of all places."

"On holidays?" asked Ebb.

"No," said Mercer.

"Staying a while?"

"Yes, I believe so."

"Eh?" said Ebb, cupping his ear.

"Probably," said Mercer louder.

"No family?"

Mercer paused. "Yes."

"Yes?" asked Delilah, motioning for them all to sit. She nestled in next to Ebb on a pink paisley loveseat, while the others squeezed into a purple couch directly across from them.

"Um," responded Mercer, "they may join me at some future date."

"I see," said Delilah and looked down.

"We have some questions about the Elizabeth Goode situation, Ebb," said Alice, raising her voice too.

"Why the hell are you asking me and the wife? Seems like an open-and-shut case. We all know who the murderer is."

"You live nearby, and we just wondered what you've observed over the last while."

"It's not strictly considered murder, at this point," added Sal, "but rather a suspicious disappearance."

Ebb and Delilah let out guffaws at the same time.

"Disappearance, my ass," he said. "Look at how long she's been gone!"

There was an uncomfortable silence for a moment; at least it seemed uncomfortable for the visitors.

"What do you want to know?" asked Ebb.

"You've lived here for a long time, haven't you, near the Goodes?" asked Sal. "That's the old Morton farm next to you here, your old place, isn't it, and your son and his family live there?"

"We've lived around here since we were born, sweetie," said Delilah bluntly. "And our parents and their parents and their parents before them. I was raised across the road and down a couple lots. My maiden name was Carruthers. Dad and Mom farmed until they couldn't farm no more, then moved into town. Mom was a Powell herself, my grandfather was Bert, and it was his son, cousin of mine, and Bertha Hunt, who lived there before you came, young fellow." She nodded at Mercer. He didn't want to even glance at Alice, for fear she was smirking.

"The Mortons and the Carruthers and Powells have known the Goodes forever," said Ebb. "I went to school with Len Goode's older brother, and his wife Irene was a few years younger. Nice people, like family, really. She was a Newman, good stock too."

"Day was," said Delilah, "when Rene and I would talk on the phone for hours at a time."

"The girl though, she was unnatural," said Ebb.

"The girl?" asked Mercer.

"Elizabeth," said Delilah. "I wouldn't say unnatural though, honey, I'd say natural, very natural, if you know what I mean." She raised her eyebrows.

"No, I don't," said Sal. "Can you expand on that, please?"

Ebb and Delilah just looked at her for a moment.

"I don't know, Del, can you expand on it?"

Delilah smiled. "They had Elizabeth later in life. She was a different sort. Rene never knew what to do with her. Oh, she did well in school, there was never any problem there, in fact, she did ridiculously well, as smart as a whip. So smart, she thought she was better than folks around here, better than her own family. They had a boy too, you know, passed when he was about thirteen, farming accident. Len always worried it was his fault. Just the two of them working together that day. Elizabeth was their only one then. She got a scholarship to some American university and went there, had some big job in the US for years before she came back. I don't think she hardly ever visited her parents once after she left, not here anyway. They may have gone down there to see her. We're talking a decade and a half. I suppose she called them."

"Snooty," said Ebb.

"But what did you mean by unnatural — or natural, I guess you said?" asked Sal.

The old couple smiled at each other.

"She got around," said Delilah.

"Got around?" asked Mercer.

"She believed in free love, I guess," said Ebb. "She had lots of boyfriends, had lots of modern ideas. Maybe girlfriends too, who knows."

"Pretty sure she's gotten over the fence in this last while too," said Delilah.

"What does that mean?" asked Mercer.

"That means —" began Alice.

"Means she was having sex with a neighbour, someone other than her husband," said Ebb, "if that's even what he is. She and that Eakins hadn't been shacked up long themselves and she was looking for greener pastures."

"Ebb Morton, that's not the way to talk, especially with visitors."

"Just being frank, Del."

"Our information is that Andrew Eakins and Elizabeth Goode were married," said Sal.

"She was having an affair?" asked Alice.

"That was the talk," said Delilah. "I can't say it's the God's honest truth, but there was some reason to believe it. With that foreign guy who lives out in the woods in that fancy place just north of Elizabeth and her man. I believe he is, was, teaching her Italian. They say he was right from Italy, a professor of some sort, but still young. Dark hair and dark complexion and one of those partial beards young men have all the time now, you know, with a few days growth on them. I don't see the attraction, though he was not hard to look at, I'll admit that. Had a tan on him in the summer that nearly turned him black." Delilah glanced at Mercer for a second. "Elizabeth went alone to his place, I've heard, and stayed for hours at a time."

Alice turned slightly toward Mercer, who tried not to look back.

"They must have been good lessons," said Ebb with a sly smile.

"Ebb Morton," said Delilah again, sternly. But then she returned his smile.

"But that doesn't mean she was being unfaithful," said Sal.

"I don't suppose it does," said Delilah, "but she and that Italian seemed awfully cozy with each other. People saw them together"

"They say Italians are like that," said Ebb. "Like lots of physical contact."

"I suppose that's kind of true, in a way," said Mercer, "but I don't know that friendliness is a bad thing."

There was silence for a moment.

"So, really," said Alice, "this is just a rumour."

"A pretty strong one though, and not just coming from old crates like us," said Ebb. "Why did she need to know Italian? Not much call for it around here. I know we shouldn't be speaking ill of the dead and maybe we shouldn't even have brought that up, but I'm telling you, many people wondered about that relationship."

"Did you two ever see them, Elizabeth and this Italian man, together?" asked Alice.

"Yeah," said Ebb, "saw them driving out the road once or twice in the same car."

Alice glanced at Sal.

"She was a modern gal though," said Delilah. "Believed in her own sort of conduct."

"I wasn't much on this Eakins either, if I tell you the truth," said Ebb. "And I'm sure he was a jealous sort."

"Why do you say that?" asked Mercer.

"Expand on it?" said Ebb.

"Sure."

"Well, I've seen some bruises on her."

Sal squirmed a little in her chair. "Where on her?"

"On her face. He wasn't a very friendly guy, not from around here, you know, never talked to anyone, not anyone I knew, sold these weird sculptures, some of them pretty sexy I hear."

"Bruises, plural?" asked Alice.

"Only ever saw one, up around the eye area, but you know what they say, if there's one of that sort, there's probably more. Men like that know how to hit where things don't show."

Delilah was silent.

"You have no evidence, real evidence though, that Andrew Eakins ever struck Elizabeth Goode, do you?" asked Mercer.

"No," said Ebb, "he was a sullen sort though, had a temper too. I remember Ben, that's my son, had some cattle in the field next to the Goode place, renting it from the Trews, you know, and one got through a gap in the fence and that Eakins guy he really blew up about it, came storming down from his place when he saw Ben fixing the fence. Ben said he thought he might hit him."

"He didn't though?" asked Sal.

"No, he didn't," said Delilah, "but a friend of mine was canvassing for diabetes and said she saw him in the barn working up his muscles, doing some sort of martial art, she figured, had the whole place rigged up for it. He was shirtless, Dolores said. He is a nicely built man ..." She cleared her throat. "Keeps himself fit and capable like as if he is always preparing for a fight. All this, and then his wife just up and disappears and he has this cockamamie story about her being with him when she wasn't."

"He had his sculpture studio in the barn too, I heard tell," said Ebb, "had some pretty gruesome weapons in it, worked with steel you know, blowtorches, an oven, and electric steel saws and the like. Heard he had a pretty good collection of guns too."

"You'd need those kinds of tools to work with metal," said Mercer.

"Not the guns," said Ebb. "I'm not a gun man myself. That's likely not in your way of thinking, sir, coming from where you do."

Mercer didn't respond.

"So, he wasn't well-liked," said Alice, breaking in, "as far as you two know. Maybe she wasn't either, around here, really?"

"I suppose they had their own friends in the city," said Ebb. "They went away every now and then. They were a different sort, no disputing that."

"They were a striking couple, I hear," said Alice. "They stood out."

"I suppose you could say that," said Delilah.

"Yeah," said Ebb, "she was a looker, in her own way, you had to give her that. A man like that Italian fellow would certainly notice, any man would, especially given her attitude too, her ways."

Delilah stared at him.

"Well," said Alice, glancing at Mercer to see his reaction, which seemed either neutral or controlled. "We should be running along." She stood up. Sal and Mercer got to their feet too.

Mercer wondered why they hadn't asked about his mysterious visitor. He certainly wasn't going to mention it. Maybe Alice wanted to explore that subject on her own, without him in earshot.

"But you haven't had any tea! It's been steeping all this time."

"She likes it strong," said Ebb. "When I first knew her, she had it so weak you had to keep the windows open so it wouldn't faint."

"You two enjoy it," said Sal. "We have to get going, have to talk to your son and daughter-in-law, and a few others today."

Delilah got to her feet; Ebb stayed seated. He reached for the remote control and glanced toward the widescreen TV across the room.

"Good to meet all you folks," he said, as if shooing them out.

"I have to ask you," said Alice to Delilah at the door, "did either of you two see Elizabeth or Andrew on the day of the incident?"

"That's a kind way of putting it, Alice dear, *incident*, but no we didn't, not that I recall. Me and Ebb, we are together all the time, and we were likely indoors almost all day that day. We often are now. We are getting awfully slow. It was pleasant to see you." She took Alice's hand and guided her out of her house, as if glad to be done with her. "Goodbye," she said to the others.

15

A Couple Apart

BEN AND BETH Morton were both home when they arrived. Apparently, Alice had called ahead and made sure they would be. All five kids were in class, bussed to an elementary school in the country and a high school in town.

Beth met them at the door, a woman nearing forty, with slightly tired looking circles under her eyes but a friendly way about her.

"Welcome, come on in," she said immediately. "Don't worry about your boots," she added, waving at their wet, snowy footwear.

There was a rubber mat though, prominent to their right by the closet with several pairs already there, and Alice and Sal immediately took off their boots, and Mercer followed suit. Beth smiled and offered to take all of their coats, which she put in the closet, one after the other, silently. Then she turned back to them, extended a hand to Sal and shook hers warmly. "Nice to meet you, Constable Haddad." She put her other hand on Alice's shoulder. "Nice to see you again too. Hope everything is good with you these days." Alice nodded. Beth turned to Mercer. "Detective

Mercer, so sorry we haven't had the chance to say hello before. Ben and I must run down to your place sometime or maybe you can come here for supper?"

"Sure, that would be nice."

"The living room is straight ahead, make yourselves at home, there's butter tarts and tea, so get right at it. I'll give Ben a call. He's in the barn." She took her cellphone out of her back pocket. Mercer didn't know what butter tarts were, but they looked awfully good, like a tart made with maple syrup and nuts.

The three of them settled into chairs in the living room, tastefully decorated with a variety of art, and pastel-toned furniture. There were pictures of their kids on display.

"She's an accountant, took a few hours off for us," said Sal quietly to Mercer as they waited. "He works as a foreman at the car plant between here and the city, and still keeps about twenty head of dairy cattle. I guess it's in his DNA."

"So," said Beth with a sigh and a smile as she entered the living room and sat down, "you must eat something!"

They all reached for some tea and the tarts.

"Ben is on his way."

"This shouldn't take too long," said Alice. "Thanks for making time."

"Oh, no problem, Libby was a lovely woman."

Mercer took out his notepad. It was not very official looking. In fact, he had bought it at a dollar store in town. "*Beth Morton ref victim in past tense,*" he wrote. He took a bite of the tart and some of the filling dripped down his chin.

"Oh, here's a serviette," said Beth, handing him a napkin. The tart tasted unbelievably good.

"How long have you known her?" asked Sal, as Beth settled herself.

"Since we were kids. I'm maybe three or four years older than her. A little younger than you, Alice. Sorry."

Alice smiled.

"She was coming into high school when I was finishing."

"I hear she was a good student," said Mercer.

"That's an understatement. She was brilliant. *Is* brilliant, I hope. Sciences were her thing. I would not have been shocked if she had won the Nobel Prize, for goodness sakes. I was surprised when she came back here, actually."

"Just because there were more opportunities elsewhere?" asked Sal.

"Yeah, that and, well, Libby was never overly comfortable here, I guess you could say."

"How do you mean?" asked Mercer.

"Hey!" said Ben as he entered the room, a friendly looking man who didn't bear much resemblance to his father. He was wearing work clothes. He started to sit down.

"Honey, maybe take off the barn jacket?" said Beth, offering him a smile.

He hesitated. "Yeah, sure, Beth." He pulled it off and left the room to put it in the closet at the entrance. There was silence while he went and came back.

"So, forgot my manners!" he said as he returned. "Did not shake a single hand! Good to see you, Alice. Hope things are going well these days." He slipped over to her, bent down and gave her a friendly hug as she rose a little to meet him. "And I imagine you are Constable Haddad?" he said, turning to Sal.

"Yes."

A quick handshake.

"And you must be Mr. Mercer from up the road. Sorry about not dropping by yet. Bad manners again. Have to work on that! Love to have you over some time."

"Sounds good."

The two men shook hands and Ben Morton sat. "Where are we at with this?"

"They were asking about Libby, honey."

"Libby, yeah, terrible thing. She was such a nice woman."

Mercer wrote in his notebook again.

"Is, I hope," Ben added quickly, noticing Mercer's reaction. "Never actually fit in here though, from an early age, really. I had gone off to agricultural college before she hit high school, but I knew her. And talked to Andrew a few times too. He seemed like an okay guy. They didn't mix a lot though."

"I hear he beat her." Mercer liked to do this sort of thing — say something shocking to people he was questioning, to see how they would react. There was silence in the room again. He could feel both Alice and Sal looking at him.

"Oh," said Beth, "I wouldn't know about that. I thought they were a nice couple, really. They just had different interests, went into the city a lot. Do you really think that went on in their marriage?"

"She had a bruise around her eye once," said Ben.

"We don't know what that was from, honey."

"Well, it was there. I thought Andrew was a nice enough fellow, as I said, but she had a facial bruise once, for sure. Not judging, Beth, just noting. I suppose, as you say, it could have been from anything."

"And she was having an affair," said Mercer. Sal and Alice shifted in their chairs.

"You must be referring to Flavio, Mr. Rossi," said Beth.

"I hear he's a handsome guy," said Alice. Mercer was surprised. He looked at her, but she was examining Beth's response.

"Yeah," she said. "He is."

"So it's true? The affair?" asked Alice.

"I doubt it," said Beth. "People are awful to talk around here. Mr. Rossi was teaching her Italian. Gossips got going about it. Libby and Andrew seemed smitten with each other. Very affectionate."

"Libby was a bit like that," said Ben. "Touchy-feely. Just her way."

"So, maybe that made people talk, if they saw her being that way with Mr. Rossi?" asked Sal.

"Yeah, likely," said Beth.

"She and Flavio were together a fair bit," said Ben. "That's true. Maybe she and Andrew had a modern relationship?" He emphasized the adjective with a smile.

"You didn't like Andrew Eakins very much, did you?" asked Mercer.

There was a bit of a pause. "Why would you say that?"

"Something about your cattle getting out, onto his property, the weapons in his barn? His temper. He had a temper, didn't he?"

Ben smiled. "Yeah, he did, but I wouldn't be pleased if a neighbour let their cattle get into my field either. I'll give him a pass on that. I don't know what you mean about things in his barn. Weapons? Really? Never saw that. Never been inside his barn at all though, never invited me. Andrew was an all-right guy, just a little different. He wasn't from around here."

"An American?" asked Alice.

"Yeah, I think so."

"We never really knew much about him," added Beth.

"Did you ever have the sense that she was afraid of him?" asked Mercer. He remembered Elizabeth Goode's odd comments about her husband.

"No, I wouldn't say that," said Beth.

"No," added Ben. "Look, I could be dead wrong, but this idea that he murdered her. Why would he do that? He didn't seem like the type."

'They never are," said Alice.

The three women nodded.

"I would say that she was more protective of him than scared of him," said Beth quickly.

"And why would she need to protect him?" asked Sal.

"Oh, I don't know. This can be a closed community and he was a foreigner in its midst. She was a bit of a foreigner here too, I suppose, given her independent ways ... She knew what it was like to feel ostracized. You know, she goes away, isn't heard from for a long time, then all of a sudden comes back, is alone in that big house for a few months, then apparently meets him in town and marries him. He stuck out here, for sure. He was, is, artistic, you know, a different sort. Sculpted kind of dark stuff, I hear, and —"

"Different enough," said Mercer, "to say that he entered a restaurant with his wife when it seems like he came in alone?"

"Yeah," said Ben, "that's quite a nut to crack. Why would he say that? What's the deal with that?"

No one answered him.

"Did either of you," said Sal, "see them the day of her disappearance?"

"No," said Beth.

"Don't think so," said Ben. "Hard to keep track of what day is what sometimes."

Their conversation soon changed to chat about local news. Mercer found himself looking out the window.

"Okay," said Alice, finally, "I think we've got enough from you guys for now. Let us know if you think of anything else, remember any strange behaviour from Elizabeth or Andrew leading up to the incident, anyone acting different around them, anyone who might have a particular dislike of them, anything like that that comes to mind."

"All-righty," said Ben and got to his feet. "I need to tend to my second job. Nice to see all of you."

Beth didn't look at her husband as he left the room. She was smiling at her guests and gesturing toward the door. Then, she somehow got to the closet first and started taking out their coats. Ben was pulling on his boots.

"We spoke to your parents," said Sal, "and they had a somewhat different take on things."

"Oh, yeah?" said Ben.

"They were convinced that Andrew Eakins was beating Elizabeth and that there was something going on with her and Mr. Rossi."

Both Beth and Ben burst out laughing.

"Of course!" said Ben as he went out. "Retirement can be awfully boring."

"My mother-in-law," said Beth, "has a vivid imagination."

ONCE THEY WERE outside, Alice and Sal walked ahead to the cruiser, and Mercer paused on the porch, zippering and buttoning up his new coat. Beth was just behind him.

"Now that I think of it," she said to him, "there was one unusual thing over the last little while around here, the last couple of months, really."

"Oh, what's that?"

"I swear a woman came by here a bunch of times, slowing down as she approached your sideroad, turning in a couple of times, but not going very far before coming back, and not always in the same car, not ones I recognized. I could never see her clearly. But I'm sure it was that same woman."

Mercer was speechless.

"May not be anything," said Beth, "just my imagination, like a ghost driving by or something, but I thought I should mention it."

"Thanks, I'll tell the others."

But he didn't.

Instead, he told them Beth had asked when he might be able to come for "supper."

THEY SETTLED INTO the cruiser to take notes before pulling out. Mercer didn't write down what Beth told him.

"Classic," he said, "for a woman to be protective of a husband who is abusing her."

"We know that, Detective Mercer," said Alice and Sal at the same time, and then looked at each other and started laughing.

"Actually," said Alice, once she had recovered, "that protective attitude of this woman toward this man is interesting, just in itself. It stands out. It may be the key to something important in this case, maybe something different than what we suppose, something kind of mysterious at this point. We all need to think about it more. Especially you, Detective Mercer."

He had no idea what she meant by that, but wasn't about to ask.

Alice pulled out of the driveway. "We have three more stops in this area. House at the end of the Goode sideroad, house almost across from the Goodes, and a beautiful little place in the woods. That will cover everyone who could have seen them out here on a regular basis, and everyone who could have observed them that last day too."

"Who are we questioning next?" asked Mercer.

"Crap," said Alice, touching her foot to the brake, "I forgot to bring my torture instruments and a hot light!" She glanced at Sal and they both grinned.

"Okay ... who are we politely interviewing?"

"Oh, gosh," said Alice, settling herself again.

"Alice?"

"Uh ... the first is just neighbours, a couple, been around for about a decade, moved here from the city. The second is an old

girlfriend of Elizabeth's, her best friend they say, and the last is ...
the Italian stallion."

They laughed again, Sal reaching over this time and squeezing
Alice by the arm.

"Very unprofessional," said Mercer.

"We'll try to do them all today, in that order."

"Looking forward to doing the Italian," said Sal.

This time they did a high-five.

"Even more unprofessional," said Mercer.

LOCALS CONSIDERED THE couple who lived at the end of the
sideroad new residents even though they had been there for nine
years. They were "city folks" who had bought and renovated their
old house almost beyond recognition. They had about an acre of
land and had built a little barn out back for the woman to keep her
rather exotic-looking chickens. Word was that they were not married. Not that anyone really cared, though a few sniffed at the fact
that they always referred to the other as their "partner." Both were
in the entertainment business: he an actor and she a set designer,
though they were in their sixties now and beginning to wind down
the work that had often taken them into the city. Images of them
online showed a couple who didn't look their age.

"They've got that pale, thin look of vegetarians," said Sal as
they tramped toward their French front doors. "Like they need
to go to a good barbecue." On the surface, the interview did not
seem to add very much to the case. The couple were pleasant and
helpful, and served up green tea and gluten-free cookies, but they
did not know much about Elizabeth and Andrew. They would see
them occasionally on their way into town, and had run into them a
few times at arts events, but their conversations were kept to small
talk. They had seen them driving past a few times too, though not

on the day of the disappearance. They both thought the younger couple were interesting people and hoped Andrew would invite them in to see his studio. They had seen his work online and thought it intriguing: dark works of anguished figures in strange embraces, almost struggling with each other. The couple were a bit perplexed about why Andrew and Elizabeth had not sought their friendship, been distant. The woman thought Elizabeth would have made a good "yoga friend." They had heard the rumours about Elizabeth and Rossi, and had seen them together more than once. They both seemed fascinated by her disappearance and the possibility that she might have been murdered. The woman even mentioned that it would make a great movie. To Mercer's relief, they didn't say anything about seeing a woman in wire-rimmed glasses.

"YOU COULD ARGUE that even the people with little to say," said Mercer as they got back into the cruiser, "even good things to say, aren't entirely pointing the finger away from Eakins."

"Or, at least, not pointing it at anyone else," said Sal.

After three interviews, it was still plausible that Andrew Eakins could have been battering his wife; she could have been afraid of him, protecting him; and they had not found anyone who had seen the couple together on the day of the incident.

"What about you and Elizabeth, Alice?" asked Mercer. He thought he would turn the tables on her a bit and maybe get something personal out of her at the same time. "You must have known her. You've lived here all your life. What was your impression of her?"

"I was well out of high school by the time she came in," said Alice, fumbling for the car keys.

"I understand that, but still, I assume you went to the same school and know something about the way things were there, how someone like her might have been treated. Maybe even if she has any long-term enemies?"

"Said I didn't really know her. And I wasn't a big fan of high school."

"I didn't know her either," said Sal. "Let's go." She gave Alice a little pat on the shoulder.

Alice immediately brightened and shook her head a bit, as if to shake something off. "Enough of my moaning." She pulled out of the driveway and gunned the car up the side road. "Next!"

"Elizabeth's friend," said Sal.

"Her only friend, it seems. Bosom buddies since childhood. She is apparently kind of different, like our victim. Lives alone. Her house is about a minute up the road from the Goode place, back from things, kind of hidden."

They began to climb the hill and could see Elizabeth and Andrew's farm to their right.

"Oh, there's Ranbir," said Sal. She rolled down the window, giving Mercer an icy blast in the back seat. "Hey! she shouted as they went by. Singh and the cadet were in what looked like a snowy garden on the road side of the barn. They were alone, digging at the hard earth, or at least the cadet was still working. The more extensive sweep of the place, the buildings and the grounds, perhaps the cistern and into the nearby forests, must already have been completed. It looked like they were finishing up. Sergeant Singh was leaning on his shovel.

"Isn't the ground frozen?" asked Mercer.

"Common misconception," said Alice. "It's usually only frozen a few inches in early winter, maybe not even that. And we've had one thaw."

Mercer was glad she didn't add — "good thing you're not in charge."

"They likely noticed a place where the snow looked disturbed and cleared it back to examine the ground underneath. I imagine Ranbir brought a pickaxe too. Just checking out the surface. Being thorough."

"Any luck?" shouted Sal.

Singh cupped his ear as if he could not hear her clearly. She waved him off.

Luck *was a rather insensitive word to use concerning finding a body in a garden, or elsewhere*, thought Mercer. A garden also seemed like a stupid place to look, even if the snow was disturbed on top of it. For one, he would have searched the indoor fireplace thoroughly with a small shovel, dug around in it. He had done that a few times on other cases and had some results. He would have swept well into the woods too, not just the near ones, all the woods and fields for many miles, with hundreds of people, or searched any nearby body of water, however small, had some diving done. Very few murderers ever dropped a corpse close to their house, no matter how desperate or amateurish they were. He wished he could get out of the car and take over. The youth of the cadet shocked him too. Alice had said he was twenty. He appeared to be about fourteen, like a kid who would either barf or run calling for his mother if a dead victim turned up.

The police radio crackled.

"Alice?" The voice had a slight accent, probably French.

Man, thought Mercer, *they are actually calling her by her first name on the police radio.*

"Alice, we have a situation back here."

Mercer perked up and leaned forward.

"A situation?"

"Clarence died."

"Who is Clarence?" asked Mercer.

Alice shushed him.

"I'll be right there."

Alice made a u-turn and put her heavy foot to work heading toward town. There was silence in the car for a while, both of the women tight-lipped. They passed the Goode place at a fast clip, neither of them looking over at Singh and the cadet, still digging in the garden. Finally, after they reached the highway, Mercer spoke up.

"We aren't going to speak to Elizabeth Goode's friend? Or the Italian?"

"No," said Sal. "Not today."

"May I ask what this is about?"

Silence.

"Alice?"

"Clarence was a dog, a lovely dog," said Sal who sounded like she was tearing up.

"A dog?"

"Mrs. Pearson's dog."

Mercer was flabbergasted. "And?"

"She was the victim of a home invasion last week. The dog was wounded. She is still in the hospital. Someone has to break the news to her."

"Can't they get a —"

"No," said Alice.

"But we're in the midst of a murder investigation."

"Alice has known Mrs. Pearson since she was a child."

"And?"

Both women turned around and glared at him.

"We'll do the other interviews tomorrow, first thing in the morning," said Alice.

Mercer stared out the window from the back seat at the bleak landscape, the lack of colour. He could hardly believe his ears or his eyes.

16

Different Stories

ALICE AND SAL didn't say anything to Mercer when they all got back to the station. The women were focused on Mrs. Pearson. Alice merely picked up the file containing the interview transcripts, handed it to Mercer, and pointed down the hallway to Chief Smith's office. Then she and Sal were gone.

He wanted to call Alice back when he got to Smith's door, since she had not given him a key. The office, however, was unlocked. He went inside and was struck by how bare it was. The desk was cleared off, other than some photos of Smith's wife and kids, and a wall, the same horrible green as in Alice's office, featured the same map she had, and nothing else. There were a few filing cabinets and stacks of CDs in several shelves, like relics from a different age, a CD player and a small speaker on the floor. He glanced at the titles of some of the albums and didn't know any of the singers or bands. There was no sign of surveillance cameras. Mercer sat down and dropped the file on the desk. It was surprisingly thin.

Soon, he knew why.

There were five light folders. What was before him were Alice and Sal's interview with Li, two separate ones for the couple who saw Eakins on the street, a file entitled "Ghost Witness Couple Inside the Café" and another with the ominous heading "Strange Visitor and Hugh Mercer." Almost all the information on every page in every file was redacted. Even names, other than the café owner's and Mercer's, were obscured. Mercer tried to look through the black ink. Opaque. Opaque like Alice and every person around here.

The only uncensored interview was the one with Jonathan Li, and only it was more than a single page. Mercer read every word. It was a professional, well-conducted interaction, Sergeant Morrow and Constable Haddad on the job. It gave Mercer nothing, however, that he did not already know, though it made him curious for more. He smiled. "Well done, Alice." He obviously could not interview anyone who was not identified, nor could he interview himself or the "ghosts." She had made the choice for him. "I will let you choose one witness to interview. One," she had said. *At least*, thought Mercer, *she is true to her word.*

He had lunch at Connie's Home Style Grill and then went to a pub half a block off the Circle that he had been to several times. He spent a long while there drinking, thinking about the case, getting more worried when he thought about whether he was still some sort of person of interest and what he had done the night that he could not remember. Just as on his previous visits, everyone was friendly, but even though he sat at the bar, they left him pretty well on his own, Afterward, he went for a long walk on a boardwalk down by the dark lake, freezing his ass off as the light faded in the sky. Streets of old houses sloped up toward downtown from the boardwalk and halfway along his stroll, he thought he spotted someone watching him from one of the cross streets.

The figure was about a block away but looked to be a woman, bundled up in what appeared to be a long grey coat and a dark toque. He thought he caught a glint of light off glasses from a streetlight. He wanted to run after her, but there was a steep snow-bank piled at the side of the street. She stood for a few moments looking his way. He stared back. Then she turned and walked away, disappearing around the block toward the town.

He knew he was still well over the alcohol limit, but he decided to chance driving home anyway. His only other choice was to walk it off for a few hours in the bitter cold. As he drove past the hospital, he could see the glow of lights from inside and wondered if Alice was still in there with Mrs. Pearson. It was very nice for her to tend to that problem personally, but they were dealing with a disappearance of over a week, a possible homicide, so not the best use of her time. He shook his head. Alice was a strange one. There was something going on with her, something in her past, he was sure of it. He thought of how the waitress at Connie's reacted and how Delilah Morton had spoken to her, both of them wary, and how Beth had inquired so earnestly about how Alice was doing.

He drove slowly even once he was out in the black and white countryside, maybe too slowly, puttering through that bleak land-scape, that *Nebraska* mood haunting him again. As he approached home, he peered at Beth and Ben Morton's place, then at Ebb and Delilah's. Their houses had that glow inside them too, that warmth and light that emanates from the interior of homes at night. He usually loved that. It made him feel good. It used to make him want to be home with his family. In this country, it seemed dif-ferent. The contrast between the outside and the inside was some-how disturbing. These homes seemed to be hiding from the outside world, their walls protecting both them and the people inside, and filled with secrets, surprises underneath the clothes.

As he headed up the road toward his own place, he could see the outline of the Goode home, no lights, a shadow on the hill.

"If she isn't dead," he said aloud, "then where is she? What is happening to her, right now? Where was she taken or where did she go?" He scanned the dark fields, the trees in the distance. "What does Andrew Eakins know?" He told himself he should take a look at the property on his own and use his instincts.

He tried to write something about Alice that night but got nowhere. When he tried to describe her and what she meant to him, she vanished like a phantom. Finally, he made one comment. "Both of us need something."

THE NEXT MORNING, he was back at the police station before the women again. Sergeant Singh was there to greet him.

"Good morning, Detective Mercer. You are a punctual man. I respect that."

They sat down together on the green chairs in the waiting area. Mercer was baggy eyed and carrying one of those cups of coffee, no doughnut. Singh looked fresh and energetic, not a libation in sight. He never seemed to be off duty.

"So," said Mercer, "turn up anything at the Goode place?"

"That is an interesting way to put it."

"Never thought of that. So?"

"So what?"

"Did you?"

"Did I what?"

Mercer sighed.

"Just messing with you, Detective Mercer," said Singh with a smile. "Although, any evidence I and my assistant Renaldo may have recovered is to be kept strictly to myself and handed over to Sergeant Morrow, on her orders. I am keeping my mouth closed, you see."

"Why am I not surprised?"

They watched the rising sun shine brighter and brighter through the high windows, somehow talking about everything except the case. Singh expertly steered the conversation away from anything Mercer wanted to hear. First, he went on about the weather, how it really wasn't so bad, that bright days — like the ones promised in the next week — were actually the coldest days, and that the winter would be over before you knew it and that the summers were lovely, much yearned for, though they also could be hot and uncomfortably "muggy." The weather here, he said, was like life, real life, with its ups and downs. Then, he launched into his views about the professional basketball team in the nearby city, the only non-American team in the NBA. He was amused, he said, about how people south of the border had been so upset when local fans cheered when an opposing player was badly injured during an important home game recently. They were shocked that the ostensibly polite fans of this country could be that way. "Didn't surprise me at all," said Singh, "that's the real spirit of the people around here coming out. There is a hardness inside us, a toughness. You know, we were killers in the wars."

"What wars have you guys fought in?"

"Are you serious?"

"Yeah, I mean, we're the ones always involved in conflicts."

"I suppose you saved the world in World War Two, right?"

"Kind of."

Singh laughed aloud and looked at Mercer as if he pitied him. "Our soldiers were combatants with whom you did not want to tangle in the big wars, the ones that mattered, before you guys even showed up to fight. The enemy knew that, let me tell you. Loved that reaction in the basketball game. Loved it! You want to win, after all."

"People around here mostly seem really nice."

"Well, they are, absolutely, but it's a good tactic, being nice."

Alice and Sal entered just as he said that. It was a full hour after Mercer had arrived. They were both carrying extra-large coffee containers and two doughnuts each. They were both in full gear with their heavy winter police coats on, neither of them done up. You could feel the cold air coming off them, so much so that it made Mercer do up his own winter coat. Alice appeared tired.

Neither woman said anything. They simply looked at Mercer and then pointed to the door. Less than fifteen minutes later, they were going up the Goode sideroad. There hadn't been much talk in the cruiser.

"Okay," Alice finally said. "Ariel Foster. She is the same age as Elizabeth —"

"Which is?" asked Mercer.

"Around thirty-three or thirty-four," said Sal. "We told you that."

Mercer almost laughed aloud. They *still* did not have her birth date, or did not care.

"She is a massage therapist," continued Alice. "Stayed here when Elizabeth left about fifteen years ago. Sal and I have probably met her a few times in the past, don't know her though."

They got out of the cruiser and walked to the front door.

"We let her know we were coming," said Sal.

Obviously, the two women were having discussions and making plans without Mercer's input.

The house was a brick bungalow, from the sixties or seventies, not very big, probably two bedrooms. Alice rang the bell and the door opened immediately. Two women were standing within arm's reach, one putting on a coat.

"Hi," said the other one, tall and athletic, in a sleeveless black sweater. "Just one second, if you will."

She turned back to her companion, hugged her, and kissed her on the lips. "Ciao," she said to her tenderly. "Next time."

"Have fun," said the other woman to the group with a twinkle in her eye. She quickly stepped outside so the three of them could enter. Music was playing somewhere in the house, some sort of South American flute music, and they could smell incense.

"A client, Miss Foster?" asked Mercer.

"Sometimes." She smiled at him and put her hand on his arm. "Call me Ariel, please, all of you. I have a boots-off, put-your-coats-in-the-closet, and make-yourselves-at-home policy here. You are all welcome in my house. Hi, Alice." She looked at Sergeant Morrow, but didn't offer her hand.

The living room was a sparsely decorated place but overflowing with plants — plants standing in pots on the floor, plants on tables, plants hanging from the ceiling as if from the canopy of a jungle.

Ariel was wearing a long gold chain from which hung a big cross and a witch's face. She sat on a big, well-pillowed living room chair and tucked her bare feet under her in a lotus position. The posture almost made Mercer grimace. She looked at them with a sense of anticipation and Alice quickly introduced the other two. Then there was silence for a moment.

"Well," she finally asked, "any word?"

Mercer wondered if she normally wore so much foundation around her eyes or if Ariel Foster was covering up recent sleepless nights.

"About?" asked Sal.

"Well, Libby," Ariel said as if addressing a child.

"No, we would have told you that immediately if there were."

"Why?"

"Why what?"

"Why isn't there any word? It's been a week! I thought you would come here with a different attitude, but the vibe I get from you is business as usual. I'm surprised too that this is the first time you've come to see me about all of this."

"Well, there's been a good deal done already," said Sal. "We're following many leads, investigating many possibilities, conducting searches. It's a very complicated case."

"Thank you for that. Such insight. Isn't there a speck of information about what might have happened to her? A clue? Isn't that what you work with? Clues? I know many people around here weren't fans of hers, but she was my dear friend. People don't just vanish without a trace."

"This may be more than a disappearance," said Mercer.

Ariel did not look pleased. "No, it's a disappearance. Andrew said it was. He went into that café with her and then she suddenly wasn't there. She wouldn't run off, not now. Someone took her, kidnapped her, lured her away."

"Mr. Eakins is a suspect," said Sal.

"Oh, please. You shouldn't even be holding him."

"Miss Foster, we have evidence of —"

"Has he confessed?"

The other three exchanged glances.

"Until he confesses, flat out confesses, I won't believe it."

"We can't find anyone who saw her with him that day, not just in the café but even around here," said Sal.

"I saw her."

Alice sat forward. "You did?"

"Andrew Eakins wouldn't harm a hair on her head."

Suddenly, Mercer felt possibilities were opening up.

"Where and when —" began Alice.

"Why do you think Eakins wouldn't harm her?" asked Mercer.

"Excuse me," said Alice, glaring at him, "I wasn't finished."

"Sorry."

Alice turned back to Ariel. "Tell us about seeing Elizabeth on the day she disappeared."

"She dropped by in the morning, like she often does. She goes for a run first thing every day."

"In this weather?" asked Mercer.

"You're from the States, right?" said Ariel.

"Yeah, New York, via Virginia," he closed his mouth.

"Go on," said Sal.

"Once, sometimes twice a week, when she does a light run, she stops here for a massage when she's done. She keeps some clothes here, showers after. That was what she did that day."

"What was her mood?" asked Sal, "Did she seem on edge, fearful about anything, say anything about Andrew?"

"Uh ... yes, no, and yes."

"What did she say about him?" asked Alice.

"She said they would just be hanging out at their place most of the day and then going into town to the Shelter Café."

"Oh."

"She seemed very happy. Couldn't wait to get back to see Andrew." Ariel rolled her eyes slightly.

"What does that mean?" asked Alice.

"What?"

"Well, you sort of said that with a slight sense of, I don't know, exasperation?"

"Libby's nuts about him."

"About Andrew?" asked Sal.

"Yes. Who did you think I meant?"

"Just trying to be clear."

"She's nuts about him and it's awfully cute, but it is also a little exasperating. She can barely stand to be away from him it seems, even if she's just been gone for a little while. We used to spend a lot more time together. We were a real team in high school. Us against the world. I missed her terribly when she moved away. She's an amazing person. Smart. Unique. Brave."

"How do you mean brave?" asked Mercer.

"Well, she dares to be different. Like me. I like that. Admire it deeply, actually. She had the guts to leave here, most people in these parts don't. You know that, Alice." Alice didn't look up from her note taking. "People who grow up here can't even imagine anything else, bitch about people from the city all the time, just down the road. She had the guts to marry Andrew Eakins too, an interesting man, an artist, not from here or like people from here. I could never figure out why she came back though, that kind of shocked me. She hated it here, just hated it, the way it was so small-time, so petty, the way people gave her grief for standing out, doing so well in school, for having so many boyfriends — bad boys, often. She hated her very name since it was so 'here,' used to say she'd change it in an instant, if she could. She used to have nightmares about being on King Street Circle and just going around and around, never getting anywhere. I thought I'd lost her for good when she went away, but then suddenly here she was, moving back into the family place, and I have her back, and a short while after that she meets Andrew, and lo and behold, they get married! Typical Libby, full of surprises."

"So, she talks about him a lot?" asked Alice.

"Yeah, like constantly, though not literally so much about him, but about the everyday things they do. She's kind of protective."

Ariel noticed the three exchanging a look. "What?"

"She isn't afraid of him, is she?" asked Sal. "Did she ever say anything —"

"Afraid of him? That's ridiculous. He's the nicest, sweetest man. Maybe a little possessive. But I'd be too, if I had Libby."

There was silence for a moment.

"She had a black eye for a while," said Alice bluntly. "People wondered about that."

"That's because they're ignorant."

"That might be a little harsh."

"I gave it to her."

"What?" asked Mercer.

"I gave her the black eye." She laughed.

"We are going to need an explanation," said Sal.

"We keep a garden together, plant all sorts of herbs and things you can't find around here. We like to cook kind of exotic stuff, you might say. I go over there to Libby and Andrew's place all the time; and we experiment. The garden is on their property. We were working one day, and she came up to me to inspect something I was planting. I was digging and didn't realize she was there. Popped her right in the side of the face with the spade. She went down like a ton of bricks and was disoriented for a few seconds, but then we started laughing so hard we were both on the ground. 'People will think Andrew socked me,' I remember she said. We thought that was hilarious too. I guess it wasn't to others."

"What about Mr. Rossi?" asked Alice.

Ariel paused for a second. "Oh, they're getting it on, big time. What woman wouldn't, with an Italian stud like that? She creeps over to his place at night, always at night. He pretends he's giving her language lessons, but he's giving her a whole lot more than that from what she tells me, lucky lady."

"Really?" said Mercer.

The three women looked at him like he wasn't real.

"She's uh ... kidding," said Sal quietly.

"Flavio Rossi is a very nice man and Libby likes to expand her horizons. She and Andrew are talking about going to Italy in a few months."

"They've been seen together out in public, her and Mr. Rossi," said Mercer.

"Well, as of today, I've been seen with you, Detective New York, are we an item?"

"I meant alone," said Mercer quietly.

"You've been talking to some of the old fuddy-duddies around here." Ariel sighed. "You know what they're like, Alice, you of all people."

Alice looked back at her without emotion, or as if she was suppressing it.

"They don't like Libby, and they don't like Andrew, and they think Flavio Rossi is unusual."

"Actually, I wouldn't say most people feel that way," said Alice. "Some do, of course"

"Well, now you know. I hit her in the head with a spade, Mr. Rossi is a lovely gentleman and respectful, Libby is very affectionate, always has been, and others took that for something else. And Andrew Eakins wouldn't hurt a flea."

"I have to tell you, Miss Foster," said Mercer, "that sometimes the gentlest of human beings, the sort none of us would dream would ever hurt anyone, are capable of really heinous crimes. I've witnessed it many times. Does Mr. Eakins have a temper?"

"He's a little emotional at times."

"His lack of control has come up in several interviews and has been witnessed by the three of us during interrogation."

"Interrogation?"

"Would you say you have an objective, unbiased view of Elizabeth Goode?" asked Mercer.

"What does that mean?"

"The two of you seem pretty close."

Ariel looked out the window and appeared a bit perturbed.

"Could you have overlooked some things about her and her relationship with Mr. Eakins?" continued Mercer. "He has not been forthcoming during our discussions. One might almost say he is hiding things about himself and his past."

"I have told you what I know. I have told the truth, the objective truth, which is my job when asked questions by the police, isn't it?"

"Yes."

"Now, if you will excuse me," — she stood up — "I have another client coming shortly."

"Of course," said Alice. "Please let us know if you remember anything else that you feel might be pertinent to this case."

Ariel moved toward the vestibule, then turned back to them. "Why would anyone kidnap my friend?"

"That's a good question," said Alice.

"One that makes us wonder," added Mercer, "if that has not, indeed, happened. There seems no motivation for it."

"I've told you though, she wouldn't run off, not now, and Andrew would not harm her, not in a million years. I am certain of that."

"Mr. Eakins has told a fabrication, Miss Foster," said Mercer. "He has made up a story about Elizabeth vanishing from the Shelter Café when others have said she was never there."

"Why would he do that? Maybe one of the others is lying?" asked Ariel.

"But there are several of them, all of them bystanders," said Mercer. "Why would they lie?"

"Why would *he* lie?" asked Ariel more forcefully. "It doesn't make any sense. Don't you see?"

"Well ..." began Sal.

"Someone has her. I know it. I can feel it. You have vibes about close friends. Don't you believe that? I hate to think of it though, what might be happening to her. What horrible things are being done to her. It takes your imagination to terrible places!"

It seemed that Ariel Foster should have been tearing up, but she wasn't. She was simply staring at them.

"WHAT SHE SAID, there, at the end," said Sal, as they all took a breath back in the cruiser, "could be true."

"But why," said Mercer, "would someone kidnap Elizabeth Goode? We don't have a ransom note or message of any sort. And if someone kidnapped her, why would they be doing terrible things to her? It isn't a realistic possibility, not at this point. Our apparent victim is an ordinary woman without any known enemies. We have to deal with facts and be painstakingly rational. I'm not considering anything else, not entertaining gruesome speculations. That doesn't get us anywhere." The same possibility, though, had passed through his mind. What might be happening to Elizabeth Goode terrified him.

"Could be true," said Alice, nodding at Sal as if she hadn't heard a word that Mercer said.

FLAVIO ROSSI LIVED in a log house a little farther down the sideroad and into the woods. It was spectacular, a shining, nearly yellow residence that appeared to have been stained and lacquered so much that it barely seemed to be made of real logs. He was a charming man with a perfect three-day growth on his somehow tanned face and perfectly unruly black hair. A little like the actor Giancarlo Giannini in his prime. Alice and Sal's reaction as soon as Rossi uttered his greetings in his Italian-inflected English pissed off Mercer to no end. They both immediately took off their parkas and handed them to him, and then sat on his minimalist, Scandinavian furniture in startlingly girlish poses. Their first questions were softballs and began with queries about his personal history. He seemed to be a well-educated man, who liked to travel and had lived in many countries. Alice and Sal used words like *explorer*, *fascinating*, and *awfully exciting* in their responses and dutifully wrote down everything he said.

"People say you were having an affair with Elizabeth Goode," said Mercer.

Giancarlo Giannini gathered himself for a moment, affecting a perfect pause. Then he started to laugh.

"What's so funny?" Mercer demanded.

"Well, I must say, modestly, Detective Mercer, that I have been involved with more than a few women in my day, on several continents." He glanced over at Sal and Alice. The former looked down and the latter kept his gaze. "This Elizabeth Goode though, would be, how do you say, a challenge of a very steep sort."

"What do you mean?"

"She loves her husband with a pure and steady passion that passes all I have ever seen. It is very romantic, yes? I would not choose to disturb such a thing, even if it were possible."

"But others —" began Sal.

"Others are fools."

"What's happened to her?" asked Alice in a suddenly hard voice, darting the question at him. She stared at him. "What's your opinion?"

"I, uh, do not know," said Rossi, looking a little unsure of himself for the first time.

"So, this challenge, as you put it," continued Alice almost derisively, "wasn't something that frustrated you? Angered you?"

"I did not kill Elizabeth Goode," said Rossi, no suave Giannini anymore. "Neither did I kidnap her. She and Mr. Eakins are my friends. I do not know why he told this story about her. It is like a movie, no?"

"We will search your grounds, sir," said Sal, no trace of girlishness left either. She examined his reaction. "Is that all right with you?"

"But ... of course."

"For a body," added Sal.

Mercer could see that this made Rossi more than a little uncomfortable. He would now try very hard to be helpful. It was a good move by Sal, and it seemed to Mercer that she and Alice had calculated exactly how to pace the interview. He doubted that they really thought Rossi had killed Elizabeth Goode, though it wasn't out of the realm of possibility, but making a subject anxious to be of assistance was always a wise idea.

"Think deeply, Mr. Rossi," Mercer said. "Did you or did you not see Elizabeth or Mr. Eakins on the day in question, or are there any other things you can tell us that might be helpful."

"I did not see either of them that day."

"Are you sure?"

"Yes."

"Well, that isn't very help —"

"But there is something I can say."

"Yes?" asked Alice, leaning almost imperceptibly forward.

"I was in the drinking establishment in town one day about a month or so ago —"

"Which one?"

"The English pub, it's the only decent one."

"Go on."

"I met someone there."

"Man or woman?" asked Alice. "Description, please."

"A woman. I cannot remember much about her. Brown hair. Sort of pale and skinny. I believe she wore glasses."

Mercer and Alice exchanged glances.

"Go on," said Sal.

"She came over and sat down beside me. I was alone. She was very friendly and asked many questions about the town and the area."

"So?"

"Well, she asked about my friends, what they were like, and when I mentioned Elizabeth Goode, she asked many more questions. Many more. It was strange. She was, I would say, forthright at first, seemed to have some interest in me, though I, honestly, I hope it is not ungentlemanly to say, had little interest in her. She changed though, once I answered her questions about Elizabeth. She just stood up, as if she had heard what she needed to hear, and left abruptly."

"Long hair or short?" asked Mercer.

"Longish."

"So, you had never seen her before? Do you think she was from around here?"

"No. She was an American."

17

Private Investigations

MERCER WAS BOTH stunned and confused by what Rossi had said about the woman in the pub. Stunned because she sounded similar to the person who had come to his door and predicted the Eakins crime, and whom Beth Morton had seen a number of times. Confused because Rossi said her hair was long and was adamant she was American. Alice believed she wasn't local and had given a good a reason for her theory. Mercer had accepted her point about the car rental, in fact felt embarrassed that he had missed something so obvious. But the woman hadn't had an American accent that he could detect, in fact had spoken like a local, made references to being from the area. Why would she lie? But the whole subject of this strange woman, what she had said to him and the fact that he had kept her existence a secret, was unsettling for him. He would rather keep her out of this, even if she somehow seemed to be involved. When the three of them got into the car, there was silence. Alice stared at him via the rearview mirror.

"You think this woman in the pub is the same person who supposedly came to your house and predicted the incident, don't you?" she finally said.

Supposedly came to his door? *What did Alice mean by that?*

"Possibly."

Alice and Sal exchanged glances.

"We've spent some time on our own trying to find her, without great results, though there have been a few people in town who've mentioned speaking with someone who to some degree meets her description. People here don't like to volunteer information. But we seem to be searching for someone who is inquisitive, curious about the town and the people in it, kind of like what Rossi said. Perhaps it's time to focus on her more."

Alice started the cruiser and wheeled out of the gravel driveway. She turned right and ripped down the sideroad, spraying snow and frozen pebbles.

"I don't think it's advisable to spend too much time on her," said Mercer, holding on to the door handle again. "There are so many other leads that we need to pursue."

"Yes," said Sal, "but she supposedly told you exactly what was going to happen. If we find her, maybe we can crack this case wide open."

Supposedly, again. *Did they really doubt that this woman came to see him, and what he said she told him?*

"As I told you before, Alice, she's more than likely just a bit of a weirdo, someone from the area who believed all the rumours about Eakins."

"But she's an American."

"Yeah, so Rossi thought."

"So did some others."

"Maybe she's just not from town or relatively new to here, so people are assuming she's a foreigner. I can see folks around here thinking that."

Alice and Sal exchanged another glance.

"I want to explore where Eakins is from," said Mercer quickly, "since I think I have a general idea, and look into his relationship with Elizabeth more and the origins of it. I want to find the body too."

"You know that Ranbir and Renaldo and others are looking after that," said Alice.

"With no success."

"It's an ongoing process. And you're still suggesting you would do better?"

"Yeah, actually, I am."

"Well, that's not your job, Detective Mercer. How many times do I have to tell you that? I believe in my colleagues."

There was silence for a while.

"I've decided I'd like to interview Jonathan Li. I'd like to do it as soon as possible."

Alice smiled.

"Good choice, Detective Mercer," said Sal.

They were on the highway now, heading toward town, rushing along well over the speed limit. They had made him park his car at the station again.

"You are going to have the day off tomorrow," said Alice, checking his reaction in the rear-view mirror.

"The day off?" he blurted out. "At this point in the investigation? What if Elizabeth is in the hands of desperate people?"

"And if Captain America doesn't swoop in and save the day, all will be lost?" Alice was smirking.

"Look," said Sal, "Libby could also be as dead as a doornail, or hiding somewhere, who knows what. We're doing the best we can, Detective Mercer. You seem stressed out about all of this."

"I'm not stressed out. I'm just being thorough."

"Well, that's a pretty wild story about an American," continued Sal, "who is supposedly not an American, who came to your door out of several thousand homes, and supposedly outlined a murder that hadn't yet taken place, not something she said to *anyone* else."

"That you then kept from us," said Alice, "but that fit right into the whole thing once it had happened."

"We know you do some writing of some sort," added Sal, almost before Alice finished, "and you've been through some tough times back home and are kind of exiled here. Maybe your imagination gets the best of you at times?"

"A rest seems like a good idea," said Alice. "Make you more capable of heroic American save-the-world kind of help when we need it?"

How did they know about his journal? He hadn't mentioned it to Alice. *Had she done some snooping around at his place?* She was always up first in the morning, so who knows what she might have investigated in his house. *But she had shared it all with Sal? And how did they know about his personal situation too?* He hadn't told Alice much.

Mercer decided it was best to keep quiet. He would take the day off. Or pretend to.

HIS TRIP HOME from town was interesting. The day was getting darker, and everything seemed particularly grey. As a homicide detective who had sent many people to jail for life, and even helped convict others from out of state who were sent to the electric chair, he had always been alert for anyone following him, watching him, for anyone about to attack. All along the roads home there seemed to be a car in the rear-view mirror, keeping pace with him. There was one when he hit the highway out of town, another as he passed through the villages, and a third when he turned down his sideroad. He stopped abruptly near the older Morton family home and watched the car zip past on the highway behind him. If that person was following, then he or she was very good. They hadn't fallen into the trap of pursuing him on a dead end road. It was almost as if they had sensed where he would turn.

He didn't take long with his meal that night, just a sausage with a little hot sauce and a bag of chips. There was too much to do, both tonight and tomorrow, his "day off."

IT HAD BEEN dark for a while by the time he emerged from the house, dressed warmly in his parka, his new tall, insulated rubber boots, a toque, and heavy yellow leather mitts with woolen liners. He paused at the spade and then the axe in the garage, but walked on past and made his way up the lane toward the Goode property, flashlight on. The sky was clear for once, and the moon and stars cast a glow over the encrusted snow, making the fields look like a white, gently undulating ocean. It was eerily quiet, only distant sounds of cars on the highway disturbing the night: It was as if he were under the dome of a majestic cathedral. At the top of the lane, he turned right, his boots crunching into the snow, sinking two feet below the surface with each step, so he had to lift his feet high to move forward. His heart rate increased, and his breathing grew louder, and soon that was all he could hear: his boots crushing the snow and his breathing. Little clouds formed in front of him as he puffed forward. At the Goode property, he had to climb the fence and it took another ten minutes to reach the house. It was barely visible, grey in the black night.

He made his way over to the half-frozen garden and saw the spot where Ranbir and Renaldo had cleared back the snow above the hard earth. They had covered everything up. And they had dug a little in other spots too. It had been a ridiculous job, so much so that Mercer wondered if Alice had had it done merely as a formality. No murderer in their right murdering mind would kill his wife and bury her anywhere near their house and then go and tell a ridiculous story about her being with him later that day when it clearly seemed she hadn't been. He supposed that it was possible that if someone else murdered Elizabeth Goode, he or she might have buried or hidden the body somewhere here to implicate Eakins. That didn't seem likely either though. It would be too obvious a set-up and whatever was going on here did not have simple answers, that was one thing of which he was certain.

He turned toward the house. When he had been inside it with Alice and Sal the other day, he had been fixated on finding clues, objects, and they had found a good one, a firecracker, or at least, it had seemed that way at first. But no murderer would write out anywhere, even inside a Bible hidden in a stairway, that he or she had committed the deed. He knew those words meant something else. Even if Andrew Eakins did kill Elizabeth Goode, he was not confessing it there. Anyway, how would he have done that? Murder her, go into town and pretend he was with her when he wasn't, then come back out and write a confession to leave in his house, meanwhile denying it to the police? This case was a puzzler, as good as anything he had pursued in New York, maybe better.

He wanted to get inside the Goode house again, sit there and feel this home, feel its spirit. He believed in that sort of thing.

Getting in was not a problem. The door and lock, like the house, were old and were a barrier only to the dimmest of criminals. In moments, he was indoors. He walked through the old kitchen, where he doubted these two spent much time — too worldly and urban — and into the living room with its more contemporary furniture and large, flat screen television. He perched on the couch, imagining Elizabeth and Andrew sitting here watching Netflix, perhaps one of those Scandinavian crime dramas that amused Alice and Sal. *Curious,* he thought, *that Elizabeth and Andrew decided to live here, nowhere, so far from where they seemed to be better suited. Why?*

Were they running from something?

That idea kept circling through his mind as he got up and moved through the house again and then left it and walked toward the barn. The wind was blowing now, whistling and moaning. Wind like that always made him think dark thoughts. He thought of the bleak Shakespearean line about life being "a tale told by idiot, full of sound and fury, signifying nothing" and the Bob Dylan lyric, the only song that ever made him cry, about the "idiot wind" that forever blows between human beings, even those who love each other. He thought of Christine. He pulled back the big sliding barn door and found another door inside, an old one with a doorknob. Locked. Again, he was inside within moments. It was surprisingly warm in there: Andrew Eakins's studio. His eyes widened. A crowd of people stood there in the dark, staring at him!

He wished he had the Glock 38. His flashlight beam swept across the group.

Sculptures.

Mercer found the light switch. Iron and steel sculptures of human figures. They were all lean and tortured looking, the heads downcast, mouths open in what looked like screams or moans. Parts of their bodies, often their limbs, had been melted, severed, and soldered so the figures were deformed. Mercer could feel the pain in every sculpture. Most were paired, with the secondary figure at the feet of the other, the primary one looking down at them, but definitely not in triumph.

The tools of the sculptor's trade, the weapons, were hanging on the walls: steel hammers, sledges, blowtorch, soldering guns. A large vice sat on a crude wooden table.

"Andrew Eakins knows about pain," said Mercer.

He walked over and examined the tools. Yes, they would work nicely if you wanted to murder someone. Eakins, though slim, was strong and fit from wielding these heavy tools every day, bending steel and iron to his will. Everything looked clean and undisturbed, perfectly in place.

There were no guns on the wall. He hadn't seen a single rifle or even a gun cabinet in the house. Mercer smiled at Ebb and Delilah Morton's fantasy of a battery of firearms and a place fitted out for intense martial arts practice. He didn't see any sign of that either. No space for it, really, unless you wanted to drop kick the sculptures. Those tools though, it was true, could be weapons — would do nicely in any physical confrontation, any attack with vicious intent. He imagined Eakins might have been spotted here by others, working hard, maybe shirtless, perhaps striking the poses of his figures, and looking like someone ready to grapple with a combatant.

Mercer sat on the base of a sculpture and looked up at a figure. It stared down at him, aghast. It reminded him of the facial expression in Edvard Munch's *The Scream*.

Who is this guy, Andrew Eakins? Mercer thought for a moment. *An American, maybe from Pennsylvania, certainly from the Northeast. He came to this area about two years ago, Alice said. Elizabeth had been away, came back. Andrew is here a little before that, and they meet and marry, according to Ariel Foster. They were not running from something. Not together, anyway. Just him.*

"We have to get more out of Andrew Eakins."

He looked down at the second figure in the sculpture. It appeared to be a woman, though not obviously; certainly smaller and wounded. A victim. Wounded by the man standing above her and looking down, aghast. He glanced at the other pieces: similar pairings.

Was Eakins beating Elizabeth? Did she keep that secret until he killed her? She was "protective of him," protecting both of them, maybe, from anyone who might discover their secret. Mercer looked over at the instruments on the wall. If they were used, it would have been a brutal death and Eakins would have the ability and the wherewithal to carve up the body and cleverly dispose of the parts. That's the key in an efficient murder: the intelligent disposal of the body. He had seen it many times. He remembered body parts plastered into walls, each in separate places throughout a home in Brooklyn: kidneys in the bathroom, genitals in the master bedroom, and the head in the office. A woman had done that. He remembered a case where human innards had been fed to a pet wolf on a farm outside Albany. He had come here to get away from all that. And more.

Mercer noticed a black object across the room against a wall, almost hidden by the sculptures in the dim glow of the few lights he had turned on. It was a big stove, body-sized, more like a furnace, or a forge, with a surface on top for hammering cast iron. He got up and walked toward it. He heard a creak near the door behind him, like a foot set lightly on the floor. He stopped. Listened. Another creak.

"Hello?" he asked. "Is someone there?"

Nothing.

Mercer smiled at himself. Mr. Paranoid. Just like imagining that car following him out on the highway. The wind had picked up outside. That was all.

He opened the door of the furnace and it squealed. Andrew's own inferno. He imagined Eakins cooking materials in here, blasting them with intense heat to force them to melt, bend, and writhe. Hammering them once he pulled them out. He imagined Elizabeth's body parts, disappearing in sun-like flames, even her bones reduced to ashes, then left to float into the air somewhere out in the fields.

There was nothing inside the furnace. He glanced back at the tools on the wall, all so pristine and in their places, even identified with perfect little name tags. He remembered Andrew Eakins in those slightly tinted aviator glasses, glowing blond hair, ironed shirt, and designer jeans. Neat freak. Mercer bet that Eakins cleaned up every day after he worked, even emptied his furnace. He pulled off a mitt, put his hand into the stove's interior, and ran a finger along the surface. He could not feel much grime and the tip of his finger looked almost unblemished when he took it out.

"No sense in even running a test on this."

He walked over to the entrance and looked back at the studio.

"And Elizabeth? Why was she living here? She hated where she grew up." He thought of what Alice and others had said about Elizabeth Goode not fitting in and wanting to get away as soon as she could. She had been destined for greatness, but somewhere else. That struck him as the dynamic, whether admitted to or not, with people in these parts. Even if they stayed, even if they professed to never wanting to leave, they always seemed to be comparing their world to the great "elsewhere." He thought of the jealousy, almost hatred, in people's voices when they spoke of Elizabeth leaving.

Mercer had a reputation back in the NYPD for not leaving a single stone unturned. He shouldn't leave this space, not just yet. He looked around the entire studio, even at the ceiling.

He started searching again. "Get behind things, under things," he told himself. He removed every tool from its place and inspected it, even took a few apart and put them back together. Nothing. He ran his hands along the edges of every part of every sculpture. Nothing. He found a crowbar, jammed it under the legs of the stove, and pried it up.

Something, under one leg.

It was a piece of material, cotton he thought, about the size of a few quarters and with two cracked buttons. He pulled a piece of Kleenex out of a pocket and picked it up. There appeared to be a pattern, blue, kind of like a peacock feather. He examined it closely and saw an almost microscopically small red dot there. *Blood?* He folded it up and put it into his pocket.

"Now how did that happen?" Mercer asked himself. Eakins did not look like the type to wear some sort of flowery pattern. "How did that get under there?" It was almost as if someone had left it for Hugh Mercer.

He left the studio and searched the rest of the barn for a while, using his flashlight, looking for secret passageways, hidden rooms, he wasn't sure what, really. His heart wasn't in that part of the search though. He doubted he would find anything more. That piece of material was an anomaly, a curious one. Anything else that might have been here was likely long gone.

When he left the barn, he didn't turn right and head back toward his place. Instead, he walked out toward the road on the far side of the Goode property. He stood there for a moment thinking about Elizabeth and why she would have come back here, almost, it seemed, against her will.

A car came up the sideroad. It slowed as it approached, and for some reason Mercer stepped back and crouched behind a spruce tree. The car slowed even more, its headlights bathing the Goodes' mailbox, the entrance to their driveway, and the wind-sculpted snow in light. Mercer peered through the branches but couldn't see who was driving. Then the car moved on, north up the sideroad.

North, thought Mercer. *That's where Ariel Foster lives.* He needed to know more about where Elizabeth had gone when she went away.

He started walking up the road in the darkness. It only took him five minutes to get to Ariel's. As soon as he turned into her driveway, the same car came by from the opposite direction. It slowed again as it passed him.

It took Ariel a long time to come to the entrance after he knocked. She peered at him through the eyehole before she opened the door. Even then, she only held it slightly ajar. She was wearing a white bathrobe and her hair looked disheveled.

"Mr. New York Detective. This is a surprise, at this hour."

He could see now that she actually looked a little anxious.

"News of Libby?" she asked and swallowed.

"No, not that."

She frowned. "What then? What do you want?"

"Just a couple of questions."

"I'm busy."

She opened the door a little more and he could see someone sitting in the living room beyond the hall, wearing a bathrobe just like Ariel's.

"I'll be quick."

"Very quick. Look, I'd let you inside, but —"

"No worries, I've got my toque."

Ariel didn't laugh.

"Uh ... just wondered if you can tell me where Elizabeth went when she left here and what she did. I'm struggling with why she would come back."

Ariel sighed impatiently. "First, she went away to university, to a couple of them, I think, six years or more, not sure exactly. Then, she got a job down there. Worked for quite a few more years."

"Down where?"

"In the States."

"Where in the States?"

"I think the first school was Bryn Mawr, near Philadelphia?"

"Pennsylvania," said Mercer.

"I'm aware of which state it's in."

"Oh, sorry, just thinking out loud."

"Look, I have to go. Libby and I are good friends, best friends, but for a while there when she was away, we weren't in touch much at all, so I'm not full of details about that stretch of her life. She wanted to leave everything around here, maybe even me, I guess, maybe even her old self. I respected that. I was pretty excited when she came back and wanted to see me again. It was like she had never been away. Though she, and Andrew, must have had a good reason to stay here, more than just inheriting the family home." Ariel started to close the door. "Anyway, doesn't Alice know all this stuff?"

He put his hand in the door. "One last thing. When did Andrew get here, really?"

"What do you mean, really? He came here a few months before she came back."

"Did she know him before that?"

"Nope."

"How do you know that?"

"That, she would have told me. Women tell each other those sorts of things." She regarded him for a moment. "Believe me." She closed the door.

He walked back down the dark sideroad and crossed the Goode property and then climbed the fence on the far side of the field and reached his own sideroad. When he got there, he noticed a car turning onto it way down at the far end, coming off the highway. As he stood there at the end of his lane, the car drove toward him. When it neared, it slowed, came to a halt, and sat there for a while. Then it pulled right up to him. For the second time that night Mercer wished he was armed. He stepped back, hands clenched in fists. In the glare of the headlights, he could not tell what kind of car it was or who was inside.

The driver's side door opened, and someone stepped out. A woman.

"Hi," said the voice, sweet and employing two syllables.

Sergeant Alice Morrow.

18

Who Is She?

ALICE WALKED RIGHT up and put her arms around him. She held him close for a moment. That was not like her.

"What do you want?" he asked.

"Company," she said, into his chest.

That was not like her either.

They got into the car and drove down the lane to the house, neither of them saying a word. When they got inside, he took her parka, toque, and mitts, and hung them up and they sat down at the table in the big kitchen.

"Was that you going up and down the Goode's sideroad?"

"Yeah."

"Why?"

"Looking for you. I came here first."

"Why?"

"I don't know."

"Yes, you do."

"I suppose I wanted to know what you were doing."

"Why?"

Alice Morrow was the sort of person you had to keep asking that question.

She sighed. "Look, I hate to admit that you might know more about the sort of thing we're involved in."

"What sort of thing?"

"This case. What did you think I meant?"

"Go on."

She sighed again. "You have lots of expertise, experience. I'm in charge and you need to know that ... but I was at home thinking about what was going through your head ... and I just wanted to know. I wanted us to put our heads together. For Elizabeth Goode."

"Really?"

"Really. Then I came out this way and you weren't here and then I found you near the Goode's place in the dark ... and then by Ariel Foster's."

"Yeah."

"Yeah? That's not good enough, Detective. What were you doing? Let's start with the Goode's house and their barn."

"What if I don't want to share?"

"This is a potential murder investigation, Mercer. You have overstayed the time you were supposed to be in this country. I did some checking. You told them at the border that you were staying for just two weeks."

She said it coldly, her manner completely changed. He knew he could legally stay longer. But could she make the misinformation he gave the border guard a problem for him?

"Okay." He paused. "If Elizabeth Goode is dead then I don't think her body is anywhere near here. That doesn't make any sense, ridiculous to consider, really." He looked at Alice, but she did not react. "I like to feel a case, as it were, to just walk around or sit at a murder scene or a key site and just take everything in.

It helps me to sort things out, get a vibe. So, I went to the Goode home. Got inside."

"Credit card?"

"Yeah. I started looking around, thinking about why they would be living here, two people like that."

"They are running from something." Alice reached across and put her hand on Mercer's hand. Hers was cold.

"Yeah. Just him though, don't you think?"

"Well, he came here first, so maybe just him. Maybe she hadn't intended to stay here, just sort out the estate, and then they fell in love. She would have been emotionally vulnerable, maybe a little needy with her parents having just died."

"Well, it seems to me that —"

"What about the barn?"

"Wanted to check it for myself. The whole building but mostly the studio. Eakins's work is about pain, between people."

"Yeah, and he has a furnace and forge in there where he could have incinerated her body. He cleaned it up awfully well."

Mercer smiled at her and took his hand back. "Why didn't you tell me all that, or let me see it?"

"I'm the boss. That was my job. You aren't officially working on this, just helping us out a little."

"But you could share."

"Sharing isn't always my thing."

"I've noticed. Look, Alice, why don't you ever talk about yourself?"

"You aren't exactly Mr. Open about everything either. That's pretty evident."

"Yeah, but you're a —"

"I'm a woman? The sharing sort?"

"No."

"Look, there isn't much to tell. What does it matter, anyway?

What does the past matter? Between the two of us? We've been having some fun together, haven't we?"

"Yeah. Yeah, sure, of course, more than fun."

She smiled. "Then there's this case. It's been interesting to have you along and work with you a little. Together, we have a better chance of solving this."

"Sometimes you act like I'm a suspect."

"Are you?"

He searched for a smile, a look of sarcasm. Opaque Alice Morrow.

"No, I'm not a suspect, not even a person of interest. You don't seriously consider me one, do you?"

"I'm a cop, Hugh. You live next door to the victim, you came here recently out of the blue, are here one might argue illegally, you would know how to do something like this, and this is a very irregular case, a fucking ingenious one. The moment you told that story about the woman coming to your door predicting a murder, you were involved in this, like it or not. Do I think you did it? No. Do I think I know what you were doing the night of the incident?" She glanced over at the bottle. "Yeah, probably. Party for one. Right here. Being Hugh Mercer. Lots of dark thinking." Then she regarded him for about as long as she ever had. "Should I ask you all the pertinent questions? Yes."

The wind was blowing outside. He felt alone and he could tell that she did too.

"Would you like to ask some more pertinent questions, upstairs?" he asked.

She crossed her arms in front of her chest. "Why did you go to Ariel's house?"

"Just wanted to get a few things straight."

"Like what?"

"Like when, exactly, Elizabeth went away, where she was, and when she came back."

"You could have asked me."

He smiled. "Well, it seems we have a trust issue."

She smiled back and then looked serious again.

"Anything else?"

"What do you mean?"

"Discover anything else at the Goode's place? I've been reading a bit about you."

"Creeping me? In addition to checking my border crossing?"

"You could say that, I suppose, but strictly professionally. Read about a few of your cases. It seems like you put in twenty-five-hour days. You are nothing if not thorough."

"I try."

"So?"

"So what?"

"Anything else?"

It was as if she knew. That was something that he had often felt about women though. They seemed to know everything about you. You couldn't hide a thing.

"No." He reached out and kissed her, with feeling. He was aware of the piece of material in his pocket, folded into a Kleenex, ready to be tested by a lab. *No lab around here,* he figured. How, though, could he get it to New York?

That was perhaps the best night they spent together. She seemed different. More vulnerable, more tender. Once, he thought she whispered a name other than his, but he wasn't sure. He wondered if he had ever done that, with her.

When he woke, she was gone. They hadn't been together for a little while, so he had forgotten what that was like — her disappearing that way. He had thought that maybe she had decided recently that they should cool their relationship because it was unprofessional for them to be intimate while working on this case. Obviously, he had been wrong. In a way, they were not intimate anyway.

He went downstairs and immediately noticed something out of place. He always left a bottle of rye on the counter, pushed discreetly up against the wall behind some things. He had often done that at home too. The current bottle was almost empty. It was now sitting about a foot out from the wall, on its own. The only other person who had been down here was Alice. He kept other bottles in the cupboard above. Had she been confirming his drinking habits? He went outside and noticed footprints going from the driveway out to the barn. She had been looking around out there too.

HE TOLD HIMSELF he would spend the rest of the day *not* thinking about the case, maybe read or listen to music, but found himself pacing the house wondering what Alice and Sal were doing, what he might be missing, worrying about Elizabeth Goode. He did a search for her in Philadelphia and New York online and turned up photos of people who were obviously not her. *But Ariel Foster was certain Elizabeth had gone to Bryn Mawr College.* A search of recent phone directories was equally frustrating — he could not find anyone with her name in Philly and "E. Goode" was listed seven times in New York, none of them noting addresses. He found nothing promising in New Jersey either. What had Elizabeth Goode done down there? She was an academic, wasn't she? Ariel had said she was "brilliant" in the sciences. And what was she was doing for a living here? Did she have a job? Did Andrew support them? He hadn't asked about that. He added it to his notes.

"JONATHAN IS WAITING for you," said Sal the next morning when he appeared at the police station, right at the stroke of nine. He was surprised to see Sal there, especially since Alice had not arrived yet.

"Where?"

"At his café. He's left the door unlocked. He said to go through the half door in the counter and you'll find him in a little office between it and the kitchen."

"Thanks." He turned to go, but then turned back. "Oh, Sal?"

"Yes?"

"One thing I forgot to ask you two. I know Eakins was tight-lipped when you first talked to him. But did he give you a description of what Elizabeth was wearing that day?"

"Yup."

"And?"

"Black leggings and a blue dress with buttons, peacock pattern."

Mercer had to use his poker face.

"Okay, thanks, just thought I should have that detail."

Mercer trudged around the Circle in the cold, his hands freezing inside his dress gloves. Time to concentrate on the Li interview. He had never considered that there might be an office in the small café and that struck him as a fault on his part. He had obviously not cased the place well enough on his previous visit. The little bell tinkled as he stepped inside. He stood for a moment and took in the surroundings again. There was the rectangular table with a bench at the window to his immediate right, where the ghost couple may have sat, and other round tables, six of them, taking up the rest of the right side of the room. The floor was varnished old wood. The counter and the display of cakes, sandwiches, drinks, cappuccino machines etc. to his left, the menus and hip photographs and paintings above them on the wall. A truncated hallway was straight ahead, the two little bathroom doors on the left. He spotted the half door at the far end of the counter again. *The office is past there somewhere? Must be tiny.*

So it was. He went through the half door and turned right, immediately in a short walkway to the cramped kitchen. He could see a refrigerator, a microwave, sinks, a counter with bowls on it with half-made egg and tuna salads. A chopping board with a big, serrated knife on it. He almost walked past the office door, even though it was open. Jonathan Li sat behind the world's smallest desk in the world's smallest office, barely big enough for one. There were two people in there though.

Alice.

"Good morning, Detective Mercer," she said. "I won't get up."

It was a clever idea to interview Li here. The tight space would make him feel uncomfortable and show his emotions writ large on his face. You could really home in on him.

"I thought I'd ask Mr. Li to talk to us here," said Alice with a smile. "Convenient for him, you know."

Very nice, Sergeant Morrow.

"Yes, well, I hope you haven't begun without me."

"No, no, we were just exchanging pleasantries, weren't we, Mr. Li?"

"Uh, yeah."

"He was telling me about how relieved he is to not have to live in a big city anymore. He's a real small-town guy now." She gave Li a lovely grin, which he awkwardly returned with a nod.

Mercer jammed his large frame down into the little chair next to Alice. The whole room now was three chairs and bodies and a desk. Mercer's leg pressed up against Alice's and she reached over and squeezed him on the upper thigh, just out of Li's line of sight, startling him.

"Are you okay?" she asked.

"Fine, yes, fine."

"I didn't know you were a cop the other times you came in here," said Li suddenly.

"Well, plainclothes, semi-retired. We've never really had a chance to chat though."

"No, we haven't."

"Just helping out Sergeant Morrow. I have a lot of experience with homicides."

"Homicides?"

"We need to consider all possibilities, Mr. Li," said Alice pleasantly.

Mercer reached into his coat and pulled out his notebook and pen. He pulled it up toward his chest.

"You have the floor, Detective Mercer," said Alice, "what there is of it."

It was a funny line, but no one laughed.

"So, Jonathan," said Mercer, "may I call you Jonathan?"

"Yes, of course."

"Jonathan, tell me about yourself and why you came here."

"Me?"

Man, this is perfect, thought Mercer. He could almost see Li sweat. He felt like he was climbing into his target's eyes and from there into his mind. Alice really was clever.

"You want to know about me? Why?" He rubbed his face.

"Just a formality. Always do this sort of thing when talking to witnesses."

"But I didn't witness anything, just an unstable man making up a story."

"We'll get to that. So, you moved here rather suddenly, it sounds like. Why this town, Jonathan, why a restaurant?"

"Café."

"Sure, café."

"I thought it was a smart business decision. I'd often driven through here on the way to other places. There was a dearth of good spots to eat in the town, nothing kind of cool. I figured a café would work."

"So, that's the only reason you came here, so abruptly? Business?"

Up this close, Li's hesitation was terribly obvious. Mercer made a show of writing in his notebook.

"Well," said Li, "there's often more than one reason you make an important move like that."

"And your other reason was?" asked Alice.

"Personal."

"Personal?" She waited for Li to say more, but he didn't.

"And you are going to share that with us," said Mercer, resting his hand for an instant on Alice's police cap jammed onto the desk.

"Uh, just personal, a breakup ...with my partner."

"And when you say partner, you mean a business associate?"

"No."

"I see," said Alice. "Well, we won't prod you about that, none of our business."

Mercer stared at her for a second, then turned back to Li. "May I ask you this?" he said in an overly polite tone, imitating the local flat accent. "Was it difficult, this breakup?"

"You could say that."

There was something about his manner, the way he looked down, put his hand to his temple as if touching a wound, that Mercer recognized.

"Was your partner difficult?"

"You could say that."

"Okay," asked Alice, putting on a smile, "as I said, no need for us to prod. The business though, here, has it gone well?"

"I'm here, am I not?"

"Can you elaborate?"

"It's going fine." He smiled for the first time. "I've settled here, haven't I?"

Mercer wrote something else in his notepad. "Now," he said, looking back up at Li, "I'd like you to describe exactly what happened on the day in question."

"I've already done this."

"I'd like you to do it again, for me."

Li sighed. "Okay." He started to recount what occurred, explaining everything in remarkable detail, even reiterating that Andrew Eakins entered the café at exactly 5:51 p.m. Mercer made notes, but not of these repeated details. He was more interested in the fact that Li was so thorough, so precise. Was that an indication of someone lying or telling the truth? Then, Mercer noticed something.

"Let me stop you there. You did what with the sign?"

"As soon as Mr. Eakins entered the café, I went out and flipped the sign on the door, to indicate we were closed."

This was a detail Mercer had not heard before. He glanced toward Alice, whose eyes widened a little.

"Why did you do that? You had nine minutes left. Didn't you want the business?"

Li looked a little flustered. "I, uh, I've gotten used to when people come in here. That was almost certainly it for the day. Another couple, as I told the police, had just left. I wanted to start cleanup as well."

"And you are sure you were on your own that day?" asked Alice cheerfully. "Owner only at work?"

"Yeah, just me."

"What do you think of Andrew Eakins, Jonathan?" asked Mercer.

There was a pause.

"Honestly?"

"That's what we're here for."

"I don't particularly like him."

"Why?"

"He is very different from her, from Elizabeth. He never talks. He's moody. Sometimes he's a bit aggressive. He, uh, he hit her." For a moment Li's eyes went steely and then he looked away from them.

"You saw him do it?"

"No, no. She had a bruise on her face once, was very self-conscious about it ... There's no proof, of course."

"What about her? What do you think of Elizabeth?"

"Very nice. Always chatting and pleasant. We get along well; we're sort of similar. She seems very protective of him for some reason. She'll order for him, look after him, almost seems to be calming him down at times."

"Temperamental artist," said Alice.

"Yeah, right."

"So, you have your doubts about their relationship?" asked Mercer.

"Only in the sense that it was a bad one, from my observation. They were always snuggling up to each other and holding hands, but when you know the rest, you figure it was an act, that she was trying to make things look good."

"What do you mean by 'when you know the rest'?"

Mercer could see Li's Adam's apple bounce up and down.

"Nothing. Just, you know, about the abusive thing."

"But you said there was no proof."

"Yes, you're right, maybe I shouldn't have said that. It's just my opinion. But you asked."

"I did indeed."

"What if I told you, Mr. Li," said Alice, "that the bruise you refer to, and it sounds like there was only one, was caused by her friend, a woman, an accident while gardening?"

Li swallowed again. "Really? You know that?"

"Yeah," said Mercer.

"I ... I guess I'd be wrong about that then, but you didn't have a good feeling about him."

"Well, that's all we want to ask you, Jonathan. Thank you," said Alice.

Mercer awkwardly shoved his notebook into his pocket, stood up, and edged out of the office. Alice followed. Li took a moment to get up and then trailed behind. When they were near the door, Mercer turned back.

"Oh, one more thing. I understand you know the other couple, the ones who saw Eakins on the street?"

"Yeah." Li didn't look Mercer in the eyes.

"Do you know them well?"

"I wouldn't say so. Just customers, fairly regular."

"And you are certain there was no one else inside the café?"

"Yes."

"Did Eakins ever stop by on his own before that day?" asked Alice suddenly.

"Eakins? No. Always with her ... except that time."

"How about a woman with brown hair and wire-rim glasses, grey coat," continued Alice, "maybe wearing a button with a feminist slogan? Anyone like that frequent this place?"

"No," said Li instantly, then glanced to the floor and then back up at them, "though maybe, that covers a lot of people."

"She likes to talk, ask questions."

They could see Li swallow again.

"As I say, I'm not sure."

Mercer opened the door and ushered Alice out before him with a grand gesture that said that it really was time to go. As she stepped through the door though, he turned back to Li.

"Why do you think Eakins made up this story?" he asked, eyeing the café owner.

"I don't know. Why would he? Why would anyone? The whole thing is pretty bizarre. But I've never trusted Andrew Eakins."

19

What If

"LET'S GO SOMEWHERE," said Alice, "we need to talk."

"Yeah," said Mercer, "there's a lot there to unpack."

"Unpack?"

"To figure out."

"I need to tell you some things too. It's time to let you in on a little more."

Progress, thought Mercer. "That was very well done, arranging to meet in the cramped office. We were a good team in there."

Alice didn't react. "I think the pub might be open or at least the owner will be in, and he'll open it for me. It'll be quiet, no one around. We can sit in a booth and not be disturbed."

Before they left, Alice led the way down a shoulder-width passageway running between the café and the next building. The back door of the Shelter opened onto an alleyway that was wide enough for a car to get through.

Five minutes later, Alice banged on the door of the pub and the owner, a guy with long hair and a black T-shirt that read "The Weeknd" let them in and brought them a couple of coffees.

"That's Jamal," said Alice as they settled in. "Talked to him yesterday about your prophetess. You'll remember that Flavio Rossi said she approached him in here."

"Oh, yeah." Mercer really did not want to get into this. The strange woman at his door was still not a good subject for him.

"He thinks he remembers someone fitting the vague description Rossi and you gave us. Your description was slightly more detailed, though you really do seem to have the nationality wrong, if it's indeed the same woman. Thought you were an expert on accents. Jamal thinks she was American too. Nothing stood out about her though. She seemed friendly, interacted with some of the regulars."

Maybe she was putting on the accent and her local knowledge, thought Mercer. He also wondered why in the world she would do that.

"Anyway, Jamal was sure her hair was long, like Rossi said, not short, and can't recall her in a coat like you described or wearing any sort of feminist button."

"So, that's probably a dead end, two different people. I really think the woman at my door was just kind of nuts. The crime happening just after that a coincidence."

"Maybe."

"Let's talk about Jonathan Li."

"Lots to unpack."

Mercer smiled. "Our café owner didn't seem very comfortable, did he?"

They went back through the interview with Li for a while and were surprised at how similar their reactions and conclusions were. It was possible Li was hiding something, but it was difficult to tell what. They both wondered aloud if there was a chance he was being paid to be quiet about what happened in his café.

"Can you get a look at his bank accounts?" asked Mercer.

"Legally, no. Not at this point. And this other couple corroborates that Andrew was on his own outside the café. No, there are no grounds for looking at his finances."

"You said you were going to let me in on more things. I'm interested in Andrew's past, and Elizabeth's as well, their relationship, why they were here. What was she doing for a living lately? Can you tell me that?"

"Online stuff, apparently."

"Well, get her laptop and let's have a look."

"Figure that's something we didn't consider?" Alice wasn't pleased. "We looked for her laptop right away, Mercer, and his. Hers is nowhere to be found."

"Stolen?"

"Maybe. Or maybe she keeps it hidden because there are things on it she doesn't want others to see, and we just haven't found it yet."

"Well, that's a whole thing in itself, isn't it? What about his?"

"Doesn't have one."

"Really?"

"He's obviously a bit eccentric."

"Yeah, but that's weird, considering his work, isn't it? Neither of them seemingly with a laptop. That could be interpreted as hiding from something, don't you think? At least one of them. What about his cellphone?"

"Believe it or not, we are on that too."

"Sorry."

"He gave it up right away. Nothing on it of interest, just business stuff, discussions of the sales of his sculptures, and lots of texts and calls to and from Elizabeth. Seems like she was just about his only friend. Sweet stuff mostly, love notes, some of it sexual. Doesn't paint a picture of a couple who were fighting or had any issues at all."

"Interesting. Maybe Andrew Eakins isn't our guy. And if he isn't ... then we really do have a hell of a case on our hands."

They didn't say anything for a while, then they took a drink at the same time, which made both of them self-conscious.

"So, let's spitball a few scenarios about what might have happened in the café," said Alice.

"Okay."

"Let's say Andrew Eakins came into the Shelter alone, having already killed Elizabeth, maybe chopped her up, and incinerated her in his cleaned-up furnace."

"In that case, she's dead and he's a weirdo with a nasty temper and hidden violent behaviour.

"Or just a man who flipped out for some reason. Happens."

"Of course, yeah, you're right. However you cut it though, no pun intended, he's our man then. That's why he's told this story, that's why he's so evasive, makes a lot of sense, and we're looking for a body or remains, and we need to find some way to break him."

"Correct. Now, let's look at the other possibility."

"She was with him when they came into that café."

They regarded each other for a moment. Mercer could feel the goosebumps rise on his arms.

"That would be something," said Alice quietly.

"... And highly unlikely, don't you think?"

"That's not what this little game is about, Detective Mercer. This is a hypothetical. We are imagining it to be true."

"So, either she was somehow invisible to both Li and the couple on the street, everyone but Eakins, or the other three lied. *All* of them."

"That's a possibility we're considering at this moment."

"And there's a phantom couple, sitting by the window of the café."

"Yeah."

"Can you tell me if you've learned anything about them?"

"We're drawing a blank. We've asked around, tried to spread the word, find out if anyone knows of anyone who might have been in the café late that day."

"But Li didn't see them. It's just Eakins who says they were there, right?"

"Yeah, but he's adamant about it, two people, right there when it happened, doesn't remember what they looked like at all, just that they were there, but Sal and I arrived within moments, and it was just Li and him. Just as Li said. Why would Eakins lie about that though?"

"And Li was the only one working. Isn't that a little strange?"

"Maybe, but remember, this isn't New York. His one kitchen help had just left and he only has two other employees. We talked to them, and one was on the job that day and he let her leave early."

"Hmm. Does he often do that?"

"A few times, apparently."

"And just after Eakins comes in, or Eakins and our apparent victim, Li flips the sign over so no one else will come in, right? He hadn't told you that before, had he?"

"No. But he likely does that every day. It was very near to closing time."

"And what about the couple on the street? What do you know about them? There wasn't a word in those lovely, redacted transcripts you so kindly gave me."

"Sorry about that, just keeping control of things as we go along here." Alice smiled. "They live out in the country, not too far from the Goode farm, name of Freeman. Their families have lived around here for a long time, in their early fifties, with kids just starting to go away for school. They're good people, a little wingy in their political views, but that's not unusual around here."

"Care to share what they told you — unredacted?"

Alice smiled again. "She had a tea, Earl Grey, and he had a coffee and they both had a scone, blueberry. She said it was 'scrumptious.' Left the Shelter maybe thirty seconds before Eakins entered for the first time, passed him on the street, recognized him. He was alone, they are certain of that. We called them right after Li told us they were the last customers he'd had. They were just getting home, so their memory was fresh. They have no business connections to Eakins, Elizabeth Goode, or Jonathan Li, laughed out loud when I asked them that. Their story perfectly fits with Li's. Elizabeth was never there. They know Elizabeth well, not him, found him distant, had heard stories about him."

"Like that he hit her? Et cetera?"

"Well, they didn't say that, just said they'd heard he 'wasn't the best' and I took that with a grain of salt — this was before we talked to Ariel."

Mercer took another sip of coffee. "Have any sixth sense about them? Do you think they could have been involved? Do you think they could have been paid to keep quiet?"

"That would be pretty wild. Sal and I swung by their place to ask some follow-up questions, nice house, maybe a bit above their station. The wife is a homemaker, he's a contractor, self-employed, "Good Man for Hire" on his business card. They were lovely to talk to in person, gave us hot chocolate. Noticed some photographs of them in Florida in front of what looked like a home, not a hotel, so they may be snowbirds, at least partial ones."

"Huh?"

"Snowbirds. You know, spread your tiny wings and fly away?"

" I have no idea what that means."

"Folks from around here who go south for the winter. These people aren't fully migratory at this point though, not retired yet, but gearing up for it."

"That would be a little expensive, wouldn't it? So, nice house, kids heading to college, big-time retirement plans on the horizon, single income."

"Yeah, but let's keep asking ourselves why. Why would they be paid and by whom, to keep quiet? And how could or why would anyone put together that scene in the café?"

"Did you ask *them* about their bank accounts?"

"Mercer ... that would be illegal and outrageous." She was smirking.

"Did you?"

"Well ... I found that they were just so easy to talk to, unlike Li, so ready to volunteer information, so I kind of vaguely hinted at it being routine to look into witnesses' financial —"

"Wow. And?"

"Funny thing is, they had no problem with it. She dug right into her purse to show me their accounts, two of them, actually had bank books, if you can believe it."

"Haven't seen one of those in a while."

"Zero detectable uptick in funds."

"Maybe they have other accounts?"

"Well, that would be interesting, and rather involved on their parts. These people aren't exactly seasoned criminals, doubt they've even had many speeding tickets. They would have to be awfully motivated, re: Elizabeth and Andrew, to be so evasive, criminally so, and involved in this.

"Yeah, you're right. Who knows, maybe they're telling the truth, or maybe something else really weird happened in that café."

"Like what?"

"I don't know." Mercer took the last drink from his cup. "You said there were no security cameras in the café, none on the street either, I assume?"

"Only cameras on the Circle are at the police station, too far away to take in the Shelter. No sign of Eakins, Elizabeth Goode, or the Freemans that we could see. Though there was one person in that five-minute period between about five-fifty and five-fifty-five, getting out of a car at the far right side of the frame, then heading in the direction of the café. "

"Really?"

"A woman in her thirties, brown hair, wire-rimmed glasses."

"What?" Mercer turned pale.

"Just kidding."

"Very funny."

"You should see your face." She laughed, then looked down at her empty cup. "There was a woman on camera at about that time though, with a man. Parked the car at five-fifty."

"And?"

"She was fairly tall, at least five foot nine, we calculated, hard to be certain, full figured. She kissed the man, and he went in the opposite direction, toward the station, looked young from his clothes and gait, wearing a porkpie hat so we couldn't see his features. She walked in the direction of the café, her back to us. We know the car is a local because we could see a monthly parking sticker in the windshield. She came back about half an hour later, approaching from the other direction, this time with her man again, arm in his, and then they left. Unfortunately, the camera angle didn't catch the licence plate."

"But you have a car make?"

"Yeah, but not the colour, the security cameras record black and white."

"This woman would have passed by the café at about the same time as Eakins entered!"

"Possibly."

"Possibly?"

"Who knows, she could have gone into another store on the Circle before she got to there. There are a few of them between the station and the Shelter. Eakins and Elizabeth Goode's car was parked seven stores to the *other* side of the café. No one else has come forward and everyone around here knows about the disappearance and where it happened."

"But this woman entered the frame coming from the *opposite* direction half an hour later! She had to have passed the café at some point!"

"Could have been after the incident occurred, Mercer."

"Maybe she saw something. Maybe she and this man are the ghost couple.

"Her man went the other way."

"And you can't find her? You have the car make and you know she is a local! You know she is about five feet nine inches tall, her build, and that she has a male significant other, wears a porkpie hat?" His voice was rising. Alice didn't look pleased. "You can't find someone like that in this little place? Are you kidding me?"

She glared at him. "You're right. We should have sent armed police officers searching the town, breaking into homes, looking for someone matching her vague description and her black and white car. All women about five foot nine with male partners to the police station, now!"

"But the —"

"We've found ten cars like that and none of the owners match the description. We've put a hundred man and woman hours into trying to find them. And looking for your phantom American accomplice!"

That shut Mercer up. "Sorry," he finally said.

Alice paused. "Sorry too. Didn't mean *accomplice*." Alice didn't look sorry though. She still looked pissed off. There was silence for a moment. "Look, sometimes it feels like you are a little fucked up about police work, like there's nothing else but it, like you don't have much perspective on it."

Hearing Alice say that made his heart pound. Christine could not have put it any better. He had thought, though, that Alice was different and would understand. For an instant, she seemed like a traitor.

"It's what I do."

"It's like you have something to prove, all the time."

When he responded, his voice was shaky. "People need us to get these things right, Professor Freud. There needs to be justice. This is a job you have to take very seriously."

"And I do. We do. But you have to take the rest of your life seriously, too."

Mercer did not respond. He stood up.

"Let's go."

He went out the door first and stood outside in the cold air waiting for her, his breath forming little clouds. He hadn't realized he was breathing heavily.

For a moment, he wondered if Alice had left some other way, but then she came out the door, still saying goodbye to Jamal behind her. She turned to Mercer. She was all business again. It almost made him smile.

"You know, every time I consider the second scenario," she said, as if there hadn't been a pause in their conversation, "the one where Elizabeth is actually in the café, I start trying to picture exactly how it went down. Were there weapons involved? Did she not scream? How was the exit managed?"

"What were the statements from the store owners next door?"

"No one heard anything."

They walked away from the pub toward King Street Circle and the police station, beside each other but a distance apart, not touching, as Alice seemed to prefer. They were both imagining that pivotal scene in the café and someone quietly removing Elizabeth Goode. They were thinking the same thing.

What if she went willingly?

20

The Art of Eakins

"LET'S TALK TO the prisoner again, together this time," said Mercer as they neared the station.

Alice paused on the first cold concrete step. She glanced back at him and then away. "Okay," she finally said. "He said he'd had enough of you. I'll go in first, soften him up."

Mercer wondered why she was allowing him this second interview, and letting him in on so much. Was she getting desperate ... or were there other reasons?

He stayed in Alice's office for a few moments. It didn't take her long to work her magic. In about two minutes, she retrieved him.

"I told him things have come up that have made you less convinced he did it, that you just need a little bit more from him."

Andrew Eakins looked much as before, everything in place, well and carefully dressed, though in different clothes, and appearing more anxious and tired. He eyed Mercer suspiciously as he entered, then his attention wandered to Alice.

As Mercer moved toward the table, Eakins turned back and met him with a steady gaze. "I can keep doing this forever, if you want, keep giving you the same answers. There's nothing new to say."

Mercer was listening closely to the way he formed his words. Definitely Northeastern states, not big city, not Boston, New York, not even Philadelphia, but somewhere not far away. Pennsylvania remained a good guess.

He always had a plan when he interrogated a witness. Usually, it started with the character he would assume. It all had to do with feel, with sensing who he needed to be and how he had to shape the conversation and push it. Today, he had decided on two characters. The first was not much different from the one he'd assumed for the previous interview with Andrew Eakins. He would see what he could get out of employing it again and then he'd move to the other. Mercer would know when to switch.

He sat down beside Alice across from Eakins, grinding his chair along the hard floor as he settled in it and returning the prisoner's gaze. He hoped his interviewee would put up with this first persona long enough.

"How you doing, Andrew?" sneered Mercer. "Ready to help us find the woman you love, dead or alive?" He could hear Alice shift in her chair.

Eakins leaned toward him. "I love Elizabeth. You know shit. You need to find her and stop barking up the wrong tree." His eyes watered a little. "I love Elizabeth," he repeated. His voice cracked a bit on the last syllable. He sat back.

"I could have sworn you wanted to hit me, just then. Did you ever hit Elizabeth?"

"Oh, man, I thought this was going to be different. I thought you were going to be different. That was Ariel, her friend. It was an accident, you idiot."

Alice put her hand on Mercer's knee under the table and then pulled it back. It was funny how he and she could communicate so well for people who struggled with each other. Sometimes he felt like they could talk to each other without saying a word, other times he did not have a clue who she was. That squeeze, he knew, as sure as if she had told him, said this was a breakthrough. Andrew had just commented on something for the first time, an important detail.

"Well, maybe you should have told us that long ago."

"Why should I tell you anything? I did not do anything. Isn't it obvious? How can I defend myself about something I didn't do?"

"To exonerate yourself? Just tell us more about who you are and about your time with Elizabeth, about why you came here, married her. We'll go from there."

Eakins looked back at him. "I gave you my name, my wife's name, and where I live. I told you what happened in the café that day. I did not do this. That should be enough. You figure it out. You need to find my wife!" Desperation appeared in his eyes.

He indeed loves her, thought Mercer. *But he's confused about something too, unsure. Is it that he can't believe she would run out on him or is it something else?*

"So, still mysterious?"

Eakins said nothing.

"You know, Andrew, I took a look around your studio yesterday."

Eakins's eyes darted to his.

"Impressive work. Lots of pain, it seems to me. Pain between two people. Always a man and a woman, am I right?"

"It's up to the individual to interpret sculpture."

"Well, thanks for that lesson in the arts."

"You're welcome."

"Yeah, I had an interesting time in your studio, went through everything, handled all your weapons, sorry, your tools. Looked under and behind and inside the entire room."

"I'd prefer that you didn't do that," said Eakins very quietly.

"Pardon me?"

"That's my workspace. It's private."

"This is an investigation into a possible homicide."

"Do you have permission to do that? Look through my things? You're an American."

Alice put her hand on Mercer's leg again and squeezed it, this time rather hard. Eakins was right, he didn't really have the authority to do that. He also hadn't told Alice exactly how thoroughly he'd snooped around.

"Yes, I'm an American, Andrew. How about you? Are you from America?"

"We don't say it that way around here."

Mercer smiled. Andrew Eakins was nothing if not intelligent. He didn't like police officers, didn't trust them. Mercer wondered why. "Do you know an American woman who was in these parts recently, about medium height, brown hair, cut short, glasses, wears a long grey coat with a black scarf?"

"Why are you asking me this?" Mercer thought he looked frightened.

"Have you seen anyone fitting that description?"

"I don't have to answer that question. I've given you what you need to know. I was told you were making progress in a different direction." He glared at Alice and his raised his voice. "*Find my wife!*"

Temper.

Mercer took his time with his next question. He leaned in close. "Andrew, are you running from something?"

Eakins sat back, his eyes shifted away, and for a moment there was resignation in his expression. But then he looked back at his interrogator. "Next question. Your last one."

Mercer stood up, walked away from the table, and turned his

back. It was time to change character. He sighed, returned to his chair and sat in it with a plunk. He looked at Andrew Eakins and smiled, a genuine tight smile. He spoke with a quieter, moderated tone.

"Look, Mr. Eakins I have some reason to believe you may be innocent. But you have to help me, help Sergeant Morrow, if we are to help you."

"You have given me no reason to trust you."

"I promise you, I will not ask you anything I've asked before. I won't push you on your past or try to draw you out on things you don't want to talk about, play any games. I just want to know some things that might help me clear you. Some things about your daily routine, who you've interacted with. It may help us find her."

Eakins looked right at him for a moment. "All right," he finally said.

Alice squeezed Mercer's leg again.

"So" — he smiled — "tell me about your sculptures. I really did like them. They're kind of haunting. It is beyond me how you do it." He paused. "I write a little."

Alice glanced at him.

"Just a journal, actually, about my life, for therapy."

Now, she was staring.

"I can't imagine what it would be like if there were even more to what I was doing, if it were a novel or something, something truly creative. I can't imagine getting my ass into that chair every day and doing that. Seems like that would be as hard as hell, really complicated, and even more emotional than what I'm attempting. But that's what you're doing too, really well, telling a story, touching raw emotions, every day in steel. Maybe that's an even tougher art? How do you do it? How do you have that discipline? What's a day like for you?"

Mercer seemed sincere. He was sincere. And Eakins looked surprised. Then, he started to talk. He told them about how early he rose every morning, before Elizabeth was up, how he stuck with it for at least ten hours every day, driven "to tell the truth about life, no matter how difficult that is." He spoke of how he thought only the arts could really tell the truth, the real truth, beyond science, politics, everything else. He said you had to have a deep-seated passion to do it. Your art had to say something. His eyes reddened as he talked.

"And yours speaks of pain."

"Yeah." A flicker of suspicion. "And forgiveness."

"Forgiveness?" Mercer leaned forward.

"There isn't much of that in the world, is there? To me, it's second to love. Love and forgiveness. If we all had those two, the world would be a much better place." He looked like he was about to cry. Both Mercer and Alice were thinking of the passage that had been underlined in the Bible. "I try to reflect what I think really matters in my work."

"I guess we all need forgiveness for something," said Alice quietly. It was the first thing she had said during the interview.

"Yeah," said Mercer, glancing at her and then back to the prisoner. "So, that makes for long days, Mr. Eakins. What do you do the rest of the time?"

"Mostly, I spend it with Elizabeth."

"You don't call her Libby?" asked Alice.

"No. I have other names for her, and her for me." He smiled, the first time they had seen him do that.

"I used to call my wife my Pillow sometimes," said Mercer quietly, "and she called me her Honey Man ... our kids were Dodger and Pumpkin."

Alice almost laughed out loud.

"Eve and the Imposter, we call our —" Andrew clammed up, and looked like he wanted to put his hand over his mouth.

Mercer leaned forward again. "Why those names?"

"No reason."

"There's always a reason. My wife was always like a pillow to me, you know, a comfort and lovely, we all need that, and I used to try to truly look after her. And my son he's always active, dodging around, and my girl, well, her hair is an indescribable colour, beautiful." He realized that he was sounding sad, tears were gathering in his eyes. He could feel Alice's presence nearby. He had to get back on track. "There's always a reason."

"No reason." Eakins's head was down, and his eyes were gazing at his hands clasped on the table.

Mercer didn't say anything. He was getting somewhere. Andrew was finally really telling him something substantial.

"It's ... it's like a band's name," Eakins finally said, so softly he was almost whispering. "I guess, like a band of our own, you know. And I have some issues, psychological, imposter syndrome, heard of it? It's when you think that you aren't good enough at what you do; it's kind of an insecurity thing."

Really? Nice catch, thought Mercer, *true or not*.

"We all have some issues, mental ones, all of us. I know I do. I'm sure you do too, Sergeant Morrow?"

She looked at him, her face blank. Opaque. "For sure."

"Struggles can draw us together," he said, still looking her way. He turned back to the suspect. "But, Mr. Eakins, we kind of got off track there. Anything else you can tell me about your daily routine? Surely, you don't spend it all with Elizabeth, though it sounds like you'd like to. You know, many people told us she seemed protective of you."

"They did?"

"Yeah, that's a nice thing from a spouse. Lovely."

Eakins didn't respond.

"Any friends? Ever go out without her?" He cupped his hand over his mouth, between himself and Alice, as if to exclude her. "A guy has to get out, right, every now and then?"

"I, uh, sometimes, go out for a drink, alone, yeah. It's important to unwind. Charles Dickens used to walk for hours after he wrote, to just get that world he had imagined so intensely out of him and return to daily life."

"Well, it sounds like you are just as passionate; have a lot of things to get out of your system. Where do you go for a drink?"

"Not in town."

"Wise choice. Not exactly great bars here."

Eakins smiled. *A touch brotherly*, Mercer thought.

"I go to this place in the next little town over, just get in the car and go west."

"Always a good direction."

Mercer stood again and picked up his notebook, which seemed to surprise the prisoner. "Well, Mr. Eakins, I want to thank you for being so cooperative. We will do everything we can." He reached out his hand. Eakins paused and then shook it. The artist's hands were strong and calloused.

Alice thanked him too. The two of them left the room quietly, Mercer turning back to look at Andrew Eakins before closing the door. The prisoner was still standing there, not moving yet to go out the rear door that a police officer was opening for him. He looked puzzled, maybe a little concerned, as if he had let the cat out of the bag.

21

"There's something I need to tell you"

AS ALICE AND Mercer walked back toward Sal's office, he wondered what she had gleaned from the interview. He had latched onto some possible ideas, but he did not want to discuss them yet. Back in New York, he was known as a bit of a lone wolf. He liked to figure out things for himself. When cases got to critical points, he didn't want to think out loud. He could do better if all the ideas, all the possibilities, could be turned over in his head.

Admittedly, he also didn't want to share his ideas because he still wasn't sure about Alice Morrow, or Salma Haddad, or Ranbir Singh, or any person around this place. He was almost certain now that Alice did not suspect him in any way — almost certain. She had let him ask what he wanted in the interview with Andrew, but he imagined that wouldn't be the case with everything going forward. She was using him, at least to some degree.

Alice was awfully proud too. She probably didn't want to ask his opinion right now anyway. A smile seemed to be hovering around her mouth as she walked beside him. Definitely deep in thought.

"You want to visit that bar, don't you?" she said after they entered Sal's office. Constable Haddad had listened in on the whole interview.

"Yeah. All right if I go on my own?"

Alice paused for a moment. "Okay. We have other things to do here anyway."

"Thanks."

"We'll keep searching for your American woman, for one."

Sal was singing a song about an "American woman," down into her desk as she wrote something in her notebook.

"There are only two bars in the place Eakins is talking about, a village really," added Alice. "Should be a snap to figure out which one he went to."

Sal looked up at her friend and nodded.

"So," said Alice, glancing sideways at Mercer, "that thing you are writing, that's a journal?"

He hesitated. "Yeah." He felt naked in front of them.

"Didn't figure you for a diarist."

"Just using it to try to figure things out."

"Figure out what?" asked Sal.

"Life, I guess."

Alice sighed. "No one ever figures that out." She took something from Sal's desk. "Here, bring this to your interview. It will loosen tongues for you." She tossed him a police badge. "But I want it back at the station tonight on your way home, and a full report right away."

"Yes, sir."

Alice did not smile and neither did Sal. Once past the reception desk he spotted someone, through the glass of the front entrance, standing at the bottom of the snowy steps. Then he realized it was two people: a woman with her back to him, kissing a man wearing a porkpie hat. Mercer stood momentarily transfixed. Then the woman started up the steps. There was a red button on her coat: "I Own My Own Body." He rushed at the door. When the woman saw him, she stopped abruptly and retreated toward the street.

"Hey!" cried Mercer as he bounced through the door. His foot slipped on a patch of ice, sending him careening down the steps, feet flying out from under him. He managed a three-point landing on the bottom step, and then tumbled on his ass to the sidewalk.

"Oh!" said the woman, turning to him. "Are you all right?"

Mercer looked up at her. Not his strange visitor. This woman was much older.

"Yeah," groaned Mercer, "yeah, I'm fine." He got onto all fours and felt her hand helping him up.

"Were you coming in?" he asked, knocking the snow off his coat. "Do you need the police?"

Alice and Sal came through the door up above. "What was that shouting about, Mercer?" asked Alice. Sal, seeing the snow on his rear end and the back of his coat put a hand to her mouth to stifle a laugh.

He motioned toward the woman. "I think this is someone you might want to —"

"Yes, I'd like to come in," said the woman suddenly, looking up at Alice and Sal in their police uniforms. She squared her shoulders, though there was trepidation in her face. In the glow of the streetlamp, they could also see the button on her lapel.

"Oh!" said Sal.

Mercer stepped toward the two policewomen and spoke in a low voice. "She just said goodbye to her friend — a man in a porkpie hat?"

"Oh!" said Alice.

"I'm Eleanor James," said the woman, "Reverend Eleanor James. There's something I need to tell you."

22

A Confession

MERCER WANTED AT her immediately, but Alice could tell that the woman was on edge and told him to wait until Reverend James had settled in her office. Alice brought a cup of tea and Sal brought her a doughnut from a pack in the kitchen, which the Reverend said she didn't want but ate anyway and wiped her trembling hands on a serviette the desk officer brought her. Then, Mercer was allowed in. As he surveyed the scene, he realized that the ladies had this woman right where they wanted her.

"There is no need to be nervous, Reverend James," said Alice in the most gentle voice he had ever heard her employ, "though I must tell you we are quite interested in the button you are wearing and in the fact that we saw you on our security cameras walking along King Street Circle toward the Shelter Café right at the time an incident took place there. A local woman disappeared. I'm presuming you've heard of the case?"

"No need to be nervous," repeated Sal sweetly.

The woman now looked even more alarmed. "You have me on camera?"

"Yes, Eleanor, we do," said Alice.

"But let's hear about the button first," said Mercer.

"Indeed, let's hear about that," said Alice. "It's of particular interest to Detective Mercer here."

"Well," said the woman, "that's why I've come. The only reason. I'm relatively new to town. Arrived here to take up my post at Grace Church about a month ago. In fact, I just got my own car yesterday. I've been borrowing cars from congregation members when necessary."

Alice glanced at Mercer with a reproving look.

"My reception at the church has been a bit a frosty though."

"Why are you telling us this?" asked Mercer. "We want to know about the button."

"He's an American," said Alice, as if that explained everything, and the woman nodded back at her.

"I'm telling you," continued Eleanor, "so you will understand why I haven't come to see you before now."

"Of course," said Sal.

Mercer rolled his eyes.

"A number of people left the church once I was hired," continued Reverend James. "You see, I have progressive views and live with my partner, who is younger than me."

"That shouldn't be —" began Alice.

"More than thirty years younger."

"Oh," said Sal and smiled. Alice smiled too.

"Even though Grace United is a fairly liberal church, the combination of my not being married to my partner and his much younger age did not sit well with some people. So, I have been trying to ease my way into my work and into the community. When I heard, you know, that the police were looking for someone wearing a button like mine, it upset me."

"Of course," said Sal.

"At first, I just thought that I had best stay out of things."

"Understandable," said Sal.

"But I know that God would want me to always tell the t-truth." She stumbled on that word but went on. "So, after thinking about it for a while, and not wearing the button, I've come here to speak to you."

"We aren't looking for you," said Mercer.

"Oh, I know. You're looking for Angela."

Mercer couldn't keep his mouth from dropping open. "Angela who?" he blurted out. "From where? What does she look like? Where is she staying? Do you have a cellphone number?"

"You must forgive Detective Mercer," said Sal, "he is not only an American, but he is also under a good deal of pressure right now. Please proceed at your own pace, Reverend James."

Mercer wanted to tell Constable Salma Haddad to fuck off.

"Well," continued Eleanor, "I'm not your typical minister, I don't completely believe in God, or at least not in 'Him' the way *men* have always positioned Him. I do believe in much of what Jesus said, who doesn't? I'm pretty liberal, socialist really; my beliefs inform my political views, and both inform my work as a minister. God is more of a spirit to me. *She*, or *they*, is everywhere."

"Your point?" asked Mercer.

"This is all to explain how I met Angela."

"Praise the Lord," said Mercer.

"I'm a feminist," said the Reverend Eleanor James.

"So am I," said Sal.

"Me too," said Alice. They all looked at Mercer. He was silent.

"I guess I'm pretty militant in my views. I think we all should be. Women are equal to men, and they need to be treated fairly, no matter who they love. I think that's what God, the spirit of life, wants. I have the right to be with a man thirty-three years younger than me. Men do that sort of thing all the time. No one, no discriminatory system can say I can't."

"And Angela?" asked Alice.

"She came to our church. She heard me speak, made a point of being nice to my partner. I appreciated that. I had given a rather strong sermon that Sunday about women's place in our world and the response wasn't very good and I really needed some support. And there was Angela, enthusiastic and kind. We talked a little about feminism."

"Why did she come to your church, do you think?" asked Alice.

"I don't know. Said she liked the name."

"Can you tell us anything more about her?" asked Sal.

"Where was she from?" said Mercer. "From here?"

"I don't know. We never talked about that."

"You saw her more than once?" asked Sal.

"Yes. She called me at the church after that first time and we went out for dinner, had a great chat. I gave her a button, one to match mine. I love her."

"Where is she now?" asked Mercer. "It's very important that we speak with her."

"I ... I don't know. I haven't seen her for a while. And I don't have her phone number."

"Is that all you talked about? Feminism?" asked Alice.

The Reverend Eleanor James took a big sip of her tea. "Yes, mostly, that and faith. Yes, I would say so."

"You would say so?" asked Mercer. "What does that mean?"

"I think she's answered the question, detective," said Alice. "Can I ask you, why were you on King Street Circle a week ago Monday, Reverend James?"

"Oh, I don't know. I was likely shopping."

"Likely?" asked Mercer.

"Well, that's a while back, sir. I'm not sure. I've been on the Circle a number of times over the last weeks."

"You would have been close to the Shelter Café when the incident occurred. This young woman has been gone now for more than a week and a half!" Mercer couldn't suppress his emotion.

"I know," said Eleanor and her eyes filled with tears.

There was silence in the room for a while.

"I don't recall passing by the Shelter Café that day or hearing —"

"But you HAD to have," said Mercer, "you appeared again on the —"

"That isn't strictly true." said Alice. "Perhaps you went into another store, Reverend James, crossed the Circle and came back without ever passing by the café? We are not here to suggest that the Reverend is lying, Detective Mercer."

"Yes," said Eleanor, "that's likely what happened, something like that."

"Anything you'd like to add?" asked Sal.

"No, that's everything. I must be getting on. Damien will be waiting for me. I've done my duty here, haven't I? Answered all your questions?"

"We wouldn't want to keep Damien waiting," said Mercer.

Reverend James got up and awkwardly excused herself. "Maybe that woman is fine. Maybe she's left for a reason, and she's free. We can only pray that's true."

"Did you ever hear that Andrew Eakins beat her?" asked Mercer.

"We don't —" began Sal.

"Yes, I know that. And it disgusts me." She said it with feeling, with a finality that ends a sermon.

23

Grace

IT WAS PAST noon by the time they were done with Eleanor James — or she was done with them. Alice and Sal wanted to have lunch on their own to discuss what Andrew Eakins and Reverend James had said. Mercer headed home, his head swimming. He was pretty sure that the Reverend was hiding something, and he was pretty sure that Alice and Sal suspected the same. There was something about Eleanor's way, her connection to "Angela," and her account of her movements on the Circle that didn't feel right. He had a sixth sense that a turning point was imminent on this case. All he had to do now was keep his wits about him, ask the right questions.

"Angela" was not just a figment of his imagination — she was here, had been here, had a name. Their prime suspect had finally talked, let down his guard, if only slightly. Maybe there were people in that bar Eakins frequented who had seen him without the mask he was currently wearing.

Mercer was guessing that Andrew had been in that bar many times. He was guessing too that it was his only place to unwind, away from everyone. He was essentially friendless other than Elizabeth, which was interesting in itself. He had obviously chosen a bar where he had a greater chance of staying anonymous. Mercer suspected that Andrew regretted mentioning the place, among other things.

"Eve and the Imposter." What could that mean?

Mercer watched some Knicks highlights while he ate dinner and it depressed him, the game more than being alone.

He set out at about seven-thirty in the evening, aware that he would reach the little place to the west in about twenty minutes. He knew he had hit pay dirt the moment he passed the community's sign. He went under a railroad crossing and saw a bar called Human and Divine immediately to his left before the road reached the main drag. There were apparently just two drinking holes here and this was likely the one. Andrew would not discriminate, not about this. He would simply stop at the first one available. Mercer would have done that himself.

It was a roadhouse and bar wrapped up in one with a u-shaped bar to the left, chairs and tables, and a dance floor and little stage to the right. No band was playing when he came in, just an old punk song on the speakers, which surprised him a little. Mercer took in the scene for a moment. Things hadn't exactly heated up much yet, though he doubted there was ever much heat. Maybe on a Friday or Saturday. Eakins likely stayed away on those nights. There were about ten people at the tables, eating late "suppers" as they often put it around here, burgers and fries, clubhouse sandwiches.

There were three people at the bar. Perfect. The bartender was a woman. Mid-forties, jeans and blouse, a bit too much makeup. She was engaged with one of the customers, so much so that she barely noticed him sitting down at the far end of the bar, out of earshot of the others. Perfect. Someone who likes to talk to the customers. At the perfect time, Eakins time. Just when he would likely be here.

When she finally noticed him, the bartender made a show of rushing over.

"Hey! What can I do for you?" She gave him a big grin.

He wasn't going to dance around this. He flipped out his badge. She actually read it, her face serious for a moment.

"Okay," she finally said, her smile returning, "what can I do for you?" He noticed that people around here were not afraid of cops like back home. That wasn't the right word. Not everyone in America was afraid of the police, though many were, certainly minorities, African Americans definitely, and with good reason. But generally, there was not the same kind of deference and caution here. Apparently, they didn't always put their hands on their steering wheels when pulled over, which seemed astounding. Cops were people too around here, at least somewhat. He wasn't sure how he felt about that.

"I have a few questions about a guy whom I'm guessing has been here a few times, probably around this hour of the evening, weeknights, always alone, slim muscular build, good looking —"

"Now you're talking."

"Longish blond hair, tinted aviator glasses, well dressed, late thirties, goes by the name of Andrew Eakins."

"Goes by the name? Who is this, an international man of mystery?"

Mercer hadn't realized he'd put it that way. He was off his game. "Have you seen him? Talked to him?"

"As much as I liked the description, he could be a number of guys."

"He's an artist, sculptor."

"Ah! Yes. Him. Been here a few times. An American?"

"As a matter of fact —"

"Like you?"

That took him aback. He had been trying to talk like a local. "Yeah, I'm American, originally, working for law enforcement here now. How did you know?"

"Please, do you think that's hard for us to tell?"

"Just that ... his accent, his attitude?"

"He let it slip once when he was talking about something completely unrelated, but I remember he moved on from the subject pretty fast. He was pretty tight-lipped about his past. It was funny, 'cause he really liked to talk, at least to me. Never spoke much to any of the guys around here. Women are more sympathetic, you know."

"Really?"

She laughed. "He just talked about his work though and about his life with his apparently amazing wife. Man, he liked to talk about her. I'm single now and he was, as you say, kind of cute, but that was a one-woman man."

"What else did he talk about?"

"Just that mostly, kind of boring to be honest. Though, the odd time, he'd mention other things."

"Like what?"

"Well, he could get a little philosophical sometimes, I remember that."

"How so?"

"Oh, I don't know. He'd start talking about human beings and how mean we all were to each other. Included himself in that. I remember those chats 'cause those ones were actually kind of interesting. I could tell he was pretty sad deep down."

"In pain, would you say?"

"That's a good way to put it, mental pain. Hard to figure, 'cause he was so happy with his home life, and here he was drinking alone. Well, not really drinking, he was careful about that, never drank too much."

"Ever let slip *exactly* where he was from? A state, maybe?"

"No. Like I said, his past wasn't a topic for discussion"

Mercer's heart sank.

"Except for one thing."

Mercer lifted his head again. "What's that?"

"I remember talking to him once about my life, telling him I'd been married a couple of times. I sensed, as I said, something sad about his past. I was trying to connect, you know, good bartender move, and he ..."

"What?"

"Well, he said something weird."

"Yes?"

"I remember he just looked at me as if he wanted to respond when I talked about being married twice, then kind of stared off into the distance and said something like: 'Marry, that's a strange name, when you think of it.'"

"That doesn't make any sense."

"Yeah, I know, eh? That's why I remember it. So I says to him, 'you mean that *marry* is a strange *word*, don't you?' And it is too, when you think about it, why do we *marry* each other? But he got pissed off, said he'd said *word*, not *name*. Then he wouldn't talk to me for a while. Marriage seemed to be a touchy subject for him, which was odd since he seemed to be so crazy about his wife."

"You think he was married before?"

"Yeah. I don't think it went well. Women's intuition. Maybe it's the source of that sadness."

"Ever see an American woman in here, in her thirties, pale and slim, wire-rimmed glasses, maybe wearing a feminist button?"

"Doesn't ring a bell."

"Ever see him, Eakins, with a woman? Even talking to one for just a moment or two?"

"Never, always alone, kept to himself."

"Anything else you can think of?"

"I think I know the first name of his first wife, if that's of any use."

"What?"

"Grace."

For an instant, Mercer had expected another name. He wrote down what she said so quickly that he could barely read what he'd written. "How do you know this? Doesn't sound like he would have offered something like that."

"Oh no, not him. But he talked on his phone occasionally, always to his wife it seemed, sweet conversations, telling her how much he loved her and what she meant to him and how much he admired her. Even referred to her as 'saving' him once. I don't think he ever knew I could hear, 'cause he would talk to her in a low voice, turn away from the bar, but women have superior hearing. Did you know that?"

Mercer smiled. "How does this relate to his first wife's name?"

"I remember him saying it during one of his phone conversations because he said it with such feeling, a bit louder than usual. He said something like, 'I'll never go back to Grace.' And I figured that was it, that was his first wife's name, right there. I think the current one is Eve. Heard him call her that a couple times."

Mercer wrote that down too.

"I get to know men well working here but I couldn't get a line on him. He was kind of deep. I sensed anger in him too. It was weird how pissed off he got when I misheard him that time, really pissed off. Then, the next time in here, he was all friendly again. Never would have gone home with a man like that, cute or not, deep or not. Has he done something?"

"We don't know."

"That sounds about right with him. I notice you keep asking about him and women, kind of creeps me out."

Mercer couldn't get anything else of interest out of her. So, they started to talk, as she moved back and forth to the few other customers, chatting mostly about married life. He told her he was single now. And she talked more about "tying the knot" twice and that the last one had ended just a year ago. He ordered a rye and coke, then another one. Her name was Amber. She had lovely hands, strong looking, rings on about four fingers, one a skull, jeans, pretty tight with a thick belt and buckle, hair with lots of highlights. She seemed as lonely as him and yes, she could talk indeed. She had a great smile too and seemed charmed by the stories he told her about life as an NYPD homicide detective. "Like the movies," she said, touching his hands when she said it. When he left, she told him not to be a stranger.

He was over the alcohol limit again, so Mercer concentrated on maintaining an even speed once on the highway. Grace was a new piece of information about Andrew Eakins. Had he really been married before? Interesting too, that Amber said he freaked out when he talked about marriage, a "touchy subject." Not a good thing to hear when dealing with a suspect in a marital crime. *Marry* IS a strange word for it though. He was right. So, Grace. Grace Eakins? It was a lovely first name. When Amber said she knew her name, for an instant Mercer expected it would Angela. But no, Angela is someone else. *Grace was the name of Eleanor James's church too. Grace United. And didn't she say that Angela had come to the church because she liked the name? What the hell does that mean in all of this? Or does it mean anything? So where was this Grace? Had anything happened to her?* He thought about the rye on the counter at home, good for when things got complicated, then pushed the thought aside.

MERCER WAS ALMOST home when he realized he'd forgotten to drop the badge off at the police station. Sergeant Morrow had been clear that it had to be returned tonight.

He cursed himself and continued past his sideroad. Speed steady and both hands on the wheel. It started to snow, soft fluffy flakes in the black night. It really could be beautiful here, sometimes.

He parked halfway around the circumference of the Circle rather than in the police parking lot. The station door creaked and it seemed deathly silent inside, but Constable Singh was there. He seemed to always be there.

"Captain America!" he said. "How are you, my friend?"

Mercer did not want to get too close to him. He imagined that Singh could smell an over-the-limit citizen at forty paces.

"Just fine." He tossed the badge, and it made a perfect landing on the counter in front of Singh. "Alice lent me that, said it had to be back tonight."

"I am aware. Would you like a cup of tea?"

"No, thanks, I'm calling it a day."

"Drive carefully."

"Yes, I will, it's snowing."

"That's not what is called snowing, but be careful anyway. Lots of folks over the limit this time of the night." He seemed to give Mercer a knowing look.

"Yeah, will do."

Out on the street, he stood for a moment looking up at the quiet brick police station. Andrew Eakins was in there in his cell at the rear, full of all the information he needed. "It's a strange thing, really, what I do, trying to find the truth, the evil inside people." It was there — he just had to dig it out. It was inside all of us.

The Circle was eerily silent, not a soul on the sidewalks, no sound of any cars, not even a dog's bark, at just eleven p.m. Then he heard a train's horn. Trains came right through the downtown.

It was a lonesome distant blast in the cold air, and it sounded to him like something that marked this area, this world.

He knew he should head right home, but then he thought of Alice. He actually had hoped she might be at the station when he dropped off the badge, but then seeing her with alcohol on his breath would not have been a good idea.

Maybe she was at home.

He drove along King East toward her neighbourhood, the whole town, it seemed, all to himself. He imagined living here. Funny thing was, it didn't seem like such a bad idea. This place somehow felt real.

He noticed two things the minute he pulled up across the street from the Morrow home. There was another car in the driveway and the lights in Alice's room were on. He lowered his window. Was it his imagination that he could see two shadows up there? He could hear music, turned up a bit, coming faintly through her window. It looked like the shadows were entwined, but he could not say for sure. The song was an old one and he recognized it. "Up on Cripple Creek." He had always loved it. He loved the woman in it. Bessie. She seemed so welcoming, so understanding. He thought of Elizabeth and then Grace. Mercer stared up at the room, wondering about Alice.

Then a face peered out the window. Mercer drove off.

WHEN HE GOT back to the farmhouse, still a little buzzed, he connected his speaker to his phone, found "The Weight" by the same band he'd heard through Alice's window, and let the music pulse through the building. He worked away on another bachelor meal, this time involving digging up a prepared, frozen bowl of rice and chicken, and making himself a rudimentary salad. He considered pouring some more rye but thought of Alice checking it and pushed the bottle back in the corner of the counter. He sat down at his laptop, thankful that he'd gotten WiFi. For the first two weeks in the house, he had actually been on dial up: it had been like living in the Victorian era.

He resisted the temptation to launch into a search for Grace Eakins.

He watched some of *The Last Waltz* on YouTube, and then idly searched Alice Morrow online and found a few photos of her at police functions, smiling as she dropped a puck for a hockey game, bowling for the local food bank. There were no personal pictures to be found of her, no identifiable social media accounts, nothing. He wondered about that. How had she managed to avoid a presence online? He thought, again, of the reactions some local people seemed to have to her, a sort of wariness.

Then, intermittently at first, he started searching for "Grace Eakins." That brought up links and photos of all sorts of women from everywhere, none of whom seemed to be from Pennsylvania. He tried "Grace and Andrew Eakins." Nothing.

He stared at the screen for a moment and then, in his frustration, turned to a favourite online pastime. He went onto Google Maps. He loved finding interesting locations all over the world — sometimes revisiting places where he and Christine had been, like Milan, where they had made love every day for a week in the beautiful apartment they'd rented, and held hands as they walked through the Galleria and toured the Duomo, as if their love would never end. He liked to search northern places too. Some of his favourites were small towns and villages in countries like Iceland and Norway, places that seemed far away from the life he'd been leading back home. It was amazing how beautiful, how sophisticated, some of them seemed, even in isolation from the rest of the world. He kept moving around on Google Maps. But something about the way Amber quoted Andrew Eakins speaking to Elizabeth Goode on his phone kept coming back to him.

"I'll never go back to Grace."

Grace, Pennsylvania.

He typed it in ... and it appeared on the map.

24

Just One More Thing
Before I Go

THE INSTANT HE saw the town appear on the screen, Mercer knew
he was going back to America to investigate. He also knew he had
to do this alone. If he told Alice about what he planned to do there
there was no way she would let him do it. At best, she would want
to go with him and essentially put him in the back seat again.

He thought about it for a moment, his heart still pounding
from his discovery. He would tell Alice that he wanted to go home
for a while. And he did. He realized that now. He thought of seeing
Christine and the kids, of the possibilities, of saying he was sorry,
frank talks with his son and daughter ... of bringing that piece of
fabric found in Andrew's studio to have it tested in New York. And
he could speak with Lauryn while he was there too.

He pulled up the Grace, Pennsylvania, phone book on his laptop. An Aiken, an Atkin, but no Eakins. No Goodes either. No
Angela anyone. It didn't matter. There was something there. He
was sure of it.

IN THE MORNING, he called the station.

"Hey," Alice said, sounding almost happy to hear his voice. "I hope things went well at the bar. Hope the local ladies went easy on you. You'd be a catch for some of them, even a catch and release would suit them fine."

"Yeah, it went okay."

"Just okay?"

"Learned nothing really. Well, not absolutely nothing. I found the place right away, found a bartender there who had talked to Andrew Eakins, several times. She had lots to say, but not anything that was helpful."

There was a pause on the other end of the line. "Really?"

He couldn't tell whether or not she believed him.

"Yeah, really. Disappointing."

"Didn't get laid either, I'm guessing."

Again, was she joking or not? Probing or not giving a flying fuck?

"Look, Alice, I'm thinking about going home for a while."

Silence.

"I'm not making a difference in this investigation right now, you two are more than capable, and I need to get back, see my wife and kids."

Silence.

"Okay?" he asked.

"Catch and release."

"Sorry?"

"Sure, it's a free country, and I guess yours is too."

She hung up.

HE SHOWERED, SHAVED, put on some cologne and had his bags packed within twenty minutes. When he got to the top of the lane where it met the sideroad, he stopped and got out of the car to look back at the farmhouse against the grey and white canvas. He wondered if he would ever come back. It had been good for him to be here for a while. He stood there for several minutes, unable to return to the car. He just kept gazing at the landscape. Oddly, this place drew him as much as it disturbed him. So did she.

He started driving and turned left at the end of the sideroad. The way to the interstate — or whatever they called them here — was south along this highway past the town. Then two hours east along the freeway before he crossed the border. He figured that crossing was a good place to enter. It was between two small towns, so not busy, then it would be straight down through New York State. He was worried about getting back into the country. He had said he was coming up here for weeks but had been in residence for months. Lying to American border officials was never a good idea. He intended to get back as fast as he could. He wasn't even sure how much he would still pursue this case when he got home. Maybe it would be best just to plead with Christine to take him back, become a better man, husband, and father, tell her his secret, that he was going to go into Manhattan and admit that he had assaulted a suspect. Forget everything up here. Forget Alice.

Then he noticed a sign in front of a house by the side of the highway: "GOOD MAN FOR HIRE — CONTRACTING."

The couple who had said they saw Eakins approaching the café alone.

He thought of Alice's game of "what if." And then the strangest "fact" of their investigation: the ghost couple.

What if …

He turned sharply off the road, squealing his tires, and pulled into the driveway. Nice house, yes, in an old-fashioned, country bungalow kind of way, recently renovated. He sat there for a moment, hands tightly gripping the steering wheel. He could still push things, take a chance.

Mercer got out of the car and slammed the door. Unlit Christmas lights were all over the roof and along the eavestroughs, as if someone had tossed them up there. There was a sign in the big picture window. "The Government," it exclaimed, "Can't Tell Us What to Do!" "We're for Law and Order!" read another above the breezeway. When he got to the entrance, he noticed the doorbell, but knocked hard instead. A little sign was stuck into the interlocking brick in the walkway, this one bright and flowery: "The Freemans — Fred and Alma. Welcome to Our Home!" Thank God for that information: Alice had not told him their first names.

The woman who came to the entrance looked out through the long, narrow, translucent window first. When she opened the door, it was just a crack.

"Mrs. Freeman? Alma Freeman?"

"Yes. May I help you?"

"My name is Hugh Mercer and I'm with the police in town." He flashed his NYPD union card very quickly and returned his wallet to his pocket. "I have a few more questions to ask you about the Goode case." He spoke firmly, keeping any expression out of his voice.

"We already answered all the police's questions. They were very nice."

"Just a couple more, won't take long."

She hesitated.

"Please, Mrs. Freeman, this is necessary. You would like us to find Elizabeth Goode, would you not?"

"Why, yes, of course. Come in please."

Bingo. Then another bingo when, after taking off his shoes (which seemed to be the thing to do around here), he entered the living room, complete with its pink and white plush furniture and found Fred Freeman just coming out of the kitchen with a beer in his hand.

"I'd like to speak to you too, of course, Fred." He was a short, beefy guy, wearing sweatpants, apparently not just a good man for hire but a man of leisure too, this weekday morning.

Fred stopped in his tracks and looked at his wife. Both of them wore big glasses. "What's this about, dear?"

"This is Mr. Mercer, honey, from the police in town, and he has a few more questions for us."

"Mercer? Don't know that name."

"I'm new."

"From where?" Fred did not sit down or offer his guest a seat.

"From up north." He tried to say it as flatly as he could. Dull it down, he told himself.

"Where up north?"

"Where it's even colder."

Fred laughed. "Sit down," he said, "we'll answer anything you've got to ask. Elizabeth was a fine woman. It breaks our hearts that this has happened."

Was, thought Mercer.

They all sat. Alma and Fred on the sofa, Mercer across from them in a soft living room chair that gave in with a sigh when he sat down.

"I'm sorry I don't have anything to offer you, dear," said Alma, smiling at Mercer. "You've caught us without a cookie or any tea made."

"Not a problem."

Mercer asked them to take him through what they were doing the day of Elizabeth Goode's disappearance and exactly when and where they saw Eakins. They immediately obliged, at times finishing each other's sentences, polite to a fault. It was the same story. He kept probing and getting nowhere, asking what Eakins was wearing, if they might be wrong about the timing. They were vague about some details, claiming it was hard to remember, but adamant that Andrew Eakins, their country neighbour, who they most definitely knew by sight, was alone. They were ridiculously helpful and of no help at the same time. He observed them closely and identified Alma as the more vulnerable. Her eyes shifted when she spoke, often looking down.

Time was running out. Soon, if he kept probing, especially doing so after they had given their statements to the police, it would be obvious that he was looking for gaps in their testimonies, errors. Lies.

He decided to go for broke, do what he promised himself he'd do when he turned into the Freemans' driveway.

What if ...

"Nice place you have here," he said.

"Thanks," said Fred. "We've dressed it up a bit lately. Can't take any credit though. I don't like to work on my own house. I had a friend in the business do it."

"I'm guessing this cost a fair bit."

Fred paused, then smiled. "Not so much."

"How is the business doing?"

"Fine," said Alma, then glanced toward Fred.

"Hear you guys are snowbirds."

"No," said Fred.

"But you go south a lot. That's what I was told."

"What are you getting at?" Fred's friendly tone had dropped for the first time.

Mercer glanced at Alma. She was looking down. It was time to pounce.

"Look, you don't need to tell me if you were paid off or not, or who paid you, but can you at least tell me if Elizabeth Goode was there that day in the café? Because you were there, weren't you, both of you, sitting by the window?"

There was absolute silence in the room.

"Who are you?" asked Fred, rising to his feet.

"Perhaps, sir," said Alma, "you should go."

"I just want to know if she was there." He gave Alma a penetrating stare and then noticed her head nod, almost imperceptibly. It made his heart pound.

"You ain't from around here," said Fred, "not from up north, are you?" He took a step toward Mercer, who got to his feet. "I need to see whatever ID you showed the wife."

Alma looked ready to cry now. "She went willingly," she whispered.

Fred stared at his wife. "She ... she's just fucking scared by all your questions. We saw that bastard on the street, and he was alone. That's it! You need to get off my property! I'm calling the police station."

Mercer turned and left the house, not looking back. He had done it now. He had opened the first huge crack in this case, cracked it wide open — and may have broken the law while doing it. He had no right to speak to them the way he had. No one at the police station had given him permission to talk to the Freemans. It was harassment, and he had impersonated local police.

He started the car and spun the wheels as he ripped out of the driveway and back onto the road. Fred would be on the phone now to Alice and she knew where he was going and probably where he would cross the border too.

25

The Home of the Free

ABOUT FORTY-FIVE MINUTES later, speeding way beyond the limit, he hit the four-lane highway and headed east. He plugged in his phone and started playing music through his speakers. He had set it for more old tunes. "The Shape I'm In" came pulsing out at him as he sped down the road. He kept looking in the rear-view mirror. No one following. Not yet. She knew his car.

About two hours later he turned off the highway and headed south toward the border, his left foot vibrating against the floor of the car. He passed over a green suspension bridge and looked down at the cold water, cold islands and cold buildings below. The US customs felt almost deserted, just three of the five kiosks were open, only three cars in front of him. For a minute he considered turning around, but then a light went on in a kiosk and he couldn't retreat. He pulled up. The agent was a heavy-set man, head shaved, with a beard, and very serious.

"Nice day," said Mercer, though it wasn't.

The officer looked down at him. "Passport."

Mercer handed it over. The officer looked at it for a while and was about to scan it when he stopped.

"How long have you been away?"

Mercer could not remember whether or not they'd stamped the passport with a date on his way up here. He considered telling the truth. Actually, for a moment, he couldn't remember the truth. Was it just past two months or three? It didn't matter: it was too long for someone who had told an officer he'd be visiting for just two weeks. He was also transporting the material from Elizabeth's dress, evidence in a crime, over the border.

"Three weeks."

The guard eyed him. "What was keeping you up there that long?"

"A woman."

The man laughed. "None good enough for you in America?"

"That's why I'm heading back."

"We do live in God's country, don't we?"

"Yes, sir."

The guard ran the passport through the scan and handed it back to him.

"Have a nice day."

Mercer had to pull over once he was a couple miles down the road, his hands still shaking a little. He sat at a tourism place, festooned with what appeared to be a hundred American flags, one the size of the state itself, it seemed. He wondered if he should call Alice, admit to what he had done, and tell her what he had learned. Maybe she would be good with that. He doubted it. He drove off.

The first question was: where to go first? He had three destinations: home to New Jersey to see his wife, to New York to get Lauryn to help him, and Grace, Pennsylvania. He ached to see Christine. That actually surprised him. Maybe he should call her. No, perhaps his showing up on the front step unannounced would surprise her in a good way. Everyone wanted to be wanted and he wanted her, and he would show it. He would tell her he was in the wrong, had been wrong for a long, long time, and tell her absolutely everything. He wondered if he could change his life.

He pulled over again and texted Keith and Stevie, sending each of them the same message: *Coming home. You and I have to get together sometime soon. Love, Dad.* An answer came almost immediately from his son. *K.* That was it. *When?* He replied. There was no answer. Stevie didn't respond at all.

Mercer got back on the road, put more music on, and raced south, trying to feel optimistic about driving straight to Christine's door. When a song called "You Don't Know Me" began playing, he started to have his doubts. He couldn't go to see his wife first. He needed to steel himself for that, get his footing back on home soil. No, he would call Lauryn when he stopped to eat, get her to meet him — that place they used to go. He didn't want anyone at her downtown precinct or his, especially his partner, to know he was back, and what he was going to ask her to do wasn't really right.

As he drove south, he noticed how different his country seemed from the world he had been living in over the last few months. There were many more billboards lining the side of the road than up north, all beckoning you to buy this or that. There were flags everywhere, hanging from houses, stores, the roofs of cars, and bumper stickers desperately proclaiming patriotism. Freedom. Freedom. Freedom. That word was everywhere. It seemed like a religion. That, and money. There seemed to be more shopping malls, more wealth, but more poverty too. He passed through Watertown and then Syracuse. He saw magnificent, gated communities in leafy suburbs in the distance and then peered down urban streets just off the interstate, filled with broken-down homes and rusting commercial buildings, signs indicating toll roads. The highway was bumpy and in need of repair. It was so interesting to see his homeland like this. It made him think about himself, who he was, and maybe who he should be. He hadn't done enough of that in the past.

Images of himself that awful night in the Bronx swirled in his mind too as he swept down into America.

He was starving, so he stopped to eat at a Bob's Big Boy and drove up past the iconic chubby dark-haired white boy in a red and white checked jumpsuit. "The Original Double Deck Hamburger." It was loud inside. He wondered if he would even be able to hear Lauryn on his phone. The waitress, a woman in her fifties with deep circles under her eyes covered by makeup, was preternaturally friendly, anxious to bring him a meal larger than all outdoors — and to be tipped substantially.

"You dig in, sir," she said with a wide smile.

Mercer dialed Lauryn, calling her cellphone this time.

"Hugh," she said blandly.

"Lauri, how are you?"

"Well, that's a better start than last time. I'm fine, and at work, so I can't really talk. How are things up in the great nowhere?"

"I'm actually back. Only a few hours from New York."

"Oh."

"Look, I want to get together."

"You do?" She cleared her throat.

"I —"

"What do you want?"

"Just to talk, mostly."

"About what?"

"I'll be honest with you."

"Always wise."

"I want to ask you for a favour."

"Work related?"

He paused. "Yes."

She paused. "I'll think about it."

"Can I see you tomorrow for lunch?"

"I don't know if that's a good idea. Why don't you come here, to work?"

"Don't want to do that."

Long pause. "Okay, where do you want to meet?" she asked.

"It's not just a meeting, I want to talk too."

"Yeah, sure."

"Let's get together at the Bubby's in Tribeca. Twelve noon. I'll make a reservation for two."

It was where they used to go.

"I don't know, Hugh."

"See you then." He hung up.

MERCER STAYED IN a Howard Johnson's near Newburgh, about an hour north of New York, and drove into the city in the morning. It was a surreal experience being back in Manhattan. He had to ramp up his nerve to enter the swarm of vehicles and people and sounds, and felt uneasy about parking his car and leaving it.

Bubby's was on the corner of Hudson and Moore, just a block south of the First Precinct police station where Lauryn worked. Mercer had met her when he came by to discuss a case involving a man who had murdered his wife after many years of abusing her. Technically, Mercer was part of Detective Bureau, Manhattan South, Homicide Squad. Lauryn had heard of him, seen him once or twice. A rising star at her precinct, she had been chosen to help him with the investigation. She was passionate about cases that involved crimes against women, and this murder had been particularly horrible. Mercer had asked her to lunch afterward to talk out some technical aspects more thoroughly, when there were really no professional things left to pursue. Mostly, he thought of it as just being supportive, as the case had clearly upset her. Bubby's had large windows looking out onto the street and they had sat there talking, starting out sticking to business and the trauma of the job, but both knew that would not last, and soon they were discussing each other: his struggles with his marriage and her trials attempting to find one good relationship. She was a driven, competitive person and so was he; but she listened too, to him. They had left it at that, listening, but when they shook hands before leaving, both hands had lingered a little. They had caught each other looking back at the other as they headed separate ways. He called her the next day, told her he had another table at Bubby's, and she had simply said "okay," like an operative being told where to meet. This time, their table was at the back, where they had a view of the restaurant, but few could see them. The reservation was for the middle of the afternoon when he knew no other cops would be around. Within minutes their conversation turned personal again and then their hands were touching. They went back to her apartment right after. She called in sick from there. He had never been with a woman quite like her, much younger than him, athletic and strong, fascinated by him like Christine had been long ago, admiring everything he said and everything he did, even when he didn't do it so well. They both felt a little embarrassed and guilty after and though he said he would call her, it took him three weeks. Then, they went back to Bubby's one last time, and over to her apartment, and after that, it ended. They knew it wouldn't last, that it was a moment in time to remember with a measure of yearning but nothing else.

SHE WASN'T THERE when he arrived, and he didn't know what to do. Should he go over to the precinct? Lauryn Jackson was destined, many thought, to one day be station chief. He knew she could arrange for the tests on the fabric torn from Elizabeth Goode's dress. She could do it and keep it quiet. He didn't want to put her on the spot, but he certainly did not want anyone in the police department to know he was here, and he didn't know how else he could get the evidence analyzed. He had cut ties when he abruptly turned in his badge. It was possible that by now, some might even know off the record that not long before, he had attacked a suspect … just a suspect. He had never told Lauryn.

Then he saw her come through the latticed door. She didn't need to speak to the maître d' to find him at their table and watched him as she approached. She looked wonderful, out of uniform, her black hair glowing, wearing a long pink coat. He wondered if he could resist her.

"Hi," she said and sat down, pulling the coat off her shoulders to reveal the dress she had worn the last time they were here.

"Hi, thank you for coming. I wasn't sure you would show."

"Neither was I. How is life in the sticks?"

"Strange."

"What do you want to talk about first?"

Straight to the point. That meant there would be two subjects to discuss: them and the favour he needed. He wondered, though, if she really wanted to talk about their relationship, if she was just as unsure as he was.

"Let's order first."

She asked for a Waldorf salad, and he got the same but with an all-dressed New York bagel and lox.

He steered the talk to work-related subjects, asking after cases that had been open when he left and new Manhattan ones, and before long, they were the way they used to be, excited about what they did, excited together, thrilled by it. She still didn't seem to know about that night in the Bronx. He remained, to her, the man who cared so much about justice. He had never been with a woman who seemed so driven by what drove him, at least not since the early days with Christine, when his young wife seemed interested in everything he said. In a way, Lauryn was so much like him. He found himself thinking about staying with her tonight. He knew that if he asked her, she would tell him the truth even if she were unsure, because she wasn't mysterious like Alice. It was such a relief.

"We aren't taking this any further, are we?" said Lauryn suddenly. He noticed how clearly she spoke, and rather loudly, unlike Alice too. She didn't look angry or even resigned. She had enjoyed their conversation too, but she knew where things ended.

"I wish we could," he said.

"No, you don't, not entirely."

"But I —"

"What's the favour, Hugh?"

He paused and looked at her, then cleared his throat. "I have a piece of a material. Some evidence." He reached into his pocket and pulled out the small plastic bag holding the little square of peacock-print fabric with the two buttons. "I need some tests run on it."

"You want me to do this? Get forensics to —"

"Bypass forensics, just take it right to the lab, ask a favour, say it matters. Your friend there, the woman from Queens who you like so much, she'll do it, won't she?" He paused. "Lauri, this is taken from a woman's dress who likely was either murdered or is, as we speak, being held, and having God knows what done to her."

"Do you have suspects?"

"Her husband, for one."

She looked down at the fabric. "This was ripped from her dress?"

"So it seems."

She sighed. "I could get into a whole lot of trouble for this."

"Your friend won't refuse. Not when you tell her what it's for."

"Why don't you just get it done up there?"

"God, Lauri, I don't even know if they have forensics in that little town. They'd likely have to send it away to a lab in the city, need all sorts of approvals. It takes forever to do things, not like here. I need to move on this now to save this woman. You can't tell me that's not important to you too."

Lauryn looked down at the bag. "I could report you for this. You've taken evidence over a border; you're obviously not complying with the police up there."

"I trust you." He took her hand. "I trusted you, when we were together, not to tell my wife. We believed in each other. I think we will always be special to one another — but there are some things that just can't be."

"That is such a crock. But, I guess, it's true too." She looked down at his left hand. "What about your wife?"

"What do you mean?"

"You still love her, don't you? You still hold out hope."

"Yeah."

"Are you seeing her?"

"Later today."

Lauryn shifted in her chair. "You and I not only trusted each other," she said, still holding his other hand like a friend. "We were always honest too, weren't we?"

"Yes, we were. That was pretty special."

"Good luck, Hugh," she said, pulling back her hand and standing, picking up the little plastic bag as she did. She had only eaten half her salad. He had finished all of his, and the bagel and lox too. "I'll text you the results," she said. She didn't look back.

26

Christine, My Love

HE DROVE UP Hudson Street after lunch, Lauryn's familiar perfume somehow still lingering. Alice Morrow had no scent, he swore, absolutely none. *How is that even possible?* He breathed in his New York love but kept moving, through the Holland Tunnel and across the Hudson River, through that bleak urban and industrial zone, through Jersey City, along the New Jersey Turnpike, barely believing the poverty he saw, and the wealth, and the industry, Springsteen playing in his head. Past the old towers of Newark with its sports palaces and then onto Interstate 280 into East Orange and beyond. Only then did things calm down. He remembered that feeling well: the decompression. The tension, the pain, seemed just to ooze out of his body every time he left that New York world behind. Why had he not kept taking Christine into his arms each day he came home? It had been like that at first. Then, life had seemed like a race to him. Even when he was with her, he felt like he needed to be moving, somehow. He needed to be getting somewhere. It was as if he were always falling behind. Maybe that was what made him try to write things down. He needed to arrest time, any way he could.

He stopped for flowers at a shop a good distance from home and it was half past two when he finally got to their street. The houses were wider apart here, room for large lawns. It was quiet, so quiet, he realized, for America. It seemed unreal.

Mercer didn't pull into the driveway. He had to surprise her. His heart was pounding, and he was feeling flush with anticipation, adrenaline pulsing through him. He felt twenty years younger. He was *really* going to tell her he was sorry, tell her that he knew he had to change, how much he loved her ... ask her forgiveness. Christmas was coming and the kids would likely be home soon. Maybe, he could just stay.

The garage doors were closed. The front door was locked but that was what they always did. She hadn't asked him for his key.

The house seemed deserted at first. Then he heard her coming up the hallway toward him, speaking to someone somewhere behind her in an affectionate tone. He recognized the name, a good friend from work, a good cop known for how much time he gave to charities and volunteering in poor neighbourhoods. When Christine saw Hugh, she froze, speechless. Part of him wanted to stay there, see them together. He wanted to take his medicine. There was no forgiveness for him, none for anyone.

Mercer turned and left the house, throwing the flowers on the walkway, the door slamming behind him. When he was at his car, he heard her call out to him.

"Hugh!"

She was standing there in her bathrobe, one he had given her for a birthday long ago, her blonde hair, not dirty blonde, a real colour that seemed full of lights, though cut shorter now. The man was still in the house, in his house. She started running toward him.

"Hugh, don't go! Not like this!" She was in her bare feet. Those feet that had made such lovely imprints in the sand on the Jamaican beaches on their honeymoon. He remembered seeing them press lightly into the wet ground, as if she were almost unreal, an angel on earth. His angel.

"I have to go," he said and got into the car.

"Hugh, we aren't together anymore, we have to face it. That shouldn't mean we can't love each other now, in a different way. We need to try, for the kids, at least."

"How long has this been going on?" He could not look at her. She didn't say anything.

"The truth, Chrissy."

"About a year."

"Behind my back."

She had her hands on the driver's side doorframe, hands that didn't touch him anymore. He pressed his foot into the accelerator and nearly knocked her down as he sped away, rushing past all those quiet homes with the big lawns and back out to the freeway and the rough world out there.

Cursing Christine, and cursing himself, not thinking about his own affair in New York, or the one up north, he headed toward Grace.

27

More Secrets

HIS HEART POUNDING and trying to calm himself, Mercer sped on, trying to somehow focus on the case. His life was in shambles but maybe, just maybe, he could help someone else, do something good.

Move forward, he told himself.

It took him a bit more than an hour to get to Allentown; then he turned south onto a smaller highway and drove through first suburbs, then farmland, Mennonites driving carriages on the side of the road, and small towns. Grace was about halfway between Allentown and Philadelphia. There were just wisps of snow in the fields.

When he got there, he wasn't surprised by the look of it. Grace was a nice town. That seemed the perfect way to describe it: *nice*. No more than four or five thousand people, mostly middle and upper class and white, a little centre of resources for the surrounding area, and a largely nineteenth century main street featuring an old courthouse. The sign for the town read "Proudly Pennsylvanian, Fiercely American. And Free."

He found another Howard Johnson's, this one at the edge of town near a new grocery store and fast-food places, and booked it for two nights. He had no idea how long he would stay. He didn't know where home was anymore.

The woman at the check-in desk was young and bouncy. "Brittany!" said her name tag. He wondered if she had added the exclamation mark.

"So, what brings you here, sir?" Eyes bright as suns, hoping for a happy answer.

He hesitated. "Visiting."

"Friends? Family?"

"Friends."

"Lovely!"

"Name of Eakins. I've known Andrew in particular for a long time."

"Hmmm." She actually tapped her finger on her chin. "That's funny. I think I know every Gracean and I've never heard of no one by that name. I know the Aikenses and an Atkins, a Perkins and even a Pickens, but not a, what did you say, Eakins?"

"Yeah. Andrew is a sculptor."

"Nope, never heard of anyone doing that around here. My gosh, YOU know someone I do NOT know in Grace. You should get some sort of prize for that!" She handed him his room card. "Have a fantastic time with us!"

He trudged up the three flights to his room on the top floor. Taking the stairs was a habit he had gotten into to keep himself in shape. Poor quality prints of art by famous Pennsylvania artists were mounted on the wall. He recognized the Warhol, the Wyeth, the Haring, but not the other two — a photograph of what looked like a balloon animal and a remarkably realistic portrait of a rower on a lake. Each step creaked when he put his weight on it; the place seemed deserted. He walked into his room, dropped his bag, and stared at himself in the mirror. He looked like shit.

He wasn't sure where to go from here. He was in Grace, but he had no truly good reason — evidence — to connect this location to the crime, or supposed crime, way up north and worlds from here. All he had was his theory that Grace was where the suspect came from, where his secrets originated.

Mercer could go to the police here, but he would have to lie about his involvement in this investigation and he had had enough of hiding the truth.

He lay down on the bed and stared up at the stucco ceiling. In the movies, homicide squads always have an evidence board where they pin photos of victims, suspects, and persons of interest, so they can get a snapshot of where they are at and where they are going with a case. Sometimes that was done in real life. He was never a fan of that process though. He liked to keep it all in his head, go with his gut. Alice and Sal, of course, had nothing other than a bad map on their walls. He found himself laughing at that, and not cynically.

He thought of all the characters in this drama: Elizabeth, Andrew, Jonathan Li, Ariel Foster, Flavio Rossi, Delilah and Ebb Morton, Ben and Beth, Fred and Alma, and Reverend Eleanor James, the man in the porkpie hat. Alice. He pictured all their photos on a wall.

"What would I tell the cops here anyway? That I'm looking for a man named Andrew Eakins who *may* be a former resident? For Elizabeth Goode? Then I'd also have to say that I know where the first one is and that the other is missing, hundreds of miles from here in another country. Or is she missing? If she went willingly from the café, then she could be anywhere. Drinking a margarita in a resort. Maybe here, under an assumed name?"

He thought about assumed names for a moment. *Elizabeth Goode can't have one up north. That's her name, everybody there has known her since birth.* "What about Andrew?" *Andrew, like Andrew Wyeth,* he thought, thinking of one of the bad reproductions he had just seen on the hotel's staircase wall, pinned there next to the Warhol. Andy Warhol. *Isn't that curious,* he thought, *the two most famous artists from Pennsylvania are both named Andrew.* He took out his phone and searched "greatest Pennsylvania painters." Warhol came up, then Wyeth ... then Thomas Eakins.

Andrew. Eakins.

"Who are you?" he said to the imaginary photo of the suspect on his imaginary evidence board. "Did you, a sculptor, a man of the arts, make up that name? Why? Why are you where you are? Why were you with Elizabeth Goode? Why was she protecting you? Why will you not tell us more when it could free you from suspicion? What happened in that damn café?"

HE HAD A shower, dressed and went out to eat.

The best place to talk to people was in the sports bars or family restaurants, places where everyone knows everyone. He didn't want to be too obvious, make it apparent he was looking for someone. Best to just chat up a waitress in the right place. At first, he considered simply going down to the hotel's restaurant, but figured that the employees there likely knew the check-in lady and he didn't want them comparing notes about his inquiries.

He drove downtown and found an eatery that was even better than a sports bar or a family restaurant, a small place where word wouldn't spread quickly about an out-of-towner asking questions, and on the main street where visitors likely often ate, didn't stand out. It was a bit trendy but not too much so, not even very small-town trendy.

He took a table for himself in the busy little room and sat against a wall so he could look out the window. He watched a few people walk by, then looked down at his menu. He would have to order something to engage the waitress.

He heard the door open and close.

"Hi," said a voice. It took him a moment to realize that this person was addressing him. He had not heard any footsteps approach. He looked up.

Alice Morrow.

Plain parka, warm for southeastern Pennsylvania in early December, a few strands sticking out from her ponytail, looking like she had yet to wash her face today.

"Hi," he said, trying not to look shocked.

"May I have a seat?"

"Sure."

She sat down, took off her coat, and put it over the back of her chair. She had that old blue hockey sweater on again.

"You've been following me since I left?"

"For sure. Had a lovely phone chat with Fred and Alma first."

"Sorry about that."

"You never noticed me on your tail, not in Watertown, Syracuse, during that interesting little conversation you had with that beautiful young lady at Bubby's in the Big Apple? Great restaurant, by the way. I ordered out from them while you two were eating. Took it with me to Christine's. I do have a question about what you gave that woman at Bubby's, and you are going to answer me."

"You tailed me through the Holland Tunnel? Along the New Jersey Turnpike too?"

"Didn't need to. Took my time. Knew where you were going."

"You know where we live?"

"Known that for quite a while, Captain America, though I must say it doesn't sound like it's 'we' who live at your home anymore.

Christine is a go-getter, not wasting any time. As a woman, I'd say 'Good for her,' but that wouldn't be very nice."

"Shut up."

"Not your turn to be pissed off, Hugh."

"Are you going to have me arrested or something? Wrestle me into your car and take me back over the border?"

"Let's eat first." She picked up the menu. "I wonder if they know how to put together a good homemade soup here. I'm frickin' starving. Comfort food for Alice." She scanned the options.

He noticed again how quietly she talked, how flat the accent was. Strangely, it stood out. Other customers were jabbering away, all their conversations public. It struck him suddenly that it made so much more sense, really, to keep things private between friends.

She found a good broccoli soup, added fries and a large diet coke, and he had an apple and cranberry salad on quinoa, and an Arnold Palmer. They didn't utter a word for a long while. He wanted to say something, but it wasn't his place, that was obvious. The next move was up to her. She had him right where she wanted him, and it pissed him off.

Finally, he spoke, quietly.

"The Freemans were the ghost couple. Alma admitted it. And she told me that Elizabeth Goode was in the café with Eakins. I'm guessing Fred didn't tell you that when he complained about me harassing them."

Alice was slurping her soup. She looked up at him. Just her eyes moved.

"Surprising what you can learn illegally."

"Look, I'm sorry, I just —"

"No, no. No cause for sorrow. Good work."

"Does this mean you aren't having me arrested?"

"We'll figure all that out when we solve this sucker."

He had no idea if she was serious or not.

"We are working on this then, here, you and me?" he asked.

"You bet your boots."

"Okay. I have some ideas."

"First you are going to tell me why you came here. You and I are like bloodhounds, and you think the blood is here. But even before that, explain what that thing was you gave Sergeant Lauryn Jackson. The lovely Lauri."

She knew her name.

"Well." He paused but didn't have a choice. He had to spill. "I found a piece of material under the furnace legs in Andrew's studio."

"And didn't tell me."

"Correct. I know it was torn from one of Elizabeth Goode's dresses, and not just any dress, but the one she was wearing the day she disappeared, because Sal confirmed for me what she had on that day. You'll recall the pattern?"

"No, dick-brain, I've completely forgotten. Though I did NOT know that you had a piece of it in your possession." She paused. "But why would the culprit not simply get rid of it, burn it? It appears to me to be something that was left there for us to find, maybe just you. We need to think about why that might be. Lauri is getting it tested for you."

"Yes."

"Illegally."

"Off the record."

"I know nothing about it, never will."

"Got you."

"Tell me the results the instant you find out."

"Or what?" He thought he would chance some humour.

"Or I'll have your balls in my purse."

He didn't want to add that it felt like she already had them.

"I came here," he said, "because the woman at the bar that Eakins frequented told me she thought he had an ex-wife named

Grace, but later I realized, from the way she'd phrased things, that Grace might, in fact be the name of a place — in Pennsylvania, the very state I thought Eakins might be from."

"And Elizabeth went to school in Philadelphia, may have even worked there. That's like, forty minutes from here."

"Yeah, Byrn Mawr College. But I couldn't find anyone online with her name and age in Pennsylvania, going back a while."

"That's curious. Maybe she just didn't have a number in the phone book or much public profile when she was in school. We need to look into the college records. But what about the ex-wife? Are you sure there isn't one?"

"Well, the woman at the bar said she was convinced he'd had one."

"Woman's intuition."

"Yeah, I guess. She said he got angry once when the subject of ex-wives came up. Said he said something weird about it."

"What?"

"Oh, nothing, really, just referred to the word *marry* as a strange name."

"Word."

"No, he said *name*."

"Well, it is a name too."

They looked at each other.

"You don't suppose," began Mercer.

"That we should be looking for someone named Mary too?" Alice paused. "The relationship with this other woman, this possible ex-wife, likely predates Andrew going north, right? Probably from down here somewhere, maybe right here."

"And if Elizabeth lived nearby in Philadelphia, maybe even after she graduated, that would be right around the same time."

"What if Andrew did live here and the name he uses up north is an assumed one?" said Mercer. "He's an artist and the name

Andrew Eakins borrows from the names of famous Pennsylvania artists."

"Makes sense. Though I have to tell you, Sal and I have been going under the assumption that he uses an assumed name for quite a while now."

"And you didn't tell me."

They both smiled. That seemed like progress.

"Damn, Alice, how the hell did you track me without my being aware of it? For days?"

"We in the north are invisible, but it's useful. Helps to be under-estimated."

She ate several more fries before she went on. "So, you've asked around about Andrew Eakins here, correct? And he doesn't appear to have been a resident?"

"No one we're looking for seems to be from here. The woman at the desk in my hotel —"

"Yeah, the Howard Johnson's. I'm in the next room."

"Oh."

"Go on."

"She seems to know everyone in town and has never heard of anyone named Eakins."

"So, as we thought, if Andrew did live here, it was under a different name."

"Yeah."

"Your next move was about to happen, wasn't it?" asked Alice. "In this restaurant."

The waitress was coming back to ask how they were doing. Mercer had been noticing how often they did that this side of the border.

"I hate that," said Alice, as the woman approached. "You do not need to make me tell you how great your food and your service is, lady."

"Helpful this time though," said Mercer. "I'll ask her if —"

"No."

"What?"

"Don't ask her anything. That's an order."

Mercer couldn't believe she just said that, but he did as he was told. The waitress, of course, was "so glad" they had enjoyed their meal here at Home Cookin' and said she would bring the credit card machine "in a jiffy."

"I've already asked your next question, Hugh, earlier today," said Alice when the woman stepped away. "And I have your answer." She eyed him for a second. "Something bad went on here about two and a half years ago."

28

First Deceiver

ALICE LEANED IN close to Mercer and spoke in an even quieter voice than she normally used. "Let's go talk outside."

He quickly paid for the meal and gave the waitress a twenty percent tip. Alice wanted some of the free candies in the jar at the counter across from the entrance. As she fished out about five of them, Mercer stood in the little vestibule by the door and glanced at the photos on the wall. Home Cookin' did a lot for the community. He imagined that was the way with many little businesses in Grace.

There were photos of the baseball and basketball teams they sponsored and the work they did with the Big Sisters of Grace. One of the images showed a couple of women standing with a number of girls in a bowling alley. "Bowl for Big Sisters!" read the caption. The date on the photo indicated that this event had happened seven years earlier. One of the women standing there, in perhaps her mid-twenties, young for this sort of thing, her arm lovingly around a girl, looked familiar. He couldn't place why though — it didn't make sense. He didn't know anyone from Grace. It must just be a resemblance to someone he knew back in the day. As a police officer who constantly examined appearances, he had often noticed how much more similar than different we all really are. Eyes could be the same, chins, or the way you stood. It cut across racial lines and gender.

"Let's go," said Alice, sucking on a candy.

It was getting dark outside. They walked down the main street in Grace not saying anything. The town seemed full of colour, many of the old buildings painted in bright hues, garish Christmas decorations everywhere. It was surprisingly loud for a small town. When they got to her car, parked across the street not far from his, she motioned for him to get in on the passenger side.

"Okay," said Alice once they were seated. "That's what you were going to try to figure out, right? That was your next question around here? Did anything remarkable happen in Grace between two and three years ago?"

"Yup."

"I asked the girl at our hotel's front desk that same question, almost. Just left out the timing. 'Has anything exciting ever happened around these parts?'"

Alice took a long pause.

"She said 'no,' and laughed that over-the-top laugh of hers. Then I said, 'Never?' And then she said —"

"What a minute!" cried Mercer.

"What?"

"I know who she is!" he cried.

"What?"

"The woman in the Big Sisters Bowlathon."

"Sorry?"

He leapt out of the car.

"It's the woman who came to my door!"

29

The Imposter

MERCER TOOK OFF across the main street of Grace into the path of an oncoming vehicle. He barely got out of the way as the driver blared his horn.

Alice stepped from her car, made sure the doors were locked, and followed him. Mercer was already inside Home Cookin' when she entered. He was standing in the vestibule scrutinizing the photos.

"Tell them you left a glove in here or something," he said to her.

"Mittens. I had mittens, and I have them on."

"Whatever."

Mercer's phone buzzed loudly, and Alice waited as he pulled it out of his pocket.

"Text from Lauryn," he said.

"May I help you?" asked the same waitress. "Oh, you two again? You must really like the home cooking at Home Cookin'!"

"Hold on a second," said Alice to her. She turned back to Mercer. "Move it so I can see the screen."

He turned his phone toward her.

Ran the tests right away. Got them in and out fast. No DNA *matches from the blood. Three sets of fingerprints on the buttons. A man and two women, we figure. No match for the man's finger- print or one of the others. The third is definitely a woman: Rebecca Prior, of Grace,* PA. *We got lucky. She had to undergo a security check to work with Big Sisters, so her prints were on file. Over and out, Lauryn*

"Rebecca Prior," said Mercer softly, staring at the photo on the wall. "Otherwise known as 'Angela.' That's her all right, younger, no glasses, hair longer, but that's her!"

"Looks very sweet here," said Alice.

"Gotcha!" said Mercer putting his finger on the woman's image.

"Do you know her?" asked the waitress.

Alice turned to her. "Do you?"

"Course. That's Becky Prior."

"We have a mutual friend," said Mercer, "and we were actually going to drop by Becky's place to say hello while we're in town. My friend, back home, had shown me a picture of her, and then I noticed this photo on the wall on my way out of your restaurant. Didn't know why I knew that face at first, came back just out of curiosity. I had her number and address on a piece of paper, but wouldn't you know, I've lost it. We'll have to look all that up and try to get in touch."

"Oh, I know where she lives.

"You do?" asked Alice.

"No use in going over there though."

"Why is that?"

"'Cause she ain't here. She hasn't been home for a long time, maybe a year? Her brother moved out too. Neighbours are look- ing after the place. Other brother lives out of state. The Priors are good people, pillars of this community. Becky has a heart of gold. This town aches for that family. We miss her. Mary too."

Oh, my God. Mercer felt like doing a fist pump. *Mary.*

"I don't understand," said Alice. "What do you mean by the town aching for them?"

"Actually, I prefer not to talk about that. Do you two want dessert or something?"

"No," said Mercer, "listen, all I need to know is —"

"Who is your friend who knows her so well?" asked the waitress.

"We should get going," said Alice to Mercer. She turned back to the young woman. "Sorry we brought this up. Sounds like Becky is a great lady and we're disappointed to be missing her. Have a great day."

She pulled Mercer out of the restaurant.

"What are you doing?" he complained as they walked back along the main street.

"The public library is just down here. We don't need the waitress to fill us in, or get suspicious. I'm betting the local newspaper will enlighten us, and in the detail we need. Even better than what we would find on our phones."

They walked quickly, saying nothing more, so excited that they both forgot about what else Alice had been about to reveal to him.

The Grace Public Library was barely a block away, a Georgian style building with big white pillars, right next to an almost identical one that was the county courthouse. It was closing in less than an hour, but the librarian told them she wouldn't lock up until they were done, if they 'didn't dawdle.' With her help, they found both *The Grace Weekly* and *The Philadelphia Inquirer*, full digital replicas. There was a search engine on the computers for names and dates going back many years.

"Prior, Rebecca."

There were many references. Mercer took *The Weekly* and Alice *The Inquirer*. They sat side by side.

Alice and Mercer hungrily consumed the stories connected to Rebecca Prior's name, huge in *The Weekly*, short reports in *The Inquirer*. They started with the first one they found and went chronologically, going through page after page. There were two stretches of news stories that referenced Rebecca Prior's name: the first told of a horrible car accident that caused her sister Mary's death, the second a murder trial.

"This is it," said Alice quietly. "This is what the girl at the hotel was talking about. She said something big happened here around this time, a death that shook up the community, but she didn't want to say more."

Based on the newspaper reports, the Priors were indeed a special family in Grace: the father, a lawyer, had served as mayor for three terms; the mother, a homemaker, seemed to run every charity in town. Both had died of cancer in their sixties and been greatly mourned by everyone. Mary, the eldest, had followed in her father's footsteps and become a lawyer, working on a number of local lawsuits against the unfair practices of big corporations; John was a respected businessman with a degree from Harvard; and Becky, a social worker who ran her business out of the large family home. Only Luke, the youngest, struggled. He had stayed at home, living with Becky. Mary became the matriarch in the absence of her parents. Despite being only in her mid-thirties, Mary was a prominent citizen in Grace, and everyone, especially her siblings, looked up to her.

The town seemed to deeply grieve Mary's death. There had been two people in the car: Mary Prior and her husband, an artist named Alex Everly. Their car had smashed into the brick wall of a building in Philadelphia at high speed.

"Are you seeing what I'm seeing?" asked Alice.

"Yeah. Everly. An artist."

There were photos of the car, crumpled like a crushed can, and a photo of Mary, a beautiful young woman, who radiated intelligence and poise. Her injuries were apparently gruesome — her skull cracked wide open, nearly decapitated from her body.

Mercer moved to the second page of the story in *The Weekly*. "Holy, holy," he said just above his breath.

"What?" asked Alice. She leaned over to look. It was a photograph of Alex Everly.

"Andrew Eakins!" she gasped. "It's him!"

Everly had survived. He was thirty-six years old at the time, had been married to the victim for three years — they were described as the perfect couple — and his work was receiving critical acclaim. He had an exhibition of his paintings set for a New York debut.

"That's weird," said Alice, "there is nothing about sculpting here. Is this his identical twin or something? Our man is a sculptor, exclusively it seems. Did you see any paintings anywhere in the studio or the Goode house? Canvases? Brushes or paint?"

"No, nowhere."

The burial at Grace Episcopal Church had been like a state funeral for the town. There were photographs of the family — Becky and her brothers, holding on to each other. Alex Everly was among them, part of them, wrapped in the arms of his in-laws, staring off into space.

They turned to the other group of stories later on, with Becky Prior's name in them.

It was a murder trial. The victim was Mary Prior.

It had electrified Grace and the entire county and many readers across the state.

The accused was Alex Everly.

30

First Murder

THE BEST ACCOUNTS were in *The Weekly*. Alice slid her chair over and they read together. There was no publication ban on court proceedings, and the local reporter had done an excellent job of reproducing exactly what transpired.

During police questioning about the accident, one officer had noticed an inconsistency in Everly's account. The accused had said that his foot had gotten momentarily jammed between the brake pedal and the accelerator and he had turned the wheel as hard left as he could to try to make the sharp turn at breakneck speed, at the same time desperate to get his foot free. It had all taken just a few seconds. The officer had then examined the car and found that the distance between the brake pedal and the accelerator seemed wide enough for more than the width of Everly's shoe. When Everly was questioned again, the officer had noted that he was very nervous, almost "frightened."

"Was your foot really jammed between the brake pedal and the accelerator?" the officer had asked him, on the record.

"Yes," was the quiet answer.

"Are you sure of that?"

"I think so."

"You think so? Mr. Everly, I must tell you, that's not a very helpful thing to say."

"Yes, then. Yes, it was." This was apparently barely audible.

"Mr. Everly, we are all interested in the truth here. It is best that you tell us exactly what happened. Your wife was a good person. You owe it to her and her memory to get this right. You owe it to her family, who are devastated. To this community."

The officer had paused for a while then. Mercer recognized the technique. The interrogator should keep quiet at this point. Say nothing. Wait for what the subject says. Let your target hang himself.

"Maybe ... maybe ..." mumbled Everly, apparently tears forming in his eyes. "Maybe it's complicated."

"How so, Mr. Everly?"

Yes, thought Mercer, *well done, say only that, lead him toward it.* There was another long pause. *Well done, again.*

"You know that thing you said about my wife being a good person?

"Yes?"

"She wasn't."

"Wow," whispered Alice. She put her hand on Mercer's arm.

"What do you mean, Mr. Everly?"

"Let's just say she wasn't."

"Let's say a little more, in the service of the truth."

"She had a lover."

Both Alice and Mercer could almost feel the tension in the interrogation room.

"Do you have any —"

"I saw them!" shouted Everly.

Alice and Mercer imagined his voice echoing off the walls.

"So, you murdered her, Mr. Everly ... for that?"

That wasn't entirely a fair question, thought Mercer, *but it's the sort of thing we cops do.* He thought of himself assaulting the young man in the Bronx again; he thought of Andrew Eakins's distrust of the police.

"Is what she did not a crime?" Everly had cried. "Why is THAT not a crime? Why is that NEVER a crime? It's among the most devastating things human beings do to each other. And yet, it goes unpunished."

"Did you purposely drive into that brick wall, Mr. Everly?"

Another leading question.

"I was confronting her about it. She admitted to it. She did not show one ounce of remorse. She said she needed it in her life. She needed him and she wondered what I was going to do about it. I swear to God ... she smiled when she said it."

"That was as you were nearing that turn."

"Yes." That answer was apparently barely audible too.

"It was a left-hand turn, wasn't it Mr. Everly?"

"Yes."

"Correct me if I am wrong, but that would put the person in the passenger seat in the most peril."

"Correct."

"Swerving as you turned left, a brick wall in front of you, would slam the vehicle into that wall at high speed and horribly injure the passenger. It would mean almost certain death for her, a painful end ... one might say?"

"Yes."

"The driver would be the judge and executioner."

The cop was putting words in his target's mouth, but he needed to do that to get a conviction.

"I suppose."

"So, Mr. Everly, can we say that you murdered your wife, Mary Prior?"

Both Mercer and Alice were thinking of the handwritten note in the Bible up north.

"I loved Mary dearly. She loved me. So she said. I believed her and I still believe her. She did love me. We were perfect. What happens to all of that?" He had looked up at the officer with tears streaming down his face.

Get him to admit it, thought Mercer. *Now is the time.* Strike. *Ask him again. Make him say it!*

"So, I'll ask again. You admit to murdering your wife?"

There was another long pause. "I don't know."

Shit, thought Mercer. *Ask again.*

"That is not a real answer, Mr. Everly. Give me a real answer."

Excellent.

"I've said everything I want to say."

Oh, crap.

"Oh, crap," said Alice.

"Maybe ... maybe Andrew Eakins did kill Elizabeth Goode after all," said Mercer. "This proves he was capable of murder, had it in him." Mercer had felt that to be true the moment the Grace police interrogator began to expose the inconsistency in Everly's story.

"I sensed that too," said Alice, "but it isn't about what we feel. It has to be about the facts."

They turned to the articles about the trial. On the strength of that interview, Alex Everly was charged with murder.

"That could be a mistake," said Alice. "Manslaughter might have been better."

"I wonder if the Prior family had anything to do with the charge? Can you imagine the betrayal?"

"Whose?" asked Alice.

"Yeah, there is something to that, but he viciously murdered her. He slammed her into that wall like a fiend would pick up an animal and drive its skull into it, in a fit of rage. Maybe even worse than that."

They read on. The trial electrified the region though it seemed, in some ways, to be just another murder case to *The Philadelphia Inquirer*. It took weeks, the lawyers jousting about whether or not Everly had admitted to the crime and Mary's infidelity constantly referenced by the defence. Everly added on the stand that though initially angry, he had gotten his foot loose and tried to correct the car before it hit the wall but had been too late. The Prior family were in attendance every day, all of them weeping, Becky cautioned for shouting obscenities at Everly several times and once removed from the premises.

A court-appointed psychiatrist was brought in to examine the accused, witnesses as to Everly's character were called upon, and a mechanic who had worked on the couple's car testified about the chances of someone having the sort of accident Everly claimed he had experienced. The Prior family were put on the stand by the prosecution, giving bitter testimonies concerning things they now recalled about Everly's temper, his devious ways. He stared at them in disbelief, though he was more than often simply a quiet, forlorn figure who looked, as the reporter said, "suicidal."

Alice and Mercer moved quickly through all the details, desperate to find the verdict, flashing past the images of the witnesses and other experts, the latter not photographed but drawn by the court artist.

There it was:

EVERLY NOT GULITY OF MURDER!

They delved into the story, written under photographs of a stunned looking Everly helped from the court and taken away under police protection as people screamed at him on the courthouse steps.

There was a photograph of Becky Prior too, standing in front of her two brothers, a look of hatred on her face. She spoke of "a murderer on the loose."

Key to the verdict, it seemed, and the "temporary insanity" defence, was the testimony of the court-appointed psychiatrist, one Dr. Newman, who spent many hours over many days with the accused. She spoke of a "decent, devastated man who in my professional opinion did not consciously decide to kill his wife, but under emotional distress and duress that any normal human being would feel, did something that he now regrets. He was not himself when he made this decision. It was not Alex Everly who did this, but a momentary doppelganger who would not do such a thing under normal circumstances." And, she had added, even in this state, he had tried to correct the car and prevent the accident.

Dr. Newman was a specialist in this sort of thing, her Philadelphia practice renowned.

Alice and Mercer turned back to an artist's drawing of Dr. Eve Newman.

Eve and the Imposter, Mercer was thinking as the image appeared.

Alice stood up and put her hand over her mouth.

Elizabeth!

Dr. Eve Newman was Elizabeth Goode.

31

If I'd Had a Gun

THEY LEFT THE library at almost a run, not even waving back at the librarian, Alice several strides ahead of Mercer. Both their minds were filled with the look of hatred they had seen on Becky Prior's face for the man who had murdered her sister and the woman whose testimony had swayed the jury.

"We have to go to the police station here," said Mercer, puffing. "Saw it at the other end of town."

"Get them to send a recent photograph of Rebecca Prior back home. I'll get Sal to put it out everywhere. Someone else will have seen her."

"We need to find out where the hell she is."

"Where she's keeping Elizabeth."

"She may not be keeping her."

They said nothing for a few strides.

"I'm guessing Elizabeth is still alive if Becky isn't home," said Alice.

"She just may be on the run."

They got into Alice's car, which was closest.

"Why would she be on the run?" said Alice. "As far as she knows, we do not have a clue she may have done this. Why would we? This is a frickin' brilliant crime, so brilliant that it seems to me we still don't know the half of it. She could try to just slip on home here to Grace soon and take up her life again."

"Wherever she is, we have to find her."

Alice put her hands on the wheel and sighed. "Newman was Elizabeth Goode's mother's maiden name. The Mortons told us that, remember? And Ariel Foster told us that she hated life so much back home that she despised the very name everyone knew her by, that she'd change it in an instant, if she could."

"Eve. That's pretty clever. She wanted to be a new person down here. So, she became the first woman."

"And it all worked out, didn't it, for a while? But then she and Andrew had to start all over again. He had to go somewhere he could be anonymous. So, he went north with her where she had just inherited her parents' home, changed his name, the two of them arriving at different times, pretending they'd just met, and she went back to being Elizabeth Goode, for him."

Alice pulled out and drove north toward the station using her lead foot.

"Both of them conveniently untraceable," mused Mercer.

"Yeah, but Rebecca Prior found them somehow and she's been hatching something for a long time back home! Planning and plotting, getting it all perfect. Imagine the loathing she must have inside her to do this."

And I'm somehow part of it, thought Mercer.

"Remember what they all said about Andrew and Elizabeth?" he said out loud. "She seemed to be protective of him."

"She even went back to the place and the name she hated to do it. That's love, I guess."

"See where that's gotten her though. She's either dead or being held somewhere." Mercer paused. "I wonder what Becky's end-game is?"

"I don't know, but I do know we have to get north on the fly."

They pulled into the Grace police station in the dark and were soon in the chief's office. He looked close to retirement, lethargic in his movements. When he took off his thick glasses indentation marks were visible on his temples. He gave the impression of being a man who didn't have anything else to do but work into the night. They introduced themselves and he listened carefully to Alice as she explained the case.

"How are you involved in this?" he asked Mercer when she was done.

"Just happened to be in town."

"Up there?"

"Yeah."

"So, really, you have no jurisdiction up there, or here, no reason to be involved in this case in any way — but we'll look the other way on those matters." He turned back to Alice. "I'll get a photo out to your colleagues before you two are across the state line."

"Thanks," said Alice.

"I knew the Priors, everyone did. In fact, it breaks my heart to think that Becky could be doing something that isn't right. What Everly did, now that's hard to forgive."

"Not grounds for kidnapping, and after Mr. Everly was declared innocent."

"Or murder, or torture," said Mercer.

"Now, hold on there, we don't know any of that. That would not be like our Becky."

"Is coming up north and taking Elizabeth Goode like her?"

The chief sighed. "No, it isn't. You got me there. If that's really what's happened. My stars though, that Everly, he got off scot-free to my way of thinking. Mostly due to this Dr. Newman, the woman you call Goode. Smart as a fox. Why, she not only got him off, but she also made sure that he could vanish. She even pushed for making his fingerprints unavailable. Try to find them, if you can. Her argument was that an 'innocent' man is an 'innocent man.' Can you imagine? The slate should be wiped clean? He would be a devil to try to trace. He is a new person up there, with no past. And then she took up with him too!"

"Eve and the Imposter."

"Sorry, ma'am?"

"Nothing. We should be going."

They stood up to leave.

"It's hard not to think that this Newman woman and that murderer aren't getting what was coming to them," said the chief. "If I were a Prior and I'd had my gun near that courthouse, I might have taken him out myself. Off the record, if she's really done this, worked it all out to nail his ass, and hers too, I feel a little bit of admiration for our Becky."

32

Racing Back

BY THE TIME Alice got Mercer back to his car it was well past six o'clock.

"Race you to the border," she said.

That was the last he saw of her for about four and a half hours. He drove like the devil, jumping on to 81 North just past Allentown and going like the wind in the dark through Wilkes-Barre, Scranton, and Binghamton, where he encountered snow, past Syracuse and then Watertown, all the way to the border. He looked in front of him and behind, but he never caught sight of her car.

As he drove, he kept thinking of what they knew and did not know. First and foremost, they still didn't know if Elizabeth was alive. And if she was alive, then where the hell was she? Were they racing against time? He sped up when he thought of that.

And how had Rebecca Prior pulled this off, and not just the buildup but the pivotal moment itself. He tried to imagine the scene in Jonathan Li's café. Alma Freeman had said Elizabeth went willingly, so not under the threat of a weapon. Why? Why, in God's name, do that? She *wanted* to go.

He called Alice.

"Hey," he said. "Where are you?"

"Wouldn't you like to know?"

"Mysterious, huh?"

"Absolutely. "

"I've been thinking about the moment in the café, when Elizabeth just up and leaves with someone. If it was Becky, then why would Elizabeth go with her?"

"It wasn't Rebecca Prior."

"How can you be so sure?"

"Two reasons. First, what you said: Elizabeth would have been freaked out. This nutbar had somehow tracked her, two and a half years later in another country and despite their changed names and everything. There is no way she leaves the café, at least willingly, with Rebecca Prior. Second, it wouldn't have been in Prior's interests either. She would not want to give away her identity, especially if she is just kidnapping her. When she lets her go, Elizabeth just says it was Rebecca Prior who took her, and boom, she's guilty of forcible confinement. We could issue a warrant for her in Grace and pick her up."

"That's why she murdered her."

There was a pause on the other end.

"Let's hope not. Let's hope we have a live body to find, somewhere. I'm trying to be optimistic. I'm hoping there's some sort of other endgame in this."

"Which means, someone else took Elizabeth Goode quietly and willingly out of that café."

"Right."

"Who?"

"Good question."

After that he tried to steer the conversation to other topics. Whenever he tried to nudge it toward personal things, she would escape like Houdini.

"Hey," he finally said, "I'm nearing the border."

"Are you, now."

"Not sure what I'm going to say if they check my movements. They will know that I only left a few days ago and am already trying to return. After I told them I'd only be up there for a few weeks. What will I do if they search all this? "

"Well, I guess you'll be shit out of luck."

She hung up.

He approached the border a few minutes later. It was nearing eleven o'clock and the dark road was almost deserted. Just a single car up ahead. Alice. It didn't take her long to go through. He didn't even see her hand the border officer anything to check. Then, the officer waved him forward.

"Passport," said the woman. She was younger than many of the border officials he had encountered and much more stern. The last time he had entered the country he had been surprised at how nice and welcoming the reception had been. This woman, however, was not friendly. She took a long time to examine his passport, turned toward him, and looked his facial features up and down. She scanned the passport and then read what came up on her computer. She frowned.

"Mr. Mercer, I do not really like what I see here."

He looked toward Alice's tail lights disappearing into the night, then back at the woman, trying to keep his eyes from appearing shifty.

"What do you mean?"

"I see that you entered this country more than two months ago, saying you would only be here for a couple of weeks, then you left for two days, and now you are wanting to return?"

"I, uh ..."

"What's the real story here, Mr. Mercer?"

"I'm really not staying long this time."

"How do we know that?"

"Well, I'm just not."

"Do you realize what the penalty is for lying to a border official?"

"Look —

"It's having to admit to Sergeant Alice Morrow that I had you worried."

There was dead silence.

"Can I go?"

She smiled. "Of course. Good luck with the investigation, Detective Mercer. In the future though, honesty is the best policy. Enjoy the snow!"

She handed him his passport, closed her window with a laugh, and waved him on.

He was going to kill Alice when he caught her. He didn't have to wait long. About a mile around the bend, he saw her car pulled over by the side of the road. He drove up behind her in the falling snow, got out, and walked up to her car.

He had never seen her laugh like that, and it made it difficult to be angry with her. There was something wonderful about seeing her so happy. It made him want to open the door and pull her out and take her into his arms. He wished to God that he knew what the deal was with her.

"Sorry about that," she said when she stopped laughing. "I couldn't resist it. Captain America with his pants down."

"More like wetting them, actually."

It was getting late. They were both exhausted. She smiled. "There's a Best Western just off the first exit after you get on the major highway. Be there or be square." She pulled away, leaving him standing by the side of the road.

SHE WAS LONG gone in the morning when he awoke. He could not believe it. How could he have let that happen again, and under these circumstances? He had slept like a rock.

"Nearly two hours to home," he said to himself as he scraped the ice off his windshield. "Home?" He looked around the cold grey parking lot and at the snow coming down. "Why the hell did I say that? "

Mercer found that he was truly anxious to get back, though he told himself it was because they were on the edge of solving this bizarre case. He turned on the radio and heard a love song called "Weak in the Knees," and it made him think of Alice or at least, of the two of them. Later, he took out his phone and called up a band he remembered Alice mentioning she liked. The songs' aggressive lyrics came pounding out of his speakers, and it made him grin. The north with its clothes off.

When he arrived at the station, he was not surprised to see that Alice was already there, huddled in her office with Salma Haddad, who had brought her doughnuts. In fact, he had the sense that she had been there for quite a while. Down at the end of the hall, Chief Smith seemed to be back, his office door firmly closed again, a song about the joys of the end of the week seeping through the crack. Leonard Ferguson was standing just outside Alice's door at the printer. He intercepted Mercer.

"Man, Hugh, this case is getting freakin' exciting. Been picking up a bit on what the girls are saying in there. Good work down in the States! You and I should have a coffee and I'll help you get to the bottom this. Eakins is behind it no matter what, don't you think? The world is too lenient these days. Let's just get his ass into court."

"Love to have a coffee with you, Leonard, but we're a little busy now," said Mercer.

"Yeah, sure, sure, Hugh. I think you promised me some New York crime stories too." He stepped aside.

Mercer entered Alice's office and closed the door behind him. Sal was pacing in the small room, obviously digesting the update on what they had learned down south. Alice had her feet up on her desk.

"Where you been?" she asked, with a straight face.

"I keep wondering if we should just let Andrew Eakins go," he said as he sat down with a sigh.

"That's a thought, but not yet. I want to talk to him first, one last time." Alice shifted her feet off the desk. "He may be a whole lot more communicative now that we know his secret. But we thought we'd wait for you."

"And he may still have done it," said Sal. She stopped pacing and folded her arms across her chest.

"I get why you might think that," said Mercer. "The first thing I said to Alice when we found out Eakins had killed Mary Prior was that it proved he was capable of murder."

"And I didn't disagree," said Alice.

"You know what else I've been thinking about all this though?" said Mercer. "I've been thinking that if you and I, Alice, thought that what he did in Pennsylvania proved he was capable of murder, if that was our instinct, if that implicated Andrew Eakins in our minds, then that's the way a jury would think too. If a jury learned what he did back in Grace and then had this café scenario presented to them, that would likely seal his fate."

Alice nodded. "If someone wanted him to be found guilty of this so-called disappearance or murder, then he or she would want his past to get out."

Sal shook her head. "Why not just tell people, then? The crime here happens, and you just say: hey, this guy was a murderer back in the States. Now, he's done it again."

"Because," said Mercer, "how could the person who revealed that history just happen to be here when the crime occurred and know all about Alex Everly, his past, his name change and everything, without being suspicious? Eakins's identity, connection to that case, everything, is protected. Only someone with a connection to the case would know — someone seeking Eakins with vengeance on her mind. Establishing the connection to Mary Prior's death had to be subtly done. Rebecca Prior doesn't want anyone figuring out she's involved up here. She just wants a crime to occur, Andrew Eakins to be accused, and to have his past history used to convict him. You've got to remember, this couple has vanished and then resurfaced with different identities in the middle of *nowhere* —" He stopped abruptly, realizing what he had just said. Alice and Sal regarded him, not looking pleased. "Sorry," he said. "I didn't mean that last part. This isn't nowhere."

"Rather be here than anywhere else," said Sal. "You know, up here we don't have a bit of interest in living in that violent, self-centred, self-deluded place down there you call your homeland. This is better than there and we all know it."

"Sorry. Really am. I don't actually feel that way. Not anymore." He wasn't entirely telling the truth. "I will admit though, that I did think that before I came here. Someone from a place like where I'm from or from Grace, Pennsylvania would think that way too. Rebecca Prior feels like she can get away with things here."

"She's been searching for and tracking Eakins for two and a half years," said Alice.

Mercer nodded. "And the waitress in Grace told us she'd been away for more than a year. That must have been when Rebecca found him, perhaps using allies in Pennsylvania, maybe in the justice system or the police force. Like a dog on a bone."

"A year." said Sal. "She's been snooping around here for a year?"

"Yup, in and out, learning about everyone, changing her appearance, homing in on the people she needs to know. Then, using them at the right moment."

"People," said Alice, "who have financial or maybe other concerns. People who might be willing to help her, like the Freemans, and Jonathan Li, and maybe the Reverend Eleanor James too."

"Yeah," said Sal, "but that's still a hell of a job. How can you convince decent people to help you do something like this? I know the Freemans, not perfect, but good folks."

"Yeah, we're all good around here," said Alice quietly.

"Good folks in need, whom Becky discovered were in need," said Mercer. "Folks who could be persuaded if you set things up properly, if you taught them how to hide the money you gave them, if you found other reasons they might want to be involved, and if you told them the *whole* story, the carefully structured, 'true' story."

"Yeah," said Alice, "of a man who murdered his former wife, who now holds his new wife, a local girl, virtually captive, beating the hell out of her, intent on someday killing her too, a man whom the police could not or would not move on. You would be doing a public service, saving an innocent woman. It would be the right thing to do, and most folks around here want to do the right thing, at least that's the vibe they give off ... Someone who spent enough time here would learn that."

"But still," said Sal, "in need of money or not, or whatever, they would have to stand by and watch this Prior woman enter that café and take Elizabeth by force, at gunpoint or knifepoint. The Freemans wouldn't do that."

There hadn't been time to tell Sal everything. "She went willingly," said Alice.

There was silence in the room for a moment.

"Why would she do that?" asked Sal.

"Because it wasn't Rebecca," said Mercer.

There was silence again.

"Someone else did this," said Alice, "probably at Rebecca's command."

"The brothers?" asked Sal.

"No," said Alice, "I don't think so. Elizabeth saw them in court every day in Grace. She would know them."

"So who?"

"Well, that's what we have to find out," said Mercer.

"Let's think about this again," said Alice. "Rebecca Prior was on this for a year here, like a snake among us, surfacing, fading, and then resurfacing. She put together an intricate plan and had all the right people involved … likely there are more folks than we've identified so far. Remember, we didn't even know she'd approached the Reverend until a few days ago."

"Next thing you know, you'll want to take a look at *my* bank account," said Sal.

Alice didn't respond.

"Oh, come on!"

"Or mine," said Alice.

Mercer didn't say anything.

"Whatever happened," said Sal, "there's a web of people in on this."

Me? thought Mercer. *She came to see me.*

"Look," said Sal, "if Elizabeth Goode is still alive, and it seems like she left the café under her own steam, then she is being held somewhere by a woman who reviles her. We've just put out

Rebecca Prior's picture, so if she's here somewhere she will likely find out we are closing in. Maybe, she'll get desperate."

"Maybe we shouldn't have done that," said Alice.

"No," said Mercer, "we had to. Standard procedure. Someone will recognize her, tell us where she is." As he said that he thought of how difficult it was to get people around here to reveal anything.

"She's pretty elusive," said Sal. "She was right at your door, Detective Mercer, leading you into this. Why did she do that? That's puzzled me for a long time."

Mercer swallowed. He thought back to that moment. The strange woman who never gave him her name coming down the sideroad, her headlights in the dark morning, then standing at his door with the short brown hair she must have cut after Rossi met her in the bar, wire-rimmed glasses, so unlike her photo with the Big Sisters, that button "I own my own body," filling out the character, the believable character of someone who was worried about Elizabeth Goode and domestic violence, someone who had learned how to sound like a local.

It suddenly occurred to Mercer why she had come to see him.

"She wanted me on the case because I'm uniquely ..." said Mercer, then stopped.

"You can say it, Hugh," said Alice. "She wanted you on the case because she was concerned that we weren't capable of figuring out Andrew Eakins's past. She knew he would thoroughly hide it, had to. It would be very difficult to discover. She found out you were here, living just across the way from the Goode home, which was perfect. It was as if you had fallen into her lap. She learned about you, your record in the Manhattan Homicide Squad, your unrelenting attitude toward your job, and figured you could be drawn in. She knew just what to say to get you interested, so you would expertly unearth Eakins's past so the man who murdered her sister could be convicted, convicted of a crime up here he did not commit, to replace the one he got away with. Justice, in her mind, not evil. Evil, to her, was what Alex Everly did in Philadelphia."

"She must have put that material under the furnace in Andrew's studio too," said Sal, "and figured you, thorough New York detective, would find it. It was put there for you."

"But she made some errors," said Mercer, "they always do. She didn't realize that her own fingerprints on the buttons could be traced, forgot that she'd been printed long ago. She is clever and dogged, but not a pro. She didn't count on us, on Alice and me ..." He looked over at her and smiled. He looked at Sal. "Everyone here. She didn't count on us connecting her to all of this."

"What's her endgame?" asked Sal. "That's important to know. Is it Elizabeth's death?"

"I don't think so," said Alice. "At least not at first. I'm guessing she just wanted Andrew convicted, even if just in the public eye. Hold on to Elizabeth until that's done, no matter how long that takes, then let her go. Elizabeth has to go through the terror of all that, frightened by what will be done to her. Maybe they even smack her around. Andrew gets his trial and gets convicted, his whole story out, enough of the victim's blood found to prove she's likely dead. Rebecca probably didn't care if Elizabeth's reappearance exonerated him of the apparent crime up here. She would have put him, and her, through hell."

"But if she let Elizabeth go, wouldn't Elizabeth just implicate Prior then?"

"Remember, it wasn't Rebecca in that café. And whoever has her now, whoever is holding her, is likely disguised. I'm sure Rebecca has set up an alibi for her own whereabouts."

"Now though," said Sal, "we've shown Rebecca's face around." She stood up. "Now, she won't get what she wants, she won't get

Andrew convicted or Elizabeth made to squirm for months. She could become desperate and kill Elizabeth."

There was another silence in the room.

"I can't disagree with that," said Mercer.

Alice stood up too. "Not if we can help it. Sal, call Jonathan Li and tell him to close his café, then call the Freemans and Ariel Foster and that fucking Reverend Eleanor James and ask them *all* to meet us there immediately. Police orders. They are to stop whatever they are doing and get there as fast as they can. We need to lay it on the line with all of them and find out either where Rebecca Prior is or where she might be keeping Elizabeth. They need to tell us who took her out of that café!" She turned to Mercer. "Come on, let's see what Mr. Alex Everly can tell us now, while the others are getting here."

33

Evil After Evil

ANDREW EAKINS TOOK the news that they knew all about him almost with relief.

"Yeah," he said, "that's why I couldn't say anything about myself. I almost told you once or twice, since I thought it might help find Elizabeth, but she worked so hard to hide us here, to help me vanish from the records, I knew she wouldn't want me to reveal anything. We'd made a vow to never give up our past, no matter what happened and go down in flames together. And I couldn't believe it was Becky, anyway! It just seemed inconceivable. And why were all these people lying about what happened? I was worried Elizabeth had just had enough anyway, had to get away, and —"

"So," said Alice, not hiding her disdain, "you murdered Mary Prior. You intentionally killed your wife."

Eakins looked at her, full into her face. His eyes filled with tears. "It was a moment of rage, of stupidity. I tried to stop. It's like it wasn't me." He stared at her. "Was it me?"

"Do you expect me to feel sorry for you?" asked Alice.

"No," said Eakins, barely audibly. "I hate myself."

"Good," said Mercer.

"I couldn't forgive. And that was lethal."

"I can't believe Elizabeth still wanted to be with you," said Alice, almost to herself.

"She shouldn't have," said Mercer.

"I love her," said Andrew, "though I don't deserve her. She lives with a man who killed his wife. She forgave what I did. She loves me. She sees into me. She knows I didn't want to do it — but I did. She holds me in her arms at night. You know, people talk about love all the time. They throw that word around. Love isn't something that makes sense though. It doesn't fit into right or wrong. It's just love. Elizabeth has taught me that. Love is for bad people too."

"We need you to help us," said Alice. "And, believe me, you will."

"Please, God, find Elizabeth! She doesn't deserve any of this." He started to weep.

"Who do you think might be helping Rebecca, supplying her, whom we might track?"

"Her brothers? They would do anything for her. I wouldn't be surprised if they're here, even now."

Mercer turned to Alice. "They haven't been in Grace for some time either."

Alice picked up her phone and contacted the front desk. "Call the police in Grace, Pennsylvania," she said. "Tell them we need images of John and Luke Prior. When you get the photos, get them out into our community immediately!"

"Describe them," said Mercer to Eakins. "We may need to know what they look like before we ever get a chance to see a photo."

"John is a big guy, respectable looking, a businessman. Short brown hair, never a follicle out of place, horn-rimmed glasses.

Luke is different, you'll know him when you see him. Shorter than John, disheveled red hair, had learning difficulties and stayed at home with Becky."

Alice and Mercer stood up and headed toward the door.

"I'm sorry," said Alex Everly. "I'm so sorry!"

Alice and Mercer stopped for an instant and then went out the door.

"Notice he didn't ask us to release him?" said Alice.

"No," said Mercer, "I think he'd be happy to stay there for the rest of his life."

Leonard Ferguson popped his head out of his office.

"Anything I can help with?" He noticed they were in a hurry. "What's going on now?"

"None of your business," said Alice. She turned back to Mercer as they neared her office. "You grab Sal and head to the café. I have something to do here. I'll be right along."

34

The Truth

"SO," SAID MERCER as he and Sal rushed out of the station and down the concrete steps into the freezing day, "what's holding up Alice? I can't believe she isn't sprinting ahead of us to the café."

"Mrs. Pearson."

"Oh, sorry to hear."

'No, no, she's not dead, just upset again."

Mercer came to a halt. "Upset? Can't that wait?"

"No," said Sal, not even turning around to look at him. "Mrs. Pearson is still missing Clarence."

"The dog."

"Yeah. Alice is giving Mrs. P. a quick call, that's all. Come on. She'll be here when she's calmed her down."

Mercer caught up to Sal. It occurred to him that she likely knew Alice Morrow better than anyone else did. The mystery of Alice.

"Alice is an interesting person," he offered. He realized as he spoke, that, somehow, he wanted to help Alice Morrow and needed her to help him.

Sal looked across at him, crunching in the snow beside him. "Oh, yeah."

"What is she like, really?"

Sal laughed. "Interesting question, coming from you. Not getting many intimate details, are you?"

Mercer actually blushed. "She doesn't talk much about personal things."

"Alice is a sweetheart. She is very dedicated to her job, believes in it, in catching the bad guys."

"Well, I have to say, that part is obvious. And I admire it."

"A dark horse too, in a good way."

"I get that too."

"She's a strong family girl. She attends a little church, Anglican, open-minded, sometimes a little too open-minded for my tastes to be honest. She goes every Sunday, volunteers with lots of charities."

"Churchgoer? That doesn't really jive with what I know of her." Some of the things she got them to do in the bedroom were things he had never even considered trying.

"Maybe you have a strange view of what a churchgoer is, at least her kind. To Alice, it's mostly just about trying to be a good person, and other than that, it's do what the hell you want to do as long as you don't hurt others. Make love, not war, you know. Don't be such a stick in the shit, Detective Mercer."

Mercer ignored that. "What about boyfriends?"

"Wondered how long til you asked that."

"Well, what about it? Does she date?"

"Date?" Sal smiled.

"Has she had any serious relationships?"

"Why don't you ask her?"

"Don't think I'd get anywhere with that."

"Yeah, she's had ..." Sal's voice faded, and she seemed to pick up the pace, as if she wanted to get away.

"Recently?"

Sal stopped. She sighed. "Look, your private life is your private life, isn't it?"

"Sure, but she and I are, well, we're, you know, involved, a bit."

"Married, as you are."

"Separated. She knows the score. What about her? I actually wouldn't be that shocked if you said she was married too, somehow. I'm not being overly nosy, I just wonder if she's had, or is maybe even involved still in some way, in a serious relationship."

"So weird that you are actually asking me this."

"Has she had anything serious going on?"

"I'm not sure I should say."

"Huh?"

Sal stopped again and turned to Mercer. "She had a guy — an important one — once."

"Once?"

"Long ago."

"And?"

"Not sure I should say."

"Come on."

"He's not around anymore." She said it in a grave voice, almost ominously.

"What does that mean?"

"It means what I said." They were at the café. "We've got work to do."

Mercer thought again of Delilah Morton's disdain of Alice, Ariel Foster's unwillingness to shake her hand, and of Alice saying how much she disliked high school, and her refusal to talk about it, or about anything from her past. Someone with her smarts had stayed in her hometown to work as police sergeant, covered up by her uniform, still living with her parents. Then he thought of her in his bed, unleashed, clutching at him, passionate. So now he knew: something had happened here long ago concerning Alice and a young man who isn't around anymore.

THE "CLOSED" SIGN was turned toward the street, just as it was the day Elizabeth Goode disappeared. Sal peered in through the window. Jonathan Li was pouring coffee into cups; Ariel Foster and an anxious Eleanor James were already seated with their drinks. Sal opened the door, and the little bell announced their presence. As it did, they heard two car doors close, and turned to see Fred and Alma Freeman heading toward them from their truck just down the street.

"Hello!" cried Sal and gave them a wave.

"Good day," said Fred. He glared at Mercer. Alma said nothing. She kept her eyes down.

Sal held the door for the couple, and they walked through without looking at either of the police officers. They made for the table and thanked Li for the coffee as they took off their coats and put them over the backs of their chairs.

They all sat down at the table. Ariel said hello. Eleanor was silent, her hands clasped together.

"Where's Alice?" asked Alma timidly.

"She's coming, dear," said Sal. "Talking to Vivien Pearson about Clarence."

"Oh," said Alma, "that's a shame. Lovely dog. It broke my heart to hear of it."

"Let's get started," said Mercer in his New York Homicide Squad voice.

"I wouldn't have come if I thought you'd be here," said Fred. "We've already said our bit. I ain't saying nothing, not one word, until you get your ass out of here, out of this town. You lied to us."

"He did?" said Ariel.

Li remained quiet, his fingers tapping on the table.

The bell tinkled and everyone looked up as Alice entered.

"Oh, thank God," said Alma. She lowered her voice. "I never thought I'd be glad to see you."

"Hold off on praising the Lord, Alma," said Sergeant Morrow. "You may not feel that way when we're done with you. Our father in heaven may want to drop your residence down a bit lower in the afterlife."

Alma's eyes widened. Eleanor looked like she might cry.

"Look, Alice," said Fred, "if this Yankee is here, then I'm not —"

"Oh, dry up, Fred," said Alice, pulling off her coat and tossing it on another table. "You and your wife, and Mr. Li here, and the good Reverend, are not in a position to tell any of us, including Detective Mercer, who, yes, can be a bit of a cowboy sometimes" — Mercer stared at her — "what you will or will not do. You are here to answer questions and to tell all of us the truth, for the first fucking time or it is going to go fucking bad for all of you!"

'Oh!" said Alma.

Mercer had never seen Alice like this, at least not in broad daylight.

"Now," said Sal in a very polite voice, "let us go over what happened on the day in question in this café. I believe that three of you, perhaps four, would like to tell us now that Elizabeth Goode was indeed with her husband and then tell us exactly, and we mean exactly, what happened?"

There was silence for a moment.

"She never set foot in this café that day," growled Fred. "This Yankee harassed the wife into —"

"Would you like that statement to go on record again?" asked Alice. "So it can add to the jail time you are about to do for aiding and abetting —"

"She was here," said Li quietly.

"Yes," said Eleanor in a voice that was barely audible.

"That's more like it," said Mercer.

"Please, go on, Mr. Li," said Sal.

"It was all set up many months ago by this woman named Ruth."

"Ruth?" said Eleanor and Alma at the same time.

"Would that be the woman whose face we've been circulating online today?"

"Online?" asked Fred.

"This face," said Sal, showing Ariel, Eleanor, and the Freemans a picture of Rebecca Prior on her cellphone. Alma gasped.

"Oh, my God," said Ariel and sat up very straight. "That woman came for a massage, several times. Said her name was Judith something. I can check. She had her hair really different though."

"I assume," continued Sal, "that you leave your clients alone in a room for a short period while they undress for their appointment?"

"Yes," said Ariel, still staring at Becky Prior.

"Do you keep personal contact information about other clients in that room? Or close at hand?"

"Well, I try to be very low-key, low-tech, no office, just open concept. Yes, everything is right there in an old card index on the desk."

"Would Elizabeth's cellphone number have been in it?"

"Yes."

"Did this woman ask about the locals, your friends? Did she get you to talk about Elizabeth?"

"Yes." Ariel's hands were shaking.

The Freemans both continued to stare at the photo too.

"Oh, Fred," Alma finally whispered, "it's Rosaline Parks!"

"It's Angela," said Eleanor.

"No, her name is Ruth," said Li. "You all have the name

wrong. It was Ruth, I'm sure of it. She came here a few times, and we talked a little."

"About what?" asked Mercer.

"About life, I guess, at first. She was very nice, very friendly, caring. I ended up telling her about my situation."

"Your financial one," said Alice.

"No, this business is fine." Li looked around the table as if he didn't want to say anything more. "Personal issues," he finally said.

'Your difficult partner? The reason you really came here?" asked Mercer.

"Yeah. There was violence in my relationship ... toward me. I had to leave, find any way to get away."

"So, he hit you?" asked Alice.

"She." Li looked toward a wall. "It's embarrassing. Humiliating."

"And this Ruth woman," said Sal, "she was caring and friendly and got you to open up, and you felt like you could share your trauma with her?"

"Yeah."

"She really was," said Reverend James. "Angela. She was so easy to talk to. That first day she told me not to listen to the idiots in town who were jealous of my relationship with Damien. She said she thought I was marvellous, brave. She liked that I wore my feminist button in the pulpit, that's why I gave her one, later on. We talked a lot, in person and on the phone."

"She was a sweetheart," said Alma, "Rosaline. I met her at the market, bumped into her, and she apologized. We talked and she offered tea and a scone. Turned up the next week too. It's like with Mr. Li here. She was the sort of person you just told things to, I guess. Truth is, we're struggling."

"Alma!" said Fred.

"We are, Fred. Now ... shut your mouth. We need to stop lying." Fred Freeman looked like he was going to have a heart attack. "Fred's business is not doing well. We had the place done up and borrowed money to do it. This woman told us she could make all our problems go away."

"I'm a good person," said Li. "I only went along with her idea because of what she told me."

"Yes," said Eleanor, "it was what she said about Elizabeth Goode."

"That's right," said Fred quietly. He still had not touched his coffee.

"She told us that she knew something about her," continued Alma. "She said that the man she was with, Eakins, who told nobody about his past, was going to hurt her. She said she had proof!"

"The bruise," said Li. "I know about bruises."

"If you are a real Christian," said Eleanor, "and a real feminist, then you help others, sacrifice for others, others in need, desperate need. You make difficult decisions. Angela and I talked and talked about that."

"It takes a mighty wallop to bruise up a woman like that. That's a coward, fit to be shot!" exclaimed Fred.

"I gave that to her, you idiots!" said Ariel, who was listening to all of this with astonishment. "It was a gardening accident!"

Alma, Fred, and Eleanor stared at her, open-mouthed.

"Well," said Li, "I didn't know that then. I have a lot of respect for Elizabeth, for her perseverance, for what she's endured. He was surly, secretive. He had a temper. I had seen it. Ruth told me that he was a murderer."

"That's right!" said Fred again.

"She told me what he had done in the past."

"And she proved it!" said Alma. "We never would have done

nothing otherwise. You have to believe us! I don't think any of us would have!"

"She showed me reports from the papers," said Li, "about what he did to his wife in the States. It was obvious he killed her, but some smartass woman got him off."

"That would be Elizabeth," said Sal under her breath.

"What?" asked Li.

"What else did she say?" asked Mercer.

Li gathered himself. "She said that it was a very tricky situation, that Elizabeth was essentially being held captive by Eakins. She lived under threats. That's why she'd returned, even though it was said she never really liked it here. Elizabeth did act weird around him, protective, so it made sense. It was obvious they had a secret. If we all let things continue the way they were then this violent man would probably kill her, sooner rather than later. Like maybe could have happened to me — Ruth said Elizabeth would one day just be a tragic bit of news."

"I just couldn't let that happen," said Eleanor. "It was my duty."

"Rosaline said she had a way to get Elizabeth out of here and away from him, to save her. She could just pluck her out of her dangerous predicament; make her vanish but also save her life. She said it was the only way to do it. That even though the police in the States knew what he had done, they could not touch him, no one could."

"She said," added Fred, "that all we had to do was say we'd seen him on the street and that he was alone. She said we'd just look like innocent bystanders, not involved at all, and others would handle saving Elizabeth. She said she had other witnesses inside the café. But the wife, she has a soft heart. She was worried about Elizabeth, wanted to be sure she was going to be all right, so we stayed in the café until Eakins came in with her the first time.

We kept our heads down, turned away from him. We left, right away after everything happened."

"I couldn't go through with it," said Eleanor. "I went to the Circle, but I just couldn't do it. I knew I would have to speak to the police, to lie. But I often imagined the scene that Angela said would transpire. She said that when the person came into the café to remove poor Elizabeth, she would go with that person"—the Reverend smiled—"that she would be glad to go, perhaps a little shocked, but overjoyed to be free and escape her fate."

"And that's what happened," said Li. "Exactly as Ruth said!"

"What cinched it all," added Alma, "what made me feel certain we had done a good deed, even if we were paid to do it, was who came to get Elizabeth."

"Who was it?" asked Mercer, the hair rising on the back of his neck.

"Why, it was Constable Ferguson," said Fred.

The three police officers stared at him. Then Sal stood up and walked away, to call Ranbir at the station. Mercer and Alice were thinking about Ferguson's wife Marlene losing her job, their upcoming trip to Florida, their colleague's tough-on-crime attitude.

"Yeah," added Fred, "that's how we knew it was going to be all right. An officer of the law, a good friend. He came in quickly and spoke to her quietly. I have no idea what he said, but she got up and went with him out the back, through the kitchen."

"He likely told her," said Alice with a stunned look, "that word had gotten out about what Andrew Eakins had done in the States and it was going to be revealed here in town, and that he would like to talk with her, outside, about what could be done for them. Elizabeth would have appreciated the officer's tact. They would talk discreetly, then she would slip back in, perhaps say she had gone to the washroom."

"When they got out the back door," said Mercer, nodding, "there must have been a car waiting for them and Ferguson shoved Elizabeth into it. Your friend, Rosaline or Ruth or Angela or whatever she called herself, is a woman named Rebecca Prior from Grace, Pennsylvania, and she may have been at the wheel, masked, or perhaps she employed someone else to do the kidnapping. Possibly her brothers, disguised too. This Rebecca Prior is the sister of the woman who was killed by Andrew Eakins in Philadelphia about three years ago. That much of what she told you is true." He paused. "We found a tiny speck of blood on a piece of material from the dress Elizabeth wore that day."

"Oh!" said Ariel and put her hand over her mouth.

"My God," said Li. His eyes reddened. He dropped his head.

"Forgive me," whispered Eleanor.

The Freemans looked pale.

"The thing I can't figure out though," said Li into the table, "is if this really happened how you said it did, then how could they possibly have gotten Eakins out of the café for just the right amount of time, and back in? It all had to be timed perfectly. Eakins could not know anything. Ruth had told us he was a beast."

Mercer thought back to the narrative of the incident as laid out by Alice Morrow in Connie's Home Style Grill. At that time, she had pieced together events according to the various witness testimonies, including that of Andrew Eakins. Though Eakins had revealed almost nothing of himself, he had provided a version of events from his perspective, starting with what occurred on the way to the café:

Andrew Eakins and Elizabeth Goode got out of their car, leaving it half a block from the Shelter Café on King Street Circle ... He had the keys. Half a dozen strides away, he turned to press the lock button, but she shook her head, smiled at him, and took his hand. Turning back to the sidewalk, they nearly ran into a pedestrian who adroitly stepped sideways and, of course, apologized, even though it was the couple's fault they had nearly collided.

"Rebecca Prior," said Mercer, "must have gotten someone who knew how to pick a pocket to nearly collide with Eakins outside the café and take his cellphone out of his back pocket, where she knew he always carried it."

Then Mercer remembered the next part of Alice's account.

As they were talking, Elizabeth's cellphone rang. She picked it up and answered but there was no response, perhaps a wrong number. Andrew instinctively felt for his own ... It was not there.

"I forgot my phone, honey," he said and got to his feet.

"Just leave it. We won't be long."

But Andrew Eakins was an anxious sort and having his cellphone in the right place and near him was important to him. He did freelance work, sculptures, impressionist metal stuff on dark subjects, and never wanted to miss a call that might mean a sale.

"Rebecca Prior," said Alice, "obviously knew that Eakins was anxious without his phone, always had to have it with him. She had found Elizabeth's private number in Ariel's office. Whoever took Eakins's cellphone simply called Elizabeth, once they knew the couple were inside the Shelter, from another cell — it would just come up as a number she didn't recognize — counting on Eakins to reach for his, discover he didn't have it, assume he had left it in the car, and leave the café to get it. It would all be very natural, completely unsuspicious. From her time here, Rebecca must have also discovered that locals took pride in not locking their cars, and rightly hoped that Elizabeth would insist on it. The person who stole Eakins's phone merely opened the car and dropped it by the front seat for Eakins to find, as if it had slipped out of his back pocket. The whole manoeuvre got Eakins out of the café on a perfect timetable."

Sal returned to the group from her phone call to the station and nodded gravely at Alice.

"All right," said Mercer. "We know what you all did, and we know what Rebecca Prior did. What we need to know now is what happened next. Is Elizabeth dead or alive? If it's the latter, then where are they keeping her?"

"You have to find her!" said Ariel Foster and Jonathan Li at the same time. Ariel looked at him as if she wanted to slap him.

"You five have to help us," said Sal. "Tell us anything you know, anything this woman might have said or anything about Elizabeth that might help us."

Ariel looked distraught. "But I have no idea where they would take her. Libby doesn't have another place, a cottage or anything that I know of where they could have taken her. The only place would be her house and you've gone through it. Elizabeth and Andrew were mostly homebodies. Did he really do that ... to his first wife?"

Jonathan Li threw his hands up in frustration as the officers looked to him. Eleanor James had her head down and her eyes closed as if in prayer. They turned to Alma. Not one of them looked toward Fred. He had been useless before because he was being deceitful; now he looked paralyzed with fear.

"Alma?" asked Alice quietly.

"I don't know," she said. "I really don't know. I wish to God I did."

"Just think again of the things that this woman talked to you about," said Mercer. "Was there anything she seemed particularly interested in? Anyone?"

Alma's eyes suddenly lit up. "The hunting camp!"

"What?"

"Fred's hunting camp. It's out in the bush, over an hour north and then east of the lake. You can't drive all the way in. There's just a footpath in and out, none this time of the year. Rosaline, that woman, she got all interested in bear hunting when she was at our place, asked Fred to show her his guns, running her hands along the barrels and the arrow on his crossbow. Sucked him in." She glared at Fred. "Touching your guns and gushing! What interest would a woman like that have in hunting bears, you ass!" She glared at him and then looked back at Alice. "She asked about the hunting season."

"When is that?" asked Mercer.

"Late summer and fall," said Alice and Sal at the same time.

"So there's no one out there now!"

"She asked all about the camp," continued Alma, staring into the distance as she remembered it. "My galoot of a husband told her exactly where it was. Exactly! How to get to it!"

Fred put his head into his hands.

Mercer's face was flushed with excitement.

"Now," said Alice, "you, Ariel, can go home. Thank you, my friend. I hope we will have good news for you soon. I hope and pray. You, Mr. Li and Ms. James, had better get some legal advice, and stay in town. The same goes for our lovely couple here," she said, turning to the Freemans. "But you, Fred Freeman, are going to do something before that and do it well and quickly! You are going to tell us, RIGHT NOW, exactly where your camp is and how to get to it!"

He did and then all three police officers fumbled their notebooks into their pockets and were out the door on the run.

35

An Eye For An Eye

THEY ALL WISHED they had driven to the café and could just leap into a vehicle and be on their way. Instead, they had to rush toward the police station first. Sal had a difficult time keeping up. Mercer's car was on the Circle between them and the station, parked along a snowbank at an old-fashioned meter he had filled with coins. They would reach it first.

"We can take mine!" he shouted.

He knew he could put the pedal to the metal on his Ford Escape and that it had some serious guts. Christine had kept the little Chevy. "Got snow tires on that thing?" asked Alice, who didn't seem to be even slightly out of breath.

"What?"

"Take mine!" yelled Sal, who'd fallen behind the other two, tossing her keys forward as she said it. Alice turned and snatched the keys out of the air before Mercer even realized what was happening.

"Perfect," said Alice. She glanced at Sal. "We'll pick you up on the way! Stand out on the street!" She turned back to Mercer. "She has a four-by-four, high wheelbase and wide snow tires. That thing will move too. That's what we need."

She slipped into the driver's seat and waited for him to get in on the passenger side, but barely, since she was already moving before he had even closed the door. He snapped on his seat belt as she squealed out of the parking lot and onto King Street Circle, and came to a screeching halt with six inches to spare between the right back door and her colleague. Sal hopped in without a word.

They careened around the Circle and turned left onto King Street West and the straightaway, using Sal's siren to get through the intersections until they reached the edge of town where the fast-food restaurants clustered near the exits to the highway. They would head north from here up into cottage country and the wilderness.

The only decent hotel in town, The Comfort Inn, where American tourists usually stayed, was coming up on their right. Alice leaned forward, peering that way, her eyes scanning the parking lot.

Following her gaze, Mercer spotted two men who looked to be hurrying toward a dirty, salt-encrusted pickup truck. "Look!" he shouted and pointed toward the lot.

One man was tall and wearing a stylish, long, woolen winter coat and glasses, and the other was smaller, with bright red hair. The bigger man was calling to him to move faster.

"John and Luke?" said Sal.

Alice swung the car across a lane, almost smashing into two vehicles as she negotiated a hairpin turn, and entered the hotel parking lot. The larger man came to a halt when he heard their car.

"Luke!" cried Mercer as he wound down the window. The second man turned and looked in his direction.

"That seals it," said Sal. "These are our guys."

Alice slammed on her brakes a yard or two from the larger man and somehow released her seat belt and jumped out of the vehicle in the same motion. The other two got out quickly too. Alice had her hand on her holstered gun. Mercer had never seen her do anything like that, nor imagined he ever would.

"John Prior?" she said, moving toward him with long strides, her feet wide apart for balance as she neared.

The man looked terrified, exhaling big clouds in the cold air, dropping a bag from his hand.

"Put your hands where I can see them."

Now, this is more like it, thought Mercer.

"Luke, you do the same, my friend," said Sal in a moderate tone. Luke immediately dropped the bag he was holding too and shot both hands into the air.

Mercer did not have a gun and it pissed him off to no end.

John Prior hesitated. Alice unsnapped her holster with a quick movement of her hand. John lifted his arms, palms toward her.

"You understand *that*, do you?" said Alice, glancing down at her weapon.

"Yes, ma'am."

"Don't call me a bullshit title, John. I am Sergeant Morrow and that is how you will address me."

"Yes ma' — yes, Sergeant."

"Hands against the side of your truck, sir, up high."

He turned and Alice slammed him against the door, nearly smashing his head into the window.

Whoa, thought Mercer.

"Frisk him!"

Mercer did as Alice stood back with her hand still on her holster but with the gun not yet drawn. *Take it out,* thought Mercer. *Don't be shy.* He had to admit though, she gave the distinct impression that she would use the weapon, and fast — and that she would not miss. John Prior certainly sensed her resolve. Mercer could feel him shaking.

"He's clean," he said. "Any weapons in the truck?"

John paused.

Sal was frisking Luke at the same time, though very gently. He had started to cry.

"Are you deaf?" Alice asked John.

"Yeah, a rifle."

"Get it, detective," said Alice. Mercer opened the door and found it behind the front seat. A simple rifle, not loaded, though there were boxes of cartridges next to it.

"I'm guessing you don't have a licence for that, Mr. Prior," said Alice.

"Alice," said Mercer, "it's just a hunting rifle, this would be easy to —"

"Detective Mercer, it would take quite a while to legally obtain that firearm here, trust me. Best not to talk about things you don't understand."

"Really? *That* rifle?"

"We don't arm the public with weapons here. It takes away our freedom — to be alive."

"I brought it from America," said John. "Brought it over the border."

"The United States?" asked Mercer.

Both Alice and Sal could not help smiling.

"Are you an American?" asked John.

"Matter of fact, I am. Just came back from a place called Grace. In Pennsylvania. Heard of it?"

John Prior looked even paler than before, as if he might faint. "Yes, sir," he said.

"Now, I'm going to search your truck further and if there are more weapons in there, then you are going to be in even deeper shit than you are right now, and believe me, you are currently in it up to your neck."

Mercer began expertly searching the car, both inside and out: in the glove compartment, under the seats, and up in the wheel wells and all around the fender and grill.

"Hands behind your back," said Alice to John Prior. Mercer heard the handcuffs snap onto him.

"Ow!" he said.

"You've got to wear these too," said Sal to Luke. "Sorry." She cuffed him and he dropped down to the icy surface of the parking lot.

"Turn around!" said Alice to John.

He turned.

"We know just about everything we need to know about you and your sister. We even know where she is keeping Elizabeth Goode. And we are going there now, and you are coming with us and will help us in every way you can. Do you understand? Am I womansplaining clearly enough to you right now?"

Funny, thought Mercer.

"The truck is clean," he announced.

"She fucking helped him," said John bitterly.

"Pardon me?" asked Alice.

"Elizabeth Goode. She got Everly acquitted. They freed a murderer because of her. We don't want to hurt her, don't want to do what she and her lover boy did to us. We just want him to get his due. We want guilty stamped on his fucking forehead. Scare her too. She deserves it. "

"Well, I can't help you with any of that," said Alice. "My job is to maintain the law in my town. What we call: peace, order, and good government?"

Sal smiled.

Alice went on. "You have illegally incarcerated a citizen of this community and attempted to frame a man who was declared innocent in a court of law. We are not going to let you hurt this woman."

"Unless you already have?" asked Mercer.

John Prior paused. "No."

"Not yet," said Luke quietly on the ground.

"What do you mean by that?" asked Sal.

"Be quiet, Luke!"

"I need you to tell me, right now," said Mercer, stepping up close to John, his face within inches of the other man's, "why you were in such a hurry to get to the truck?"

"We saw the pictures," said Luke, "of Becky. They're everywhere."

"I told you to be quiet, Luke!"

"So," said Sal, turning Luke to look directly at her and away from his brother. "Were you running to get out of town?"

"No, we would never do that. We couldn't leave Becky behind."

"So where were you going?"

Luke tried to look toward John.

"Don't look at him, just answer the question."

Luke was silent. "It's bad," he finally said.

"What's bad?"

"Becky's mad. She's really, really mad."

"And where is Becky now?"

Mercer put his hand over John Prior's mouth, so hard that his victim didn't bother attempting to speak.

"She's heading out there, out to the woods. She left awfully fast in her vehicle. She was spittin' mad. She said there was no way Alex was going to pay now, that he'd get off free again ... and that one of them had to pay. Becky has been awfully upset. She's not really been herself. She went down into the maintenance place in the basement here in the hotel when we were trying to calm her down. We were telling her that we just needed to go, get out of here. We didn't know why she was going down there. She busted open the maintenance room door. I didn't even know she could do something like that ... She found a sledgehammer and took it with her." He sobbed.

"And where was she going?" asked Sal calmly.

"Miss Elizabeth Goode is tied up in that little camp building, way out in the woods. She can't move. Becky brought a sledgehammer!"

"Everyone in the car!" cried Alice. "Mercer, you're in the back with Mutt and Jeff."

"We had to get our clothes and boots," said Luke in a monotone. "Becky just ripped out of here. She's been gone for maybe ten minutes now!"

"In the car!" repeated Alice.

They all got in. Mercer somehow ran the seat belts in and around his two fellow back seat passengers, ingeniously tying their handcuffed hands down so they couldn't even move them to the side. He'd seen someone do that in New York.

"Why the sledgehammer?" asked Sal as they squealed out of the parking lot, the siren on. "Why not just take the gun?"

No one said anything.

"Becky," said Luke finally in his same quiet manner, "she has reason to be so mad. Mary's head smashed against that brick wall in Philly, you know. You have no idea. Becky saw a picture. Becky talks about that a lot. She says Mary's skull was split open like a melon, her head nearly off, the insides oozing out. Our Mary."

All of the police officers were thinking the same thing but not saying a word as the car raced northward on the salt-encrusted, icy road.

Elizabeth Goode is helpless. Becky Prior is coming for her with a sledgehammer. Mary's head exploded when it hit that wall.

36

Hunting Becky Prior

IT TOOK THEM barely an hour to make the one-and-a-half-hour trip to the jumping off point in the woods to the hunting camp, but they never once saw Becky's vehicle, the make her brothers told them she was driving, not even in the distance. They drove through a heavily forested area for nearly half an hour before Luke Prior pointed to the turnoff onto the snowy dirt road from the highway that would lead them to the camp. It was a crude passageway and Sal's vehicle slewed in the snow but kept moving, Alice powering it forward at a dangerous speed. Still no Becky in the distance.

Who are we really saving Elizabeth Goode from? thought Mercer. He noticed Alice glancing at him in the rear-view mirror. *From a woman who simply wants justice?* Alice appeared to be trying to read his thoughts and he imagined how she would respond to him. She would say life is complicated, that we are all guilty of something, we all make mistakes, but they had to stop this particular brutality, no matter what. "We can't change the past," he imagined her saying, "but maybe we can affect the present." He gazed into the mirror and their eyes fixed on each other.

Maybe the old style of justice was best, thought Mercer, *like in the Wild West. Let Rebecca Prior do this to Andrew Eakins and to the woman who let him go free. Would that not make things even?* But he imagined Alice saying "We can't live in a world where people take the law into their own hands, no matter what the cause is. We have to stop this. You know it." He didn't think anything for a while, then he nodded at her, and she nodded back.

They got out of the four-by-four where the road stopped at a circle in the woods. Becky's vehicle was there, another one she had rented, likely from out of town, this one a small truck. They could see her footprints in the snow, leading along a winding path through the woods that was barely a path. Sal pulled a pair of boots out of the back of her vehicle and tossed another pair to Alice.

"I always keep a second pair. These should fit you."

Alice looked over at Mercer as she pulled on hers, setting her socked foot down on the snow for an instant without any apparent discomfort, that naked toenail painted red. "Sorry," she said.

Mercer had outdoor wear on his feet, but they were barely boots. Instead, they were the short-cut, trendy hiking things he had worn when he went back to America. He looked toward the path they had to walk, packed down by treks the three Priors had been making out here, but narrow. Here and there, Becky's footprints had sunk a foot into the snow, and she weighed about half of what Mercer did.

"Let's go!" said Alice emphatically but careful not to shout. "If the brothers make a warning noise, turn and put your gun to their heads!" she said to Sal. "If they make another one, shoot them!"

Off they went, Alice in the lead, followed by Sal, then the two Priors, trying to rush in the snow with their hands cuffed behind their backs. Mercer brought up the rear.

Alice was soon running up front, forcing the pace, Sal puffing as she kept up, and Mercer cursing under his breath as his feet sank into the snow every five steps or so. It took about twenty minutes to get to the camp. Through the lines of the trees, they could see several perches, hunting blinds, where Freeman and his fellow hunters would sit in their camouflage clothing to take down a black bear with a gun or crossbow. They could hear crows cawing and Mercer looked up to see three of them following. He wondered if there were other creatures watching. The camp itself appeared almost out of nowhere in a small clearing. The whole building was no more than twenty feet long and about ten feet wide. It was made of some sort of corkboard without paint, insulation visible here and there. There was chopped wood and an axe near the door. Thin wisps of smoke were beginning to rise from a crude metal chimney on the roof, obviously a wood stove inside. A little generator, now turned off, sat outside.

They could hear voices. Alice held up her hand and everyone stopped. Mercer figured they were about the distance from a pitching mound to home plate.

It was difficult to tell what was being said, but it was obvious it was two people, women, and both sounded desperate.

Then they heard a scream, followed by the thud of something heavy punching a hole in the wall.

They all started to run. In the movies, the police would call out to Rebecca Prior about now. That, however, would be a mistake, and Alice, Sal, and Mercer knew it. Becky was enraged. A warning would make her do the job even faster — if it wasn't done already.

Alice reached the door first and kicked it in with a boot, a flying bottom-of-the-heel shot that looked like something used in an MMA cage. She still hadn't unholstered her weapon. Sal had hers out now, and Mercer would have drawn his, if he'd had one. In fact, he would have had it out long before now.

They stepped inside the crude building.

"BECKY!" cried John and Luke at the same time, in a sort of howl.

Rebecca Prior looked like hell. She appeared to have not slept for weeks, her hair was even shorter, stringy and matted. Her glasses had slid down to the very tip of her nose, her face bathed in sweat. Her coat had been tossed to the floor and the sleeves of her sweater pushed up above the elbows, so she could swing her weapon with maximum effect. The muscles in her thin, bare arms stood out like twisted rope as she pulled the sledgehammer out of the wall where it had indented a hole the size of a cannonball. Elizabeth Goode, chained to a chair in front of her, her eyes wild with fear, was looking to duck a second time to save her life. She was wearing a puffy black coat over the peacock-pattern dress, which still did not seem enough cover in the cold room.

Becky bared her teeth like a wolf as she glanced toward the door and cocked the big hammer again, taking aim. "I'll explode this bitch!" she cried.

Elizabeth screamed again.

"Miss Prior!" shouted Alice. "Drop your weapon!"

Sal was shaking and couldn't raise her gun.

Mercer could not believe it.

Becky started to swing, aiming lower this time, to meet Elizabeth Goode's temple as she dropped her head to save her life, split that skull wide open like a melon, take it off at the stem, let the insides ooze out.

Mercer rushed in. This was his chance to make things right, at least for Elizabeth Goode. He was too far away though, and he tripped and then hit the floor at Rebecca's feet, only the tips of his fingers reaching her big black boots.

The sound that came then was like nothing he had ever heard before. First, it was like a click, a barely audible whoosh, and then a bang, so loud and near him that it nearly deafened him. He knew the last part. The blast of a gun.

Alice Morrow had pulled her weapon from her holster and shot Rebecca Prior in the neck as quick as a gunfighter. He doubted she had aimed carefully. Police officers rarely do in moments like this. You draw and fire. The sledgehammer dropped and the business end clanked against Mercer's knee making it feel as if it had knocked off his leg, but he didn't feel the pain because he was staring up at the blood spurting from Becky Prior as she writhed on the floor, her brothers looking on in horror, Luke screaming.

Mercer struggled to his feet and turned to see Alice. She was standing there with no emotion on her face — just blank, the gun still pointed where she had aimed it. Mercer thought of Ranbir Singh saying how lethal the people from around here were in wars.

Sal yanked off her coat, threw it over Becky Prior, and knelt down to apply pressure to her neck.

"No!" gurgled Becky. "No!" She struggled to speak. "Leave me. God will take me now! God knows."

"NO! BECKY!" cried Luke dropping to his knees, pressing his head to her neck too, blood smearing on his face and red hair, squirming, with his hands still cuffed behind his back. He toppled on his side, weeping. John just stared at the figures on the cabin floor, his mouth open.

Mercer and Alice bent down toward Rebecca. She was having trouble breathing.

"She's done," whispered Mercer. "Seen this before."

"I," murmured Becky, as they all listened, "I do *not* forgive them ... God knows." With that, her head fell back, and she went silent.

37

The Secret Chord

HE COULD NOT believe that she slept with him that night. He also could not believe that she did not seem shaken by what had happened. Once Rebecca Prior had uttered her last words and John, weeping, collapsed to the floor beside Luke and his dead sister, Alice had holstered her gun and turned to what needed to be done without emotion. Mercer had wanted to take her into his arms, but she had given him a look that said, "back off." They had released Elizabeth Goode from her chains and Alice had taken off her coat and given it to her, putting it over Elizabeth's own coat as she shivered, doing so before Mercer could do it himself. They forced John and Luke away from the camp and Becky's body, closed the door securely, and made their way back out to the vehicles. On the way, Alice called the station and arranged for the crime scene to be secured and inspected. The keys were still in Becky's car, so Mercer drove it back to the station with Elizabeth Goode in the back seat. She did not say a word as they traveled the one-and-a-half-hour trip, though she occasionally sobbed. When he asked if she was all

296 I SHANE PEACOCK

right, she merely nodded. He could see the inner toughness of
Dr. Eve Newman and the brilliant Elizabeth Goode.

They all arrived at the station at the same time. Chief Smith's
door was still firmly closed at the end of the hall, another loud
song softly pulsing inside. Leonard Ferguson was in a cell, and
Jonathan Li, Eleanor James, and the Freemans were in a room
giving statements to Ranbir Singh. The Prior brothers were taken
into custody too. Andrew Eakins was kept out of their sight, but
was brought into the reception area when the others were gone
and when he saw Elizabeth, returning from a brief medical exam-
ination, he broke down. She ran toward him and leapt into his
arms, and they hugged each other and wept. It seemed as though
they would stay like that forever. They formed a little world within
the room.

"Thank you," said Andrew finally, over his shoulder to Alice
and Mercer, who both had splats of blood on their clothing.

"I don't have much use for you," said Mercer. "And I do not
accept your thanks."

Alice said nothing. She just stood there watching.

"I understand," whispered Andrew.

Elizabeth turned toward them. "I don't blame Becky," she said.
"She simply tried to do what Andrew did, just with premeditation."

"I didn't mean to," said Andrew. "Good God, I didn't mean
to!" He could not look at anyone, not even Elizabeth. She took
him by the hand and led him out the door.

MIRACLE OF MIRACLES, Alice was still there when they awoke in
Mercer's bed the next morning. She smiled at him too and let him
hold her. It felt like their last night.

"You think you're pretty tough, don't you?" he said, putting
his hands on her tattooed hips and pulling her closer.

"Not really."

"You haven't shed a tear."

"Why would I do that?"

"Or expressed any regret, any concerns. Are you sure you're okay?"

"I'm fine. I did my job. And I'm glad to be rid of Fergie."

They laughed and she pulled him closer, but she looked away too, over his shoulder, beyond him. She only looked right at him in bed at the height of her passions. Then, she would stare intensely into him, with what was almost a questioning look.

"I was just imagining what was going through Andrew Eakins's head," she said.

"When he killed his wife? Momentary hatred, I would say."

"Ever feel that?"

"Not like that."

"But you've felt it in some way."

Mercer paused, the memory flooding him, of his fists raining down on the young man in the Bronx.

"Yeah."

"When Elizabeth and Andrew were embracing, I had a 'there but for the grace of God go I' kind of feeling."

"Killed someone, have you?"

She didn't answer.

"Alice?"

"Well, I killed Rebecca."

"That's different. I meant otherwise. Another time?"

"You're getting awfully personal."

"Is that a crime?"

"Not one with a sentence."

He stared at her. She looked down to his chest. "Tell me about yourself, Alice Morrow. I really want to know. Tell me about your life, your past. Who are you?"

"I'm just Alice." She paused. "Who are you?"

"I grilled Sal about you, you know."

"I do know."

That surprised him a little, but it shouldn't have. "So, you had a special guy, once? Long ago. He's gone? How is he gone? Where is he?"

"You know, I was looking at Elizabeth and Andrew holding each other, and it seemed to me that somewhere in his face he was saying to us, asking us 'Please, please, forgive me.' It was like he was also saying, 'if you can forgive me, then you can forgive anyone. Even yourself.'" For a second, Alice looked Mercer in the eye and then her gaze shifted away again. "Elizabeth loves him so much. I wish I had an Elizabeth."

Sometimes Mercer held Alice in his arms and felt she was somewhere else. She had a way of making you feel you were alone or at least sending you away. His thoughts wandered and for a moment he was with Christine, but he heard Alice's voice repeating "then you can forgive anyone, even yourself."

He wanted to tell her how much he cared for her, loved her, and hoped she cared for him, but he fell asleep and when he woke again, she was gone. There was a note on her pillow that read "Enjoyed our time together. Catch and release." She had drawn a broken heart. "Remember me," was lettered along the crack.

He lay there looking at the note for a long time. He eyed the curves of the letters and traced them with his fingertips. He smelled the note. There was no scent.

HE KNEW HE had to go home. Home did not necessarily mean Christine. Maybe it did. He didn't know. He had to go back to America though, there were so many things he had to do there, make right. Pulling his bathrobe tight around him, and counting each of the seventeen steps, Mercer descended to the kitchen. He could not stay here in this neutral land of grey and white. It was such an ordinary place, no colour, no ambition. Ordinary, like Alice Morrow.

He tried to write in his journal that morning but couldn't. Maybe he was fooling himself. What did Alice say? Something about never figuring things out. This case, though it had thrilled him to his soul, certainly didn't have any answers, no clear good guys or bad guys. He had gone through a journey in this cold country, though he wasn't sure what it really was or what it meant. Maybe that was always true in life. You are always in between. That was how he felt here, with Alice: without answers, in between. And that seemed very real.

He packed up his bags again, put the keys on the table, and left.

He drove up the lane and could see the Goode farmhouse and barn rise into view as he ascended the slight incline. He thought of Andrew's sculptures, how frightening they were at first, a crowd of lonely figures trying to be couples, in pain. Mercer pulled the car over at the top of the lane to look back at the farmhouse. Then he got out and looked down the road toward the highway. He thought of Christine past the end of that road, of his kids, of Lauryn, of Christmas in America, God's country. Alice Morrow was the other way ... distant, passionate, and incomprehensible. He thought again of the ingenious crime they had solved together. He thought of his terrible secret, his own crime. Maybe he should just keep it to himself, try to do better, *much* better. The car was running, and a door was open, the radio set on a local station. "Hallelujah" came on, a cover of the song by Leonard Cohen. He loved the lyrics, though he did not have a clue what they meant. He had heard that Cohen was from up here too. He wondered if that was true; it didn't seem right. Mercer looked toward the farmhouse and the bleak snow-covered landscape again as the words began, sung by a pure and somehow northern voice, each word enunciated yet unknowable. A woman. Her voice did not ornament the melody as so many women's voices did on American radio. It was straightforward, clear as a bell, and yet as mysterious as hell. It told the truth.

He couldn't go. Not yet.

"I'll just stay a little longer," he said to himself, his words appearing to form in the air with his breath.

Acknowledgements

THIS STORY IS in many ways a departure for me and yet in other ways not different at all. It is my first crime novel for adults after many novels for young adult readers, though many of those were a little dark, a little adult, and some, like The Boy Sherlock Holmes, were focused on crimes and mysteries.

I set out, with this novel, to discuss forgiveness, in a world where that seems to be greatly needed and yet is often in short supply. I also wanted to set the story in the northern country where I have lived my whole life, a place renowned for its decency and politeness but in reality a more complex and often darker place, a place of iceberg personalities and secrets. I wanted to show our reality to the world. And perhaps also show how we are like all of the rest of you. I paired my local protagonist with another protagonist from our large neighbour to the south, so they could be compared to each other and give us their views of each other.

As always with novels, there have been many people helping me realize the book's vision. Essential people. The very first person to encounter the manuscript was my son, Sam Peacock, a smart guy who read the first chapter in raw form and immediately encouraged his dad to go on. Such advice from someone like him was something to be heeded. My agent, Hilary McMahon, was quickly supportive and gave the manuscript several readings and suggested important revisions. And then Marc Côté, fearless and thoughtful publisher of Cormorant Books, embraced the book's vision too and allowed it to be fully born. Attila Berki gave it a thorough edit, and Gillian Rodgerson a perfect copyedit. Barry Jowett guided the manuscript as well. Other folks helping at Cormorant were Sarah Cooper, Sarah Jensen, and Luckshika Rajaratnam. Authors Andrew Peacock and Eric Walters also read the manuscript at various stages in its development.

Absolutely essential in all of this was the input of Sergeant Janice MacDonald of the Cobourg (Ontario) Police Services, who not only read the manuscript (and quite liked it!) but also corresponded with me and met with me in person to help make the activities of Sergeant Alice Morrow (who isn't Janice, I promise!) and Detective Hugh Mercer realistic and believable. Thanks also to David Sheffield for putting me in touch with Sergeant MacDonald.

And finally, as always, thanks to my family, Johanna, Hadley and Sam, whom I hope I pay more attention to than Hugh Mercer does, and my dear wife Sophie whom I love with all my heart.

The author respectfully acknowledges that this novel was written while he was living on land located in the traditional and treaty territory of the Michi Saagiig (Mississauga) and Chippewa Nations, collectively known as the Williams Treaties First Nations, which include Curve Lake, Hiawatha, Alderville, Scugog Island, Rama, Beausoleil, and Georgina Islands First Nations.

We acknowledge the sacred land on which Cormorant Books operates. It has been a site of human activity for 15,000 years. This land is the territory of the Huron-Wendat and Petun First Nations, the Seneca, and most recently, the Mississaugas of the Credit River. The territory was the subject of the Dish With One Spoon Wampum Belt Covenant, an agreement between the Iroquois Confederacy and Confederacy of the Ojibway and allied nations to peaceably share and steward the resources around the Great Lakes. Today, the meeting place of Toronto is still home to many Indigenous people from across Turtle Island. We are grateful to have the opportunity to work in the community, on this territory.

We are also mindful of broken covenants and the need to strive to make right with all our relations.